Archimedes Nesselrode

Justine Graykin

DOUBLE DRAGON PUBLISHING

It is inadvisable
to bring your
bat-winged
star nose
mole

to your
dental
appointment.

best
wishes,

Justine
I'll never
forget your
Beowulf

Archimedes Nesselrode

Copyright © 2013 Justine Graykin

Double Dragon Press

An Imprint of
Double Dragon Publishing
PO Box 54016
1-5762 Highway 7 East
Markham, Ontario L3P 7Y4 Canada
http://www.double-dragon-ebooks.com
http://www.double-dragon-publishing.com

ISBN-10: 1-77115-130-7
ISBN-13: 978-1-77115-130-6

A DDP First Edition October 15th, 2013

*

My humblest thanks to the following: Eric Mulder, Dana van der Bijl, and the late, great Deerfield Writer's Group, for their invaluable assistance to me in the creation of this octopus. Your criticisms, suggestions, and tireless ferreting out of typos are deeply appreciated. To Trisha Wooldridge, Elaine Isaak, all my fellow Broads, for their support and encouragement, without which I would have been as lost as Mr. Nesselrode in Manhattan. And of course to Larry, for laboring long and mightily on the cover art that graces this work, for all those hours of recording at Panama-on-Lamprey, and for, well, all the rest. 143. And lastly to all the other fans of Archimedes Nesselrode who pestered me to keep trying, convinced of its inevitable success. Bless me in Latin, it seems you were right.

CHAPTER ONE

The Housekeeper

"He's an artist. And he desperately needs a housekeeper."

Frank Shekle had other clients, but none of them occupied his time and efforts as much as Archimedes Nesselrode. As the sole agency for Nesselrode's work, the prestigious firm of *Shekle and Kronor* enjoyed considerable prosperity. But Nesselrode was rather high maintenance, and Frank's father, the venerable founder of the agency, had put Frank in charge of the account. It was very nearly a full-time job, requiring him to act as agent for far more than just the artist's creations. Frank was wearing one of those other hats now, trying to find someone to manage what had to be one of the most chaotic and woefully neglected households imaginable. It wasn't easy, but enough money could buy anything. In time. He hoped.

This was the seventh applicant he had interviewed so far that morning. He'd been at it for a month and a half.

"Miss Mare," he began.

"*Ms.* Mare," she corrected him firmly. "You have my references."

Frank opened the folder on his desk. The remaining pool of acceptable applicants was discouragingly small. Nesselrode was very particular about the qualifications. But never mind what that lunatic wanted; the real challenge was to find someone who would put up with *him*. Out of well over a hundred applicants, only a fraction had passed muster, and none of them so far had lasted more than a few hours with their prospective employer. For most, it had been a matter of minutes.

The woman sitting prim in the chair in front of his desk was wearing a severely conservative navy skirt, ivory blouse and jacket. She was tall, her dark hair braided and pulled back into a bun (whoever did *that* nowadays?) with stern, brown eyes and a firmly set mouth. She had a brisk, masterful manner (she'd need it). Not an exceptionally attractive woman, but pleasant enough to look at. A healthy thirty-two, unmarried, no children (lesbian?).

Her employment history listed some prestigious households and her references included a letter of recommendation from a literary celebrity. She was, all in all, the most hopeful prospect he had left.

He glanced through the folder again. "Impeccable." Clasping his hands over the neat, orderly paperwork, he said, "You've heard of him, of course."

"He makes things," she said with indifference.

Frank pointed with a pen to a small Lucite cube on his desk. It contained a black-spotted, orange salamander, curled up around a white and grey marbled stone. Frank tapped the cube lightly. The salamander opened its golden eyes and flicked a long tongue from its mouth. A fly emerged from behind the stone. The salamander's tongue darted out and caught it. Then it crawled on top of the rock and regarded them both thoughtfully.

"My word!" Ms. Mare exclaimed. "Is it alive?"

"Not exactly."

"Some sort of holograph?"

Frank shook his head.

"What is it, then?"

"No one knows."

She scowled at the cube. "How does he make them?"

"No one knows that, either." And Mammon only knew how many multiple millions *that* secret was worth!

She picked up the cube and the salamander slid off the rock. It glared at her. "Hasn't anyone ever tried to take one apart?" she asked.

"Oh, yes," Frank assured her.

"And?"

He shrugged. "The image disappears. The cubes are empty." He took the cube from her, setting it back down on the desk. "Lovely, whimsical little mysteries which can't be mass-produced, and thus are fantastically expensive."

"How intriguing! I shall take the job," she said.

Frank raised both eyebrows. "I haven't offered it to you yet."

"Is there any reason why you should not?" she challenged him. He confessed he could think of none. Ms. Mare rose from her chair. "Then it is settled."

"But, we haven't discussed your terms of employment—wages—duties—"

"I am sure they shall all be satisfactory. When do I begin?"

"There are some details about this position that you should be, shall I say, *warned* about. It's not your usual household."

"All the better. You shall have to inform me of all the particulars."

"But, Miss Mare—"

"*Ms.* Mare," she reminded him severely. "Ms. Vivian Mare."

***

Transportation was arranged to the nearest city of reasonable size proximate to her prospective employer's location, and she called for a taxi to take her the remaining distance. The taxi did not arrive promptly, which annoyed Ms. Mare, but this was a small city and one couldn't expect the sort of conveniences to which one might be accustomed. The cab finally pulled up to the curb, driven by an enthusiastically smiling Asian man who spoke with a heavy accent. She was at first concerned that he might not be knowledgeable of towns outside the area. She told him where she wanted to go and he consulted one map, then another, all the time cheerfully assuring her with bobbing head, "I find it, no problem! Get you there quick! No problem!"

With a little help from Ms. Mare, he located their goal on a third map. "Ah!" he exclaimed with comprehension and delight, "Very simple! Get you there, no problem!" He started the taxi and pulled away from the curb, engaging the meter.

It was rather a long drive, and so to pass the time, Ms. Mare made conversation with the young man. She found out that he was Korean, and his name was Kim Sam, although she wasn't sure which was his first name and which was his surname. He had come to the United States to work for his brother, who owned the taxi business. Unfortunately, his knowledge of English was mostly limited to what was necessary to do his job, and her knowledge of Korean was negligible, so she was not able to ask him the more interesting questions about his homeland and experiences that she might have wanted to ask. Resigning herself to the resultant silence, she settled herself as comfortably as she could on the seat, which was stained and had been repaired in one spot with duct tape, and she considered the adventure ahead. This brought a smile to her lips. Whatever its challenges might be, her new situation ought to be most interesting.

She had become accustomed to interesting situations growing up. Her mother had been personal maid and secretary to Esther and Erasmus Galbraith, the celebrated travelogue writers. The couple traveled the far corners of the globe and managed to find pockets of romance even in the modern, twentieth-century world. Ms. Mare's mother had traveled with them, assisting them in their work, sharing in their adventures, until one adventure got a bit too romantic for her and Catherine Mare found herself inconveniently in the family way. But the Galbraiths were loyal employers, childless themselves, and they welcomed the baby as simply another adventure. Vivian Mare's childhood experiences included being swaddled like a papoose on her mother's back while riding a pony across the plains of Tibet, falling out of a canoe on a river in Brazil and narrowly escaping a school of piranha, and dressing up in male garb to wander the back streets of Tunisia disguised as a boy. When as an adult she had ventured out on her own, seeking service in an interesting household, she had nearly despaired at equaling her mother's good fortune. People seemed to have terribly ordinary lives nowadays.

Her suitcases were in the trunk of the taxi, containing all her worldly possessions. She traveled light, a habit acquired in her youth by the necessity of traveling nearly constantly. Her purse was on the seat beside her, and Frank Shekle's instructions were folded neatly next to her purse. They included directions to the house and an emphatic warning to wait at the gate when she arrived. Under no circumstances was she to attempt to open the gate or to venture alone up the driveway. When she asked why, Shekle made references to Nesselrode's "security system." He would not elaborate.

She knew she was close when they came to the long, dense hedge of hemlock and juniper. It ran for almost half a mile along the side of the road. Then the high hedge stopped and she saw the gate. It didn't seem terribly forbidding, just a wrought iron gate about seven feet high with bars and an ivy design. A bit rusty.

"This is it, yes?" Kim Sam asked, stopping in front of the gate.

"I believe so, yes," Ms. Mare said, and she got out of the taxi. As she did, a flock of brilliantly colored birds rose from the hedge with a startling commotion. She shaded her eyes, watching them take off. How lovely! Unlike any sort of bird she'd ever seen before.

The gate was locked, and there was a small sign which read, "Private Property, no trespassing under any circumstances. Warning: Intruders will be eaten."

"Eaten?" she echoed to herself. "How droll." She'd been warned that her prospective employer was more than a bit odd. But that was exactly the point, wasn't it? Precisely the reason that the position appealed to

her. To work for an artist must surely be different from anything she had
done before, a departure from the usual run of chief executive officers,
senators, and management consultants. Frightfully boring, all of them.
Even the household scandals had been predictable and tedious. No
imagination, any of them.

Ms. Mare checked her watch. She was early; in spite of his tardiness
in responding to her call, Kim Sam had done an admirable job of efficiently
navigating the route. She peered through the gate at the wild tangle of
garden beyond. Mr. Nesselrode ought to have a gardener, she thought
with a sniff. One would think an artist would have more aesthetic sense
than to let his grounds go like that. The driveway curved and disappeared
behind a line of unpruned boxwood, arbor vitae, and wildly undisciplined
yew. Disgraceful. A second rank of ancient oaks further conspired to
conceal what lay beyond. To her disappointment, she could gain not the
slightest glimpse of her prospective employer's house.

Kim Sam rolled down his window. "You want I wait?"

"Yes, please. I believe we are expected."

He shrugged. "Meter ticking. Person you wait for paying, I hope."

She didn't have to wait long. She had observed something blue some
distance away on the lawn, and was trying to make out what it was, when
she noticed a vehicle approaching along the driveway.

"Ah!" she remarked to Kim Sam, "Here comes someone now."

"Good!" he said, popping out of the taxi. "I get bags ready."

The vehicle, some sort of large, silver monstrosity, drove ponderously
up to the gate and stopped. The passenger's side door opened and a man
got out. He was slender, dressed in a baggy blue cotton shirt with the
sleeves rolled up, and tattered khaki pants. His hair was quite long, a
reddish brown color. A rather disheveled-looking individual, but he had a
pleasant smile. "Miss Mare?" he inquired.

"*Ms.* Mare, if you please," she corrected him politely as she walked
over to him. "Do I have the pleasure of addressing Mr. Archimedes
Nesselrode?"

"You do," he replied with a slight bow. "You are here to interview for
the position of housekeeper?"

"I am. I have all my references with me, and—"

Nesselrode waved his hand dismissively. "I'm sure Frank looked into
all that business. What matters is whether you're suited to the position,
and we'll learn that soon enough. Rather a lot to deal with, I'm afraid."

"So I've been informed," Ms. Mare replied briskly. "I am sure I shall be equal to it."

"We'll see," he murmured. "Well, now, mustn't keep you standing there. Allow me to open the gate."

As he tugged at the latch and swung the metal frame to the side, she looked past him at the car, expecting to see a driver behind the wheel. There was none, which startled her momentarily until she realized that the steering wheel was not where she expected it to be. She approached, and walked around the vehicle in awe. "My word! A Daimler, is it?"

"Rather old, I'm afraid. Nineteen sixty-something. I'm fond of it, though, and it does run well."

It was in mint condition, not a bit of rust, which she supposed would make it quite valuable. But it was one of those awfully German sort of cars with everything in the wrong place and on the wrong side. To her relief, it appeared to have an automatic transmission. Should she have need to drive it, it wouldn't be too much of a bother.

"Put bags in trunk now?" Kim Sam offered.

"Yes, please," Ms. Mare murmured. Leather bench seats, wooden dashboard; the car was a classic.

"You'd better wait on that," Mr. Nesselrode said.

Ms. Mare looked up. "I beg your pardon?"

"The bags," Mr. Nesselrode said, "just in case."

"In case of what?"

He smiled apologetically. "In case you decide not to stay after all."

She drew herself up. "And why should I decide that?"

"Most of them don't," he said. "Stay, that is. Come up to the house, and perhaps you'll understand why."

Ms. Mare sniffed dubiously. "If you say so. Kim Sam, would you please follow us?"

The taxi driver shrugged. "Your dime," he said with a grin.

"Kindly get in the car," Archimedes Nesselrode said, "and I'll lock the gates behind us. Just as a precaution."

Eccentric, indeed, she thought as she settled herself in the Daimler as instructed. The taxi drove in and waited. Watching the gates close behind him with a clang appeared to unsettled even the buoyant Kim Sam. As the artist got back in behind the wheel he explained, "I can't be too careful, you see. I used to have a dreadful problem with intruders, but not any more. Now I have to make certain that no one innocently blunders in here." He backed the car up to turn it around, edging past the taxi with somewhat nervous, unpracticed care.

"Mr. Shekle mentioned your 'security system'," she said, glancing over at him as he settled into navigating the Daimler back up the curving driveway. His profile emphasized a long, rather crooked nose and prominent Adam's apple. His skin was smooth and fair over fine bones, and his eyes were pale grey, almost silver. It was difficult to estimate his age.

"Yes, my security system," he chuckled. "It is quite effective, I must say. Sometimes a bit too effective, I fear."

They passed through the line of shrubberies and the grounds opened up into broad lawns being trimmed by a flock of sheep. Very small sheep, in assorted shades of blue, explaining what she had caught sight of before. "What unusual animals!" she exclaimed.

"Unique, and useful," he replied. "They keep the grass down. Ah, you were curious about my security system. Here she comes now. I'll introduce you."

There was a screeching of brakes as Kim Sam came to an abrupt halt behind them.

Vivian Mare stared in speechless astonishment at the creature which came trotting across the lawn to meet them. It was some twenty feet long including its whip-like tail, with blazing red eyes, green scales, sharp claws and fierce fangs. It crouched in front of the taxi and growled menacingly. But as soon as Archimedes Nesselrode got out of the Daimler, it went to him, a rumble strangely like a purr coming from its throat. It bumped its broad, flat head against his legs affectionately.

"Come on," he motioned to Ms. Mare.

She emerged from the car slowly, staring at her prospective employer as he stroked the scaly head of the monster. He grinned, his silver-blue eyes twinkling mischievously. "This is my basilisk. I assure you, once she knows you are part of the household, she'll protect you the same as she would me." He hesitated. "That is, if you still intend to become part of the household."

"Your basilisk," she said, mustering her wits with difficulty. She glanced back at Kim Sam, whose eyes and mouth were both wide open, and who was gesturing to her frantically to get back into the taxi and flee with him to safety. Ms. Mare turned to face the beast, thinking, *I have braved greater dangers in my time!* Although honestly, at that moment she could think of none to quite compare. "One of your creations?" she inquired, keeping her voice calm.

"Yes, indeed."

She took a deep breath. "Well, then. I needn't be afraid of burglars, need I?" Bracing herself, she took several steps towards the beast. It stopped purring and sniffed her tentatively.

"Good girl," he cooed to the basilisk. "Ms. Mare has come here to look after us. That is, if we don't frighten her overmuch." His gaze returned to Ms. Mare, awaiting her reaction with amused curiosity.

The basilisk resumed purring and thrust its nose towards Ms. Mare, who stood her ground, assuring herself that it did seem tame enough. She reached out a tentative hand and petted it gingerly. "Must cost a fortune to feed."

Archimedes Nesselrode laughed delightedly. The first test had, evidently, been passed.

They returned to the Daimler and he drove around to the side of the house, parking in front of a barn desperately in need of paint, whose sliding door had fallen off its track and hung half-way open. The house itself was in reasonable repair, but beginning to look a bit worse for wear. He accompanied her up to the side door. Kim Sam remained solidly in his taxi, making a point of reaching over to lock all doors before hunkering down to wait.

"I hardly ever use the front door," Archimedes Nesselrode said as they went up the steps. "I don't think I could even get it open. It sticks dreadfully. This goes directly into the kitchen. More handy for you, I'd guess."

"Most likely," she agreed. She stepped into the entryway, the door closing behind her. She caught her breath. The condition of the interior was appalling. She walked into the kitchen, expecting the worst, and was greeted by a scene beyond her expectations. They surprised half a dozen black monkey-like creatures tearing apart a loaf of bread on the kitchen table. Mr. Nesselrode shooed them away and regarded the mess unhappily.

"Are they your creations, too?" she asked.

"Oh, yes," he admitted. "They're terribly naughty, I'm afraid."

"Can't you do anything about it?"

"Not really," he said with a sigh. "All my creations have some measure of independence once I've made them. The marmosets have a bit more than one might prefer."

Ms. Mare surveyed the rest of the kitchen. The sink was piled high with dirty dishes, although a few clean ones in the drainer testified to a half-hearted attempt to tackle them. The stove was caked thick with burnt spills. Every surface was yellow with grease and every knob and handle was dark with fingerprints. She shuddered to think what horrors awaited her behind the grime-bespotted door of the refrigerator.

The floor hadn't been cleaned in weeks, perhaps months. Perhaps years. She peered into the dining room and the living room. There were broken dishes on the hutch. The windows were grimy and the curtains were soiled; on the sills were sadly overgrown and under-watered potted plants covered with brown leaves and dead branches. The corners of every room were thick with cobwebs and every unused surface was covered with dust.

"Dear, me," she murmured in dismay.

"I hope you don't find it all too, ah, *daunting,*" her prospective employer said.

She took a deep breath—which made her want to cough; the place was in dire need of airing out—pulled up her sleeves and folded her arms across her chest. "There is no task," she declared, "that I am not equal to, given sufficient time and resources." She turned to face him. "Where am I to stay?"

"Ah," he said eagerly, "you should find your room quite pleasant. Heron and I worked hard to get it ready."

"Heron?"

"Yes. You'll be meeting her presently. She's a bit stern, but don't let her intimidate you."

"I am not easily intimidated, Mr. Nesselrode."

"So I see. Well, this way. Mind the starfish."

"Starfish?" Sure enough, there was a enormous starfish in the middle of the hallway, a sort of cinnamon gold color with blue spots along the ridge of each arm. It was as big around as a good-sized throw rug and high as a hassock. "Starfish," she confirmed aloud to herself, eying it warily as she circumambulated it. It made no threatening gestures.

On the table in the hallway sat a long-haired, orange and white cat who stood up, stretched, and jumped into the artist's arms as he walked by. It climbed up onto his shoulder, purring.

"Is that one of your creations, too?"

"Oh, no!" he laughed. "Madam Beast is just an ordinary cat." He stroked her head. "Forgive me, my lovely. I shouldn't call you ordinary, should I? No. You are hardly ordinary, are you?" He started up the stairs. "I have seven cats at the moment. All acquired in quite the normal way. Strays. They wandered in and made themselves at home. My basilisk didn't prevent their entry. In fact, I rather suspect she encouraged them. She's fond of cats. She got that from me, I suppose. On the other hand, the Bishop dislikes them. He spends most of his time in the silver teapot on the dining room table, contemplating the Divine nature or some such thing. But he insists on blessing all the meals. He comes out of the teapot, muttering Latin, and everyone must put down their forks. The cats ignore him, of course. That annoys the Bishop to no end. But you simply can't tell a cat what to do. Not even if you are a bishop. Cats are thoroughly Pagan creatures."

"Yes, of course," Ms. Mare replied as she threaded her way carefully up the stairs, which were piled high with stacks of envelopes and papers. "What *is* all this?" she asked, catching a tower which started to fall when she brushed against it.

"Oh, mail mostly," he said cheerfully. "Don't worry, it's not important. Frank Shekle's office takes care of the important things, and disposes of the disturbing matters. He sends the rest to me. Dreadfully dull, most of it. Copies of documents, accounts, nonsense. Letters from people I don't know. I'm not sure quite what to do with it."

"One generally either files it away or throws it out," Ms. Mare said.

"Oh. Yes. I suppose one would." The notion had evidently never occurred to him.

They reached the top of the stairs and went to the end of the hall. He opened the door and led her in. "Here we go!" he said, and shooed a large, emerald green lobster off the bed. It clacked its claws irritably.

Efforts had indeed been made to welcome her; the room was clean, aired out and uncluttered. It was a pleasant room, rather old-fashioned in its decor. A spacious wardrobe made up for its lack of closet space. There was a dark cherry wood bureau and a matching dressing table with seat, an ornate mirror hanging over it. Two tall windows overlooked the lawn and another overgrown flower garden. Ms. Mare made a mental note that she would have to do something about that garden. She couldn't abide having to look out on it every day in its current state of neglect.

"The bath is through here," he said, opening a door. She inspected it. The tile was new, an agreeable shade of blue. The fixtures looked charmingly antique although the plumbing appeared to be in good repair; a test of the faucet produced a robust stream of water without any ominous clanks or shudders. She noted with approval the deep, claw-footed tub. She enjoyed a proper bath. There was a medicine cabinet and small but adequate linen closet. The towels had seen better days. They were white with pink trim. She detested pink.

Returning to the bed chamber, she said, "It will do, although I wish I had a proper writing desk."

Nesselrode frowned. "A desk. Of course. By all means, do look into it. Something nice that will go with the room. How much do you think it would cost? Would a thousand cover it?"

Her eyes widened. "Well, I hardly think—"

He waved his hand in dismissal. "I have no head for the cost of things. I'll leave it to you. Just have the bill sent to Frank. Oh, and do let me know when they plan to deliver it. I'll need to give the basilisk the afternoon off."

"Yes. Of course," Ms. Mare replied, "It would hardly do to have the delivery men eaten by a basilisk."

"Then," he inquired hopefully, "you will be staying?"

"I believe so," she said, nodding.

"Praise the numina!" he exclaimed, jubilant. "I'll assist you with your suitcases!"

"I should think not, Mr. Nesselrode," she said, marching past him out of the room. "That is *my* job."

"Oh, yes," he said meekly, standing aside.

"I shall require compensation for the driver. I expect he's due a handsome tip."

She followed Kim Sam down to the gate in the Daimler. She wouldn't have minded riding down in the taxi and enjoying a brisk walk back after letting him through the gate, but she was not yet quite certain about the basilisk. As he drove past her, Kim Sam rolled down the window and said to her with heartfelt sincerity, "Good luck, lady. You gonna need it!"

Later, as Ms. Mare was unpacking her clothes, she noticed she was being observed by a stern heron about four feet tall wearing spectacles and a hoop skirt with a very large bustle. Ms. Mare greeted her politely. "You must be Heron. I am pleased to meet you."

The heron sniffed with disapproval, fluffing her feathers, and sailed away from the door with a highly superior air. "Well!" Ms. Mare exclaimed to herself, "At the very least, I expect I shall have no fear of boredom."

CHAPTER TWO

The Household

Ms. Mare spent the next few days familiarizing herself with her territory. Mr. Nesselrode hovered about, alternately solicitous and nervous at her presence. The house was rather old, a three-storey New Englander with a connected back house which was used for storage, and a barn, which belonged to the sheep and the basilisk. A converted carriage house next to the barn served as a garage for the Daimler. The house was reasonably sound, although the exterior could use a good scraping and a coat of paint. The shingles on the roof were a bit worn in spots. When she asked him, he admitted that in the ten years he had been living there he had done not a thing for maintenance. Ms. Mare clucked and shook her head. He certainly did need a housekeeper in the largest sense.

Her territory did not include the third floor. The door at the top of the back stairs was boarded up and the door at the bottom of the front stairs was shut tight. His studio was on the third floor and he did not require her services up there. She was informed of this quite firmly. As to the running of the rest of the house, he was at a loss. He offered her no instructions aside from respecting his creations, evidently content to let her use her own judgement.

"I understand that a vehicle would be available for my use," she said. "That wouldn't be the Daimler, would it?"

"Oh, yes! I hope you don't mind. It's a very good car. Never given me a speck of trouble. That's fortunate, since I don't know the first thing about mechanics."

Rather an extravagance, she thought, such a car being used for common errands. "Well, I expect I'll get used to it. Could you be so kind as to instruct me where to find basic services in the nearest town?"

He looked puzzled. "What do you mean?"

"Where do you do your shopping, Mr. Nesselrode? And do you pick up your mail or is it delivered?"

"Everything is delivered," he said. "I never go out."

"I beg your pardon?"

"Ms. Mare, I never leave the grounds of this estate. This is my sanctuary."

"You never leave?" she echoed incredulously. "Why—what about the car?"

"I drive it down to the gate to pick up the delivery of my mail and groceries. Periodically, a man comes and takes it to a garage where they fill the tank with gasoline and do whatever it is one does to cars, and they return it."

"And you never leave the property?"

"I haven't for ten years," he explained. "Whatever I need, I call and I arrange to have it delivered. You see, I can't leave. It isn't safe for me out there."

"I see," she said, not really seeing at all, her curiosity further piqued. But her employer chose not to elaborate.

The most daunting task that faced her was figuring out where to begin. In the first week she made three trips to the local transfer station, the trunk of the Daimler filled with bags of trash. It was clearly a trip that neither the Daimler nor any vehicle acting on behalf of the Nesselrode household had ever made before. The job was complicated by the fact that the towering piles of mostly unopened mail on the stairs were an indiscriminant mixture of junk and possibly important documents and receipts. She contacted Frank Shekle's office and was assured that they were quite aware of her employer's lack of appreciation for proper record-keeping, and a complete file of all necessary documents was kept on his behalf by the firm.

And, by the way, how was the situation working out? they tactfully inquired. Ms. Mare told the secretary to inform Mr. Shekle that the situation was just fine, quite adequately under control, thank you very much.

There were personal letters, also mostly unopened, some with intriguing return addresses. Her employer seemed to have blithely ignored some significant individuals in the art world and beyond. When she brought these to his attention, he dismissed them as unimportant. Anything he cared about he had already taken upstairs. So into the black plastic bags it all went, along with the cereal boxes she found behind the couch, the trimmings from the neglected house plants, and the cushions which the cats had shredded and soiled.

A reconnaissance of the town was necessary to locate such things as the supermarket, bank, library and drug store. Most businesses were conveniently within a few blocks of one another except for the supermarket, which was in the next town. However, there was a charming Mom and Pop market with gas pumps out front which would do for any small item she might need in a hurry. She stopped at the post office to explain that she was newly in the employ of Archimedes Nesselrode, showing documents to prove it, and informing them that she would now be picking up his mail. The postmaster regarded her with a mixture of pity and awe. She received the impression that as soon as she departed, the postmaster and his assistants would be gathering in the back to take bets on how long she'd last.

Admittedly, she did have her moments of doubt, such as the first time the winged snake flew past her through the living room. Its sudden appearance startled her so badly that she dropped a bucket of wash water and then stumbled over it. Sitting in the midst of the soapy mess, Ms. Mare questioned whether she really did enjoy being in a household quite this interesting.

It was not so different from any other household in that there was dusting to do, windows to be washed, rugs to be vacuumed and floors to be swept—but her first efforts at these normally routine tasks brought the Augean Stables to mind. Her initial shopping trip included purchasing many of the elementary tools of her trade, which seemed never to have existed in her employer's house. A mop, for example. Dust cloths and furniture polish. A non-fossilized sponge.

Once she had excavated its components from their sediment of dirt and debris, the household proved unusually tricky to manage. She learned that she needed to keep the cabinets tightly closed or the black marmosets would get in and tear open the cracker boxes. She couldn't leave food unattended in the kitchen; the cats were nearly as undisciplined as the marmosets. She had to be careful not to trip over the starfish which crawled leisurely along the floor from room to room. And the repeated appearances of the winged snake drove home the futility of having any sort of breakable dish or vase on display.

Her employer, if not much of a help, was at least not a hindrance. When she could track him down for approval of a decision on some household matter, he deferred to her. Apart from the health and welfare of his cats and his sundry creations-in-residence, he seemed utterly indifferent to anything that went on beneath the third floor.

Heron, on the other hand, made her disapproval clear in spite of the fact that she never spoke a word. It was remarkable how much meaning she could communicate with a squawk, clack of the beak, or avian glare. She did not like the way Ms. Mare positioned the furniture, nor how she arranged the linen closet, nor how she organized the kitchen, right down to the order of the silverware in the drawer. The household possessed no clothes dryer, things apparently meant to be hung on a clothes line and dried in the sun, a healthful practice which Ms. Mare had no quarrel with. She found it most convenient to store the bag of clothes pins on a hook to the right of the washing machine. However that was not, to Heron's mind, where they belonged, and Ms. Mare consistently found them moved to the table by the utility room door where they had been before. Similar subtle rearrangements occurred with the linens and the silverware. Ms. Mare suspected that Heron was in league with the marmosets.

Archimedes Nesselrode could not care less where the linens or the clothes pins were kept. He didn't care if his clothes were ironed or not, although most of what he wore an iron would be wasted on. Ms. Mare adjusted to the impossibility of trying to make his bed, since her employer kept extremely irregular hours and was as likely as not to be in it. She learned not to bother to fix breakfast or lunch until he appeared and asked for it. He ate like a bird at meals, but evidently was in the habit of raiding the kitchen in the middle of the night. So she tried to make certain there was always an assortment to raid from.

Dinner, curiously enough, was a daily ritual never to be missed. He sometimes showed up at the last moment in his dressing gown and slippers with his hair tousled, but he always appeared. The requisite evening meal was to be served in the dining room, and was always blessed by the bishop in the silver tea pot. The cats—all seven—ate with them, each with his or her own dish served on a place mat on the table. Dinner was one of the few things her employer did care about, so she made every attempt to cooperate with his requests, unorthodox as they seemed to her. But then again, why should dinner depart from the general chaos and unorthodoxy which seemed to be the norm for the household?

For instance, her employer insisted that Ms. Mare join them at the table for the meal, in spite of her protests that this was quite irregular. He sat at one end of the table and she at the opposite end. He always waited politely for her to finish serving and did not began eating until she was settled in her place, an arrangement which took her quite a bit of getting used to. Heron and the winged snake also joined them at the table. They ate politely, but of course never spoke, which left the conversing to Ms. Mare and Mr. Nesselrode. Generally, they made small talk. He often asked about the weather or, curiously, the phases of the moon. She discussed with him matters concerning the running of the house. She asked if the starfish could be induced to go somewhere other than living room when she needed to clean there, and was there something that could be done about the marmosets? The condition of the curtains was really quite deplorable, and did she have leave to replace them? Could the little striped emus be put outside? They kept trying to nest in the flower pots. Should she air out his room, and did he want his bed changed? If so, when could she count on him not being in it?

He promised he would have a word with the marmosets—not that he expected it would do any good—but the starfish pretty much did as it wished. The flower pots were expressly for the use of the emus, and they should not be disturbed. By all means, purchase new curtains; whatever she thought was best. And Tuesday around two o'clock she could do his room.

As much as she might have wished to, Ms. Mare could not very well bring up the issue of her conflicts with Heron while the bird was sitting there at the table. It would simply have to wait until she had an opportunity to speak to him in confidence.

One evening, she brought up the subject of hiring more help. "A cook, for instance," she suggested.

"A cook?" He looked up at her puzzled. "I can find no fault with your cooking."

"You are very kind to say so," she replied. "However, I am not accustomed to the role. Every household in which I have previously served has been fully staffed, including a cook. And, I may add, when there were grounds to be looked after, the staff included a gardener."

He waved his fork dismissively. "I don't much care about the condition of the grounds. The sheep keep the lawns mowed, and the hedges are welcome to grow as dense and wild as they please, the better to discourage intruders."

"Well, I suppose that is your affair," she said with thinly veiled disapproval.

"Ms. Mare, it was difficult enough finding you. Besides, I do not think Heron would approve. She only grudgingly accepted the necessity of hiring a housekeeper in the first place." He nodded towards the bespectacled bird, who agreed with a stern bob of her head, and a glance towards Ms. Mare which communicated that she was still not entirely persuaded on the wisdom of it. He returned to the precise task of placing equal portions of stuffing and sole onto his fork to be conveyed to his mouth.

"Your confidence in my abilities is flattering, however, proper management of a household of this particular sort requires more than one person."

He regarded her with frank sympathy. "It is a difficult household, I know." He brightened. "Perhaps you could ask Heron to help you out a bit more. I know she has been feeling rather at loose ends of late, since she used to do much of what was done around the house before you came. Oh, I know, she isn't really well suited to some tasks, but I'm sure she could be of service."

Ms. Mare and Heron looked at each other dubiously.

"And perhaps the marmosets could be taught simple chores," Mr. Nesselrode continued, oblivious to the cool reception his previous suggestion had gotten. "They are really very clever, you know, and useful occupation might help to keep them out of trouble."

"I am rather skeptical of that," Ms. Mare understated.

"Oh, well. Simply do the best you can, Ms. Mare, and don't bother yourself with the rest. I am quite happy with all you do, since quite frankly, it is far better than having no one at all."

Well, that certainly could not be denied. He was adamant, so she resigned herself to the situation. In some ways, it *was* easier simply to handle things herself. Dealing with even a small staff could be a terrible trial, since it seemed very few people had a proper work ethic and pride in service nowadays. Always ready to complain about the slightest inconvenience or perceived violation of their "rights," never willing to go even an inch out of their way, over their time, or outside of their job description. She'd had a dreadful time of it in other positions, trying to supervise inadequate and incompetent help, finding no one worth a damn to replace them no matter how hard she searched. Very well then, she would do it all herself. Since her employer had very simple expectations, she could work at her own pace, and needed only to satisfy herself. Really an agreeable arrangement she had to admit.

But if Mr. Nesselrode's expectations weren't demanding, Ms. Mare's were. There were certain standards she felt it necessary to maintain, and it was not easy to maintain them. It often strained her patience.

Finally her patience was strained to the breaking point.

The normal routine had been disrupted by the delivery of the desk she had purchased. She had spent a day hunting in second-hand shops. Certainly something new would never do; modern furniture had no personality and was made cheaply, never mind what one actually paid for it. Besides, Mr. Nesselrode had specifically said it should go with the room. So she settled on a charming Queen Anne style desk which was in excellent shape, except for a small chip off the back leg, a few scratches and slight tarnish on the hardware which a bit of stern polishing could no doubt remedy. The finish was not too dissimilar from what was in her room, and the price was most reasonable. The pigeon holes would require a thorough cleaning. But then it would be quite serviceable. She made arrangements for delivery.

But the basilisk refused to leave her post until Mr. Nesselrode himself came down to order her away to the pond. Then the poor delivery men nearly tripped over the starfish as they carried the desk through the hall, and the black marmosets were horrible, stealing the shorter man's hat and trying to ride on the shoulders of the taller one. Most embarrassing. In the end, the desk was installed with only one additional scratch, due to a cat running underfoot and upsetting their balance. Ms. Mare tipped the delivery men handsomely for their trouble.

Fuss and bother, and still her chores to be done with half the morning wasted. She hurried to the laundry room, pausing to lean out the window and scold one of the marmosets, which she spied up in the maple tree, still sporting the poor delivery man's hat. The insufferable little imp chittered back at her in deliberate mockery.

Slamming the window down and cursing most unbecomingly, she continued on to the next task on her list. Her progress was again interfered with by a puddle of cat vomit which she discovered in a most unpleasant way, necessitating going outside to clean her shoe off at the tap, then returning to clean up the remainder of the puddle.

Archimedes Nesselrode

"And here it is a Tuesday, and past two o'clock, and if I don't get up there to attend to making Mr. Nesselrode's bed, I'll have lost the opportunity for yet another week. How a person can be so indifferent to basic sleep hygiene, I shall never comprehend!"

She went to the linen closet to fetch the sheets, discovering that once again everything had be reorganized, sorted by color instead of by type. Fuming, she dug beneath the towels in search of sheets and a pillow case, finally having to pull the whole business off the shelf in order to get what she needed.

At which point she dropped it all with a scream. There was a spider sitting on top of the linens. Not just an ordinary spider, but one as big as a cat and just as shaggy, with red, white and gold bands all along its body.

Ms. Mare could not abide spiders. She had once suffered a traumatic encounter with a goliath bird-eating spider in South America. The guide and Mr. Galbraith had left camp to search for firewood, and little Vivian had followed them. She spied an armadillo rooting about in the leaf litter and darted after it. Tripping, she fell very nearly on top of the monstrous spider, which hissed at her and gave her a nasty bite. "No danger to humans," the guide assured them soothingly as the child sobbed in her mother's arms, but the bite swelled up and stung terribly for days, and she got a horrid itchy rash from where she had touched the thing.

Ms. Mare had learned to steel herself against the common pests she inevitably encountered in the course of her duties, and had had a great deal of practice in her battles with the accumulated cobwebs in that particular household. But this nightmare aberration was far beyond anything with which she could reasonably be expected to cope.

"Mr. Nesselrode!" She charged to the bottom of the attic stairs. "Mr. Nesselrode!"

"Gracious," he said, hurrying down the steps, "What is the matter?"

Ms. Mare led him back to the linen closet. "Is <u>that</u> one of <u>yours</u>?" she demanded.

"Ah, yes. Isn't she a beauty? Perfectly harmless, of course. Aren't you, Arachne?" He picked the spider up, petting its back.

"Get rid of it, if you please!"

He gaped at her in astonishment. "Get rid of it?"

"Yes. Un-create it, put it in a cube and sell it, whatever! But I will *not* have that horror in the house!"

Archimedes Nesselrode bristled. "I beg your pardon. I do *not* un-create things, nor would I put my lovely Arachne in a cube and sell her! Those cubes are mere bubbles I blow to amuse the public! A sacrifice of trifles to satisfy the likes of Frank Shekle! Arachne is *not* a trifle!"

"No, she is a dreadfully monstrous spider! Mr. Nesselrode, I have tolerated the black marmosets stealing the potatoes for dinner, the winged snake knocking the dishes off the hutch, cleaning up after the cats, tripping over the starfish, finding the lobster in my bath, and putting up with Heron criticizing everything from my choice of curtains to the arrangement of the flowers in the vases, and undoing my work behind my back. But I cannot tolerate this! Either she goes, or I go!"

"You can't be serious!"

"I most certainly am!" She folded her arms across her chest and regarded him severely.

"Pish!" He put the spider on his shoulder and sailed aloofly out of the room. "I'll not be told what I can and cannot create in my own house!"

She demonstrated to him just how serious she was when she came down the stairs with her coat on and her bags packed. Heron hastily fetched the artist, who met Ms. Mare in the front hallway.

"Ms. Mare! You can't leave!" he cried in alarm.

"I can, and I will."

"B-but, how will I manage?"

"That is your affair. I am calling a taxi."

"Oh this is dreadful! A calamity! Ms. Mare, you mustn't leave! What if I kept Arachne in my studio? Yes, yes, she'd be no trouble to you there. Would you stay then? Please? Oh, please, you simply *must* stay!"

His hands were clasped, his expression desperate, his silver-blue eyes pleading. Behind him, the marmosets were peeking out anxiously from behind the drapes. The Bishop lifted the lid of the teapot, frowning, and Heron was watching from the kitchen doorway with concern.

Vivian Mare sighed. "I do apologize for the remark regarding your spider. Naturally I could not expect you to un-make one of your creations. Keeping it in your studio would be an acceptable compromise."

"Very well. I'll see to it immediately. Now, where has she gotten to?" He spotted Arachne under a table. Ms. Mare shuddered at the sight of it. He coaxed it out, then picked it up, setting it onto the table and kneeling down to look straight in its eight shiny black eyes. "Arachne, my lovely, you must listen carefully."

The spider regarded him solemnly.

"Ms. Mare dislikes you, I'm afraid," he said with regret. "Some people are terribly afraid of spiders. That's simply the way it is. We must be understanding. You must promise me that you will not come back down again. If you do, Ms. Mare might leave us. We cannot allow that to happen. Do you promise, Arachne?"

The spider gracefully waved its two furry front legs in acquiescence.

"She promises," he said, looking up at the housekeeper hopefully.

"Thank you." Ms. Mare paused. "However, it is more than simply the spider."

"What else, then?" he asked solicitously.

"You intend for me to be in charge of this household, am I correct?"

"Absolutely. Yes, yes, that was the arrangement."

"Then I am going to need to have my authority respected. Not only by the basilisk, but by your other creations as well."

"Has there been an issue?" he inquired with surprise. "Oh, well, I know the basilisk was reluctant to leave her post, but that is only because she is so protective of me, and has not quite adjusted to you yet. I shall speak to her. But, what other problems could there be?"

Ms. Mare shot a meaningful look at Heron, who ruffled her feathers and affected a look of aloof incomprehension. "I must insist that my decisions regarding the organization of this household not by undermined by those in it. That includes the kitchen, the linens, and the laundry room!"

"Oh, dear me. Heron, have you been a bother?"

The bird clacked her beak indignantly.

"I know," Mr. Nesselrode said, "and I do appreciate that, but if we expect Ms. Mare to do her job, we must allow her to do it as she sees fit."

Heron squawked defensively.

"Of course, you have your own ideas, and when it was your job, I know you did the best you could. Really, it's my fault. I was not terribly sensible when I created you. I might have given you hands or something. But that wouldn't have been right, would it? No, I made you to be just as you ought to be. You are Heron, and perfectly so. It is as we discussed: we need someone who can take care of us all, someone admirably suited to the role, as you are perfectly Heron and the basilisk is perfectly the basilisk. Yes, yes, do you see? Ms. Mare is just as she should be, and we mustn't go about fussing that she ought to be different."

Heron summoned her dignity and straightened the folds of her apron with her beak.

Ms. Mare added by way of diplomacy, "I would, of course, welcome assistance from the more experienced members of the household. It is, after all, a great deal to manage and one sometimes wishes one might have help."

Heron regarded Ms. Mare with a kind of cool graciousness which implied a willingness to give the matter consideration.

Archimedes Nesselrode smiled broadly. "There! It's all understood. Is this satisfactory to you then, Ms. Mare?"

"What about the marmosets?" she asked him sternly.

His smile faded and his shoulders sagged slightly. "Oh, dear."

"Never mind," Ms. Mare said, putting down her suitcases, "One can't expect everything. You have been most gracious, Mr. Nesselrode. I believe I shall stay." She took off her coat and folded it over her arm.

The Bishop withdrew into the teapot, Heron sailed away into the kitchen, and the marmosets disappeared, no doubt off to seek mischief.

Ms. Mare went upstairs and unpacked. The lobster assisted her.

CHAPTER THREE

Discoveries

"What is this delightful concoction you have set before me?" Mr. Nesselrode asked, sampling the dessert.

"Peaches in wine syrup with a sweet yogurt sauce," Ms. Mare explained. One of her more ambitious culinary efforts, she was quite pleased at how it came out. "It's a Spanish recipe."

"Ah, Andalusia! A most romantic and intriguing land!"

"I quite agree. I wish I'd been older when I traveled there. I was far too young to appreciate it. Did you know that 'Andalusia' comes from the Arabic, 'Al Andalus' which means 'land of the vandals'?"

"Goodness, no!" he exclaimed. "Really? And I understood it to be such a civilized place under the Moors!"

"Well, Cordova wasn't built in a day. I believe when the Moorish Arabs first settled in southern Spain it was every bit as nasty and brutish as the rest of Europe. Within two centuries, though, it had become the most civilized place in the world. They had books and libraries, lovely gardens, paved streets and decent plumbing. It was the Arabs, by the way, who first introduced peaches to Spanish soil."

He gazed at her with admiration. "How on earth do you come up with such interesting facts?"

"I read up on Spain last year," she explained. "You see, the Galbraiths—they are my mother's employers—toured the Iberian Peninsula, and I always like to find out about whatever part of the world they find themselves in."

"How fascinating! Let me see now, Galbraith, hmm...." He cocked his head. "Don't they write books? About going to all sorts of exotic places?"

"Why, yes, that's right. Have you read any of them?"

"No," he admitted. "But I have heard of them. I wasn't always so very isolated from the world!"

Ms. Mare seized this opening. "It must be very interesting being an artist. I expect you've led quite an eventful life."

"Hardly!" he snorted. "Dull as dishwater! I've never even been out of the country! Do tell me about your visit to Spain!" He leaned forward on his elbows avidly.

"As I said, I'm afraid I was quite young at the time. My most vivid memory is being dragged through the Museo Thyssen-Bornemisza in Madrid, my mother and the Galbraiths breathlessly admiring the artwork, which mostly seemed to be endless interpretations of the Virgin Mary. All I wanted was to escape outside and run through the dusty streets to the market and get some fried pastry. Oh, and the Prado. I recall looking at this portrait of an astonishingly ugly man and wondering who would ever want to paint his picture."

"One of the Hapsburgs, no doubt," Nesselrode murmured. "But, do tell me more!"

As she did the washing up in the kitchen after dinner, she thought to herself that it really was quite understandable. Ten years of solitude in this house, with only his mute creations for company; no wonder the poor man was starved for intelligent conversation. It was rather to be expected that he might want his housekeeper to join him at the dinner table. Not really so extraordinary after all. And it was quite pleasant, sharing her reminiscences and interests with such an appreciative audience. He was well-educated, if not well-traveled, or at least he was able to converse as if he were. A congenial companion. For all his eccentricities, quite a delightful gentleman.

She stopped herself, realizing that she was smiling and thinking in far too familiar terms about her employer.

This, she told herself sternly, would never do.

* * *

On Thursdays, Ms. Mare went into town. It was agreed to be her day off, but she found it convenient to run household errands and do the shopping while she was out on her own time. There was so very much to do at the house, she disliked taking more time from it than she had to.

She also disliked driving the Daimler, and muttered very uncomplimentary things about it whenever she was behind its wheel. Although she had learned to drive in Great Britain, that had been a very long time ago. Most of her adult life had been spent driving in the United States, in cars adapted for the right side of the road. Having the steering wheel where she didn't expect it caught her nearly every time she got into the car, requiring a tedious circumambulation to the other side. The alternative was sliding across the seat, which twisted her skirt uncomfortably. Also, being an antique, it was missing many of the amenities, or had them located in unexpected places.

She did have to admit, however, that it was a quite reliable car, and as she grew used to it, her slanders against it grew fewer. Like most everything else in the Nesselrode household, it grew on her.

Today's errands included a trip to the public library. Her mother and the Galbraiths were currently in Belize. Ms. Mare was delighted to find a very good article on the country in a current issue of National Geographic, which she had borrowed and was now returning. The Galbraiths didn't go adventuring as much as they used to, but they still liked to find exotic parts of the world to lodge for a few months at a time, moving on when the spirit urged them. Ms. Mare corresponded with them faithfully, although occasionally their letters did a bit of adventuring on their own as a result of frequent moves by both parties.

Ms. Mare had always left her employers on good terms, and made certain she gave no cause for complaint, but she found she could not remain in one place for very long. As soon as the challenges of a new position lapsed into routine, she became bored, and Ms. Mare could not abide boredom anymore than she could abide a dirty dish. Fortunately, she lived in an era where competent domestic help was in great demand, and she had no difficulty finding new situations. As a result, her address changed nearly as often as her mother's did.

While she was at the library it occurred to her that perhaps she should do a bit of non-geographical research. She had never really had the leisure (or, truth be told, the interest) to follow current events all that much, and had only the most superficial awareness of the popular phenomenon of Archimedes Nesselrode and his creations. As much as her employer loved to hear her talk about her own lively past, he was reluctant to talk about himself. Mr. Shekle had implied Archimedes Nesselrode was quite famous, so the chances were excellent that his own reticence had not been matched by the press. She asked at the reference desk, and was well-rewarded for her efforts. The better part of the afternoon was spent satisfying some of her curiosity concerning her employer.

On her way home, she stopped at the drugstore for stationery. She must write to her mother and the Galbraiths about this.

Her day's duties completed, the cabinets secured against the marmosets, the refrigerator restocked with delicatessen items for her employer's late-night raiding, her latest conflict with Heron settled (the order of the cats' placemats on the dining room table was not to be changed, and Ms. Mare acquiesced; one must choose one's battles), she settled at her Queen Anne desk, took out the stationery and a good pen, and began to write.

"My dearest Mother,

"Your last letter, though tantalizingly brief, was welcome in that I now have a reliable address to send you mail. I expect my last letter will catch up with you eventually, so I will not repeat at length everything that was in it. Suffice to say that I have finally found a position that provides a genuine challenge to me, in the employ of the artist, Archimedes Nesselrode. It is the most extraordinary household (details in my other letter) and I have sole charge of it. Let me say that some of the more egregious irritations I mention have since been addressed, at least in part, so do not allow them to concern you.

"Today I did a bit of research about my employer, who is highly unusual, even for an artist. No, I was not snooping, which of course would not be appropriate. As Mr. Nesselrode is a public figure, I confined myself to what was available in the press, and that was more than enough. I expect you have heard of him, but not knowing how much, I'll share what I've learned about it. It's all quite intriguing!

"The Nesselrodes were an aristocratic family who emigrated to the United States from Europe and became prominent figures in the exclusive New York upper class. They made and maintained their fortune through the importation and authentication of works of art. Young Archimedes had governesses and tutors and all manner of privilege. He was described in one article as a wayward child with a fantastical imagination, gifted at an early age. He was, of course, sent to the very best academies of art, where he frustrated everyone by refusing to follow the prescribed curriculum, instead taking full advantage of the opportunity to play with every artistic medium he could get his hands on. One former instructor spoke of how the young man was failing academically, but producing astonishing pieces with very little effort. To watch him work was intriguing and baffling. He seemed able to coax clay into any shape he liked with a casual touch. He blended pigments in the most haphazard and technically incompetent manner imaginable, yet they turned out precisely the way he wanted them to. He wielded a hammer and chisel in a fashion that made his instructors grimace and gnash their teeth, yet the stone invariably broke perfectly. Even after he had flunked out and ought to have been sent packing, he was permitted to continue puttering around the academy workshops simply because he was such an anomaly. Apparently, he eventually floated off of his own volition.

"There was a period of some years where he seemed to be doing nothing in particular that anyone could trace, at least I could find nothing specific about it, just that he was orbiting erratically in his parents' circles, causing them no end, it was implied, of grief and despair at his inability to apply himself usefully to anything. Then the first of his "creations" appeared on the market. They were an overnight sensation. He became a celebrity, a state of affairs which didn't suit him very well. He couldn't handle money, had no sense of responsibility and never showed up where he was supposed to, all of which meshes quite plausibly with my employer as I've come to know him. There were scandals, lawsuits, and raging controversy, ending in the artist's abrupt disappearance from the public eye.

"I could find no photographs of him any more recent than ten years ago, which supports his claim that he has not left this house in over a decade. The ones I was able to find are quite singular. At the height of his notoriety, his flamboyance rivaled the antics of Dali and Warhol. He sported hair half-way down his back, outrageous outfits and make-up, and quite frankly, looked more like a rock star than an artist. Experts have speculated feverishly on his methods, all without success; futile efforts have been made to debunk him as a fraud. High-brow circles dismissed him as a charlatan at worst, and at best, a mere pop-culture phenomenon. His parents disowned him and left the country. His name was linked romantically with an astonishing assortment of actresses, heiresses, singers and assorted flotsam, including the famed operatic diva Zarah Trebbiano, to whom he became engaged. Abruptly, before the engagement could progress to its ultimate consummation, he dropped out of sight. He surfaced nearly a year later in the house where he is presently living, now the fanatic recluse in whose employ I now find myself."

She paused, looking up and reflecting on the magazine photograph of the youthful Mr. Nesselrode, eye shadow and glitter on his face, posing in an emerald green tuxedo and black cape next to a large Lucite cube containing a grinning griffin with golden wings. The expression on his face was almost mocking; grand, mysterious, canny and cool, Archimedes

Nesselrode as a superior being privy to secrets unattainable by the ordinary mortal. This monstre sacré was utterly unlike the gentle, timid soul she knew, and yet, unmistakably, it was he.

She returned to her letter.

"I must get to bed now. Do please give the Galbraiths my love, and write to me as soon as you can. I am reading all about Belize, and look forward to your account of it.

"love always,

"Vivian."

***

Ms. Mare was recounting a boating trip she had once taken up the Prince Regent River in Australia to visit King's Cascade, a spectacular waterfall quite remote from civilization, which was more recently the site of a famous attack on an American model by the deadly Australian estuarine crocodile. Her employer listened, rapt, until finally she said, "Really, Mr. Nesselrode, it is getting late. I ought to clear."

"Ah, yes," he agreed unhappily with a glance at the clock on the wall. "I suppose you must. But, tell me, do you play backgammon?"

"Yes, of course," she said, standing up and commencing to stack plates and gather silverware, "although I confess I haven't done so for some time."

"Would you join me for a game after you've taken care of things? I believe there is a set in the living room somewhere."

Ms. Mare considered. "There is a games table in the corner near the glassed-in bookcase. I recall coming across it when I was cleaning in there. It polished up quite nicely. Its drawer contains a number of game pieces, quite possibly including backgammon."

"Excellent!" he said, rubbing his hands together. "I shall go and see!"

"I had planned on getting a number of other chores done this evening," Ms. Mare said hesitantly, "but if you insist..."

"Surely your chores will keep until tomorrow," the artist said. "I would be so pleased if we could play!"

Playing backgammon with her employer! She shook her head as she rinsed the dishes off and put the pan to soak in the sink. First she was expected to dine with him, then to play games with him. All highly irregular. And yet, it seemed cruel to deny what was, after all, a harmless enough request.

"I shall consider it simply a part of my job," she decided. "He is lonely. An ordinary game of backgammon to pass the time. No harm in it at all. And it will be a pleasant diversion. Certainly I have earned it."

He had found the table and dragged it out into the room, and was putting in place a peacock chair piled with cushions for himself. The table had an inlaid playing surface which could be lifted and turned over, a chessboard on one side and a backgammon board on the other. He had it set up and gestured to her eagerly.

"Come, come! Oh, this is such fun! Can I pour you a brandy perhaps?"

"No, thank you, Mr. Nesselrode," she declined politely, selecting a comfortable seat for herself and bringing it over. Settling down, she examined the board, trying to recall how to play. "I see that I am brown. Where are my dice?"

"Here in the cup. Wait a moment, I need someone to roll for me. The Bishop? No, he would not approve of games of chance. Heron could, I suppose, although her beak is not well-suited...Snake! Snake, would you roll for me? You can manage a dice cup with your tail, surely."

The winged snake slithered over and demonstrated that she could.

"Why must you have someone roll for you?" Ms. Mare asked curiously.

"It wouldn't be fair if I rolled the dice myself," he replied. "It would completely eliminate the element of chance. Now then, let us begin!"

***

One evening an event of surpassing strangeness occurred, which in that household was an achievement indeed. Ms. Mare had been asleep and dreaming—one of those improbable dreams where she was hurrying through rooms that never existed in a house where she had not been in years, answering a summons which she could not remember hearing but which she suddenly realized she had shamefully neglected. She heard music, and was startled to find herself in the midst of a dance in a small village in Croatia.

Then something woke her. She sat up in bed, gradually recollecting where she was, the dream fading except for the music. It was a warm evening so her window was open, and she could clearly hear something going on outside. Curious, she got up and looked out.

The moon was high and bright in the sky, illuminating the extraordinary scene below. A sea horse, balanced on its tail, which coiled to make a pedestal on the ground, was playing some sort of horn, while a plump badger with an elegant plumed hat played upon a flute. An iguana with a great, glittering crest beat upon a drum, and dancing about waving a ribboned tambourine was a creature with an armadillo head and a terrapin body, reminiscent of the mock turtle out of Alice's Wonderland. The music they produced was a gay medieval air to which her employer, wearing only a dressing gown and slippers, was dancing. His partner was a fox in a billowing skirt, twirling on her hind feet. They were surrounded by an entourage of fabulous creatures: several birds with beautiful plumage leaping gracefully on long legs; a tall squirrel with long curling hair who carried her fluffy tail like the train of a formal gown; a frog in motley who croaked with laughter and did tumbles across the grass.

Ms. Mare crouched down at the window, afraid that she might be observed spying on this impossible scene. But surely she must be dreaming. Even her enigmatic employer couldn't create anything so fantastic as this! Could he? And this wild revelry, why it was completely unlike him. Yes, she was certainly dreaming, and yet it seemed—

The music ended and the artist bowed to the fox, who curtseyed daintily. He spoke to her, though Ms. Mare couldn't make out what he said, and the vixen lowered her eyes and looked away coquettishly, pulling out a fan and partly covering her face. Then he spoke to the others who clapped their paws and clacked their beaks and otherwise made a merry noise, and with a wave of his hand he signaled the musicians to strike up a minuet. Taking the fox's paw he led her out across the lawn and the rest of the party followed. They all danced away around the corner of the house and the sounds of music and laughter gradually faded.

Ms. Mare sat on the edge of her bed for several minutes. Then she arose and went into the bathroom, splashed water on her face and dried it, and concluded finally that no, she was not dreaming. She was awake, and remained awake for several hours more, unable to get back to sleep, uneasily listening for strange music in the night and, occasionally, hearing it.

CHAPTER FOUR

Cultivating the Garden

Ms. Mare overslept and woke up feeling distracted and out of sorts, haunted by what she had seen the night before. Mr. Nesselrode, acting in a perfectly ordinary fashion as if nothing at all had happened, showed up in the late morning requesting a soft-boiled egg on toast with juice. Ms. Mare had been in the middle of cutting up haddock to bake in a casserole with a mushroom cream sauce and breadcrumb topping for dinner, and had to put it all aside and wash her hands.

While her back was turned, the marmosets got into it and began tossing bits of fish down to the cats, enticing them up onto the counter where they began helping themselves. By the time she had gotten her employer settled comfortably at the little table by the window in the living room where he liked to take his breakfast, she returned to the kitchen to find the fish had been spoiled. The calico cat, who had wolfed down entirely too much too fast in her greedy delight, had thrown up all over the floor. Ms. Mare had no sooner gotten all this cleaned up and figured out an alternative entrée for dinner, but Heron alerted her that another cat had gotten ill in the laundry basket all over the clean clothes. In the end she found Mr. Nesselrode had fallen asleep in the chair, his nice breakfast gone cold and he hadn't touched a thing.

After such a trying morning, following a poor night's sleep, Ms. Mare decided to put off her plans to clean out and repair the kitchen cupboards. Some healthy activity outdoors in the fresh air and sunshine would suit her much better. The eyesore of a garden beneath her window had been bothering her since she moved in. Several clumps of pink and white phlox were bravely attempting to bloom among the weeds, and she would enjoy rescuing them. It was a lovely afternoon, the sun was warm but with a breeze to cool things and keep the insects away. So she changed into loose pants and an old shirt, found gloves and tools in the barn, and went to work.

Several cats supervised her labors, including a shy, slim black one who chased butterflies while the grey Manx napped in the sun. The basilisk came over, curious and clumsy.

"No, no," Ms. Mare shooed her away from the flower bed. "This is a garden. You may not go rooting around in it."

The basilisk lashed her tail back and forth, looking longingly at the freshly turned earth. Ms. Mare stood with her hands on her hips, looking it sternly in the eye. Then she said, more kindly, "But you may stay and keep me company, if you wish. I shouldn't mind that at all."

That resolved the matter. The beast settled with a great, grunting sigh on the grass next to the garden, content to be consoled with a gentle word from the mistress and a pat on the snout.

"There's a good beast," she said, returning to her work. Her thoughts wandered back to the night before, and she murmured aloud to the basilisk, "I suppose if he can create the likes of you, he could create blessed near anything he wanted to, couldn't he? Mock-turtles and dancing foxes and frogs in motley. For all their strangeness, they all seemed quite tame. You're about the most fearsome of the lot, and you're really a love, aren't you?"

The basilisk raised her head and thumped her long tail, for all the world like a great, scaly dog. Ms. Mare smiled. "Let's be practical. It is really none of my affair if your master wants to cavort at midnight on his own lawn with whatever creature takes his fancy. I'll just mind my own business, then, shan't I?"

Feeling that she had settled the matter adequately in her mind, she returned to pulling grass out from among the phlox, thinking how nice a border of primrose might look.

She had been at it for about an hour when she heard a voice behind her, startling her out of a pleasant bucolic reverie.

"Why, Ms. Mare, bless me! I hope you don't feel obligated to tackle the gardens, too, what with everything else you have to do around here."

"Good afternoon, Mr. Nesselrode," she said, turning and shading her eyes, looking up to see the silhouette of the artist standing next to the basilisk, stroking the beast's neck. "You are feeling better, I hope."

"Somewhat improved after my nap, thank you," he replied, but there was a listlessness in his voice undercutting his usual buoyancy.

"I'm glad to hear it," Ms. Mare said, getting to her feet, "As to the gardening, it is quite my own choice. I am doing it for the pure pleasure of it. Not to mention the satisfaction of how it will look when it is finished." She glanced down at herself, all grubby with fresh dirt and bits of weed. "Gracious!" she exclaimed, "I do look a fright."

"Nonsense. One can hardly remain immaculate while weeding a garden."

"I suppose not," she admitted, brushing grass from her pants. "Are you wanting your lunch?"

"Not at all! I wouldn't think of disturbing you if you are enjoying yourself. Do you mind a bit of company?"

He plunked himself down onto the grass cross-legged. Ms. Mare was about to admonish him that he would get his clothing soiled when she realized that the clothes he was wearing would hardly suffer from the experience. Like most of what he wore, both pants and shirt had seen better days. Then she noticed that he was holding a glass of what was presumably white wine—if the stemware had been filled with the substance appropriate to its design—some of which had slopped onto his sleeve and pant leg when he sat down. This she could not refrain from commenting on.

"Mr. Nesselrode, is it not a bit early for that? And you without a proper meal in your stomach."

"I seldom pay much mind to what o'clock it is. Often noon is my midnight, and midnight my noon."

She frowned at the note of sadness in his voice, trying to gauge his degree of intoxication. "There is a bit of cold roast," she said, taking off the gloves and brushing a stray bit of hair out of her face. "I could come in and make you a sandwich."

"I won't hear of it," her employer insisted. "Particularly after the trouble I put you to this morning. The afternoon is lovely and I urge you to enjoy it. I don't believe you get enough fun, Ms. Mare."

"I am not in your employ to have fun," she replied with dignity. "I am here to execute my duties efficiently and in a manner which I hope you find satisfactory."

"Oh pish!" he exclaimed. "Everyone needs to have fun, even in the execution of one's duties. And may I assure you, your performance has been exemplary. I couldn't be more pleased. I hope I've made that clear."

"You've given every indication of satisfaction," Ms. Mare replied. Not wanting to be standing while her employer was seated, she knelt back down next to the flower bed. She noticed that the moccasins he was wearing badly needed repair, or better still, replacement. The stitching had come loose in several spots. She pulled a clump of grass from the garden, shaking the dirt from its roots.

"And you, Ms. Mare?" Mr. Nesselrode said, somewhat anxiously, "I hope you are satisfied with your situation?"

"Most satisfied," she assured him.

"Since that business with Arachne, I have tried to make it clear to everyone that your authority is to be respected."

"The situation is much improved." She saw no point in mentioning that the clothes pins were on the table again. The linens, at least, had remained where she had put them. "At the moment, it is the cats that I am most annoyed with, but never mind. It's all in a day's work."

"Good, good!" He sipped his wine. The marmalade tabby came over, tail in the air. Ms. Mare glared at her briefly, as she suspected her to be the one who had thrown up in the laundry. But it isn't sensible to hold grudges against cats, who are quite oblivious. Ms. Mare returned to pulling grass and sorrel. The tabby rubbed against her master's knee and he stroked the fur along her back with fond obedience to the purred command. "This weeding and grubbing about," he said, "You really enjoy it?"

"I find it a pleasant diversion," Ms. Mare replied, sitting back on her heels. "I have only rarely in my life had the opportunity to garden. Normally my situation doesn't allow for it." She shifted over to a different spot, working her way around the clump of white phlox. "When I was in my teens," she continued, "my mother and the Galbraiths settled for an entire year in Little Dorset, a delightful country village north of London. They liked it so much that they rented a cottage, and Esther Galbraith did a garden. I've always loved gardens. I don't necessarily mean the gloriously elaborate affairs that one often sees around temples and palaces, although I have seen some extraordinary ones and enjoyed exploring them. It's the quaint little cottage gardens that I find particularly charming. I should think it a marvelous hobby to have in one's retirement, puttering about, tending one's flowers, herbs and vegetables, perhaps putting up a bird feeder or two among them. That summer when we were in Little Dorset, we had a lovely garden, with primrose and foxglove, morning glories and petunias, as well as tomatoes, peppers and, oh my! All manner of things. Mrs. Galbraith swore she enjoyed it so much that she might just settle in Little Dorset permanently, but of course, we didn't. Within a year we were off to Egypt."

"Well, perhaps this time you can enjoy the fruits of your labors," Mr. Nesselrode said. "You won't be compelled to go running off to Egypt or some such place. You may stay here as long as you like."

"Thank you," she said. "I generally don't stay very long in one place, a habit of my up-bringing, I suppose. I am restless by nature." She glanced up and saw the worry in his face, and she smiled reassuringly. "Don't concern yourself, Mr. Nesselrode. You see, I found my previous positions to be all, well, rather tedious after a time. I think this position may be different. It certainly is unique."

"I hope so!" he said fervently. "Things are very much better since you've come. I confess I wasn't sure about, well, the *intrusion* of having a stranger coming to live here, but it has been quite delightful. Not to have to worry about things, such exquisite meals, and wonderful conversation. I had forgotten how nice it is simply to talk to someone."

She looked at him with sympathy. "In the ten years you have lived here, have you had no one to talk to?"

"Not really, no. I mean, I talk to Frank, but that is all business. Delivery people, merchants, service people—" he flipped his hand dismissively. "I suppose it had begun to prey on my nerves. I hadn't created anything for Frank in a very long time. I suppose he was becoming worried about it. Perhaps that is why he insisted I must hire someone. I think he was rather alarmed at the state of things the last time he came out."

"You mean, you haven't created anything to sell?" Certainly there had been no dearth of creations, she thought, particularly last night.

"Not in months. Perhaps even a year or so. I just haven't felt up to it."

"I don't expect an artist can always control when the muse will strike," Ms. Mare said, digging at the deep and stubborn roots of a dandelion. "It is not like housework, where one simply does what must be done without thinking too much about it. Nor, I would imagine, is it even like the work of a craftsman, which takes a great deal of thought and care, but which follows a prescribed course of procedures. For a true artist, there must be inspiration, the infusion of the spirit, which does imply a rather mystical element."

"Oh, yes!" he exclaimed excitedly, "Quite so! How very perceptive of you!"

"Thank you," she replied modestly, "but it is hardly an original thought. I'm sure I read it somewhere."

"Nevertheless, you have an understanding of what you read, a retention of the ideas. Although it is so much more complicated than that. Art, I mean. That is, the cubes I give to Frank to sell, they really are common craftwork—well, in a way they are, and in a way they are not. Certainly they aren't like Arachne or Winged Snake. But on the other hand, I cannot just crank them out, as if they were widgets on an assembly line. Each must be unique, special, unlike any other. It can be quite exhausting!"

"I see," she said carefully, weighing the appropriateness of the question begging at her lips. He was in such a candid mood, and it seemed no harm to ask. She would take it quite gracefully if he refused and discreetly drop the issue if it made him awkward. But she was so very curious. "Mr. Nesselrode, if I may be so bold, how do you create these things of yours?"

He gave a short little laugh. "So many ask! I find it difficult to think of an answer! Strings and sealing wax, marzipan, dew from fairy circles gathered in the full moon—it is simply impossible."

He emptied his glass and sighed, gazing off across the lawn where the little blue sheep placidly grazed. The breeze stirred the hair around his shoulders and shifted the branches of the maple shading them, the bright sun dappling through. He blinked, glancing up at the shifting glare, and shaded his eyes. Unaccustomed to bright sunlight, Ms. Mare thought, a fact attested to by his pale complexion. More accustomed to moonlight. What a fascinating man! No wonder all those glamorous women fell in love with him. He was no male paragon by any means, but he had such an air of exotic charm about him. Quite handsome, really, if one found that sort of refined delicacy appealing, and Ms. Mare would have to admit she did. A true artistic genius—no, much more than that, a sorcerer, a conjurer of marvels, an utterly indecipherable mystery who had confounded all the experts.

He was also hopelessly irresponsible and in need of looking after, particularly in light of present circumstances. He would need a good dinner, something easily digestible, after having eaten nothing all day and indulged most unadvisedly in spirits. Ms. Mare stood up and brushed herself off. "This has been very pleasant, but I really must see about dinner. It is getting rather late."

"Is it really? I suppose it must be. I have no conception of time." He sighed and accepted assistance from the basilisk in getting to his feet. "It is always such a pleasure talking with you. You are so very kind to me. Very kind indeed. You've accomplished so much in so short a time. Why,

I'm sure I'd be absolutely devastated if I ever lost you. That is—" he stammered, suddenly awkward, "if-if you decided to seek another position. Surely a woman of your qualities—that is—an individual of your exceptional abilities—I mean, well, you are so very...." The sentence hung unfinished.

She found herself feeling flustered, not sure how to respond to his praise—no, not sure how to respond to the warm glow it inspired in her. This wouldn't do at all. She must maintain a safe distance. "I am simply doing my job," she said with cool aloofness.

"Of course," he murmured. "Your job."

"But I enjoy my work a great deal," she said quickly, thinking perhaps she had sounded a trifle too aloof. "I find you a most interesting employer."

"Do you?" he asked eagerly. "I've been told I can be most irritating."

"Oh, I don't find you so at all. Not in the least bit."

He was looking at her in an odd way, as if there were something he wanted to say. She found herself caught and held by those silver-blue eyes, their color made even more pale and unearthly by the bright sunlight which had shrunk his pupils down to dots. Dear me, I don't know what to say! she thought helplessly. It is highly inadvisable to be looking at my employer this way—

Then, suddenly, the basilisk gave her master a powerful nudge with her head, knocking him off-balance and right into Ms. Mare. She caught herself and kept them both from toppling onto the grass. In holding him to keep him from falling, she felt for less than a heartbeat a strikingly contradictory strength and delicacy in his limbs, a warm vitality radiating from his body. He was staring into her face, mortified, then he hastily straightened himself up and pulled away, blushing bright pink.

"Good heavens, forgive me! I—I—"

"Quite all right, Mr. Nesselrode," she gasped.

He spun furiously on the basilisk. "Shame on you! What on earth possessed you to—?" Several marmosets leaped chittering gleefully from the basilisk's head. "You!" he shouted at them. "You little monsters put her up to it, didn't you?"

The basilisk was hanging her head guiltily, but there was a distinctly unrepentant gleam in her red eyes.

"There, there, it was just a harmless prank," Ms. Mare soothed him, struggling to control her own distressing agitation. "No harm done."

"You are most understanding," he replied, flustered. "Well, I should—I should leave you to your duties. I—I'll see you at dinner." He retreated, not quite running.

"Well!" she exclaimed when he was out of sight. "Well!" And then, as she attempted to focus her attention the task of tidying up her gardening tools, "Dear me!"

CHAPTER 5

Confidences

Dinner had been awkward at first. Her employer showed up at the last minute, talking too fast and too brightly, still unsettled by that afternoon's incident. Ms. Mare was determined to put him at ease, and behaved in an entirely normal and professional manner, as if absolutely nothing out of the ordinary had happened. She had a nice broth with bread, a custard for dessert, and she entertained him with a story about her and her mother when they were in Ireland. They had asked the son of a friend to drive them to town in his father's car. He was a shy, mild-mannered lad. However, when seated behind the wheel, entrusted with all that power, freedom and speed, he turned into a positive maniac.

"He sent the car tearing over the narrow lanes," Ms. Mare said, "nearly loosening our teeth as it bounced through the ruts. He tooted the horn wildly at every hill and bend in the road to warn away sheep and pedestrians, with varying degrees of success, occasionally necessitating some heart-stopping swerves. We arrived in town intact, barely, with nothing wedged in the car's grill. Mother and I needed a strong cup of tea to settle our nerves before we could go about our business, and Mother insisted on driving on the return trip home. The poor young fellow was quite baffled and disappointed. He was under the impression that he had done a marvelous job."

Mr. Nesselrode laughed with delight at the story, enjoyed his meal, and was quite himself by the end of it. He declined an invitation to play backgammon, pleading exhaustion, which was just as well with Ms. Mare. The last twenty-four hours had been a bit of a trial, and a good night's sleep was a most inviting thought.

Later that evening, in the privacy of her room, Ms. Mare prepared for bed. She had taken her bath and now sat before the mirror, taking her hair down and applying cream to her face and arms. The latter she did not do so much for the cosmetic effect as for the pleasure of the scent and sensation to her skin. It was one of her few indulgences. No matter how difficult the work day, how unpleasant the tasks or how boring and tedious, she could look forward to a nice bath, perhaps with a lovely scented oil, and the smooth, cool sensation of rich cream massaged into her skin. Her mother had taught her that bedtime rituals were important. One could endure nearly anything if one had a good night's sleep, and the key to a good night's sleep was a relaxing, soothing ritual before bed.

She regarded her face in the mirror with satisfaction. A strong face, with character, much like her mother's. Not pretty, not a trifle for a man's pleasure, but the face of a woman who knew what she wanted, who had her pride and dignity, and was quite happy with her lot in life. Capable and competent. Trustworthy. Self-sufficient. A good face.

She reflected on the day, and thought again of her employer. Such an exceptional man, a fascinating man. Utterly helpless in many ways, quite in need of someone such as herself. It was satisfying to know that he appreciated that fact. He was most anxious to be sure she would be staying with him. Most anxious, indeed. It was really quite touching. Might there be some deeper feelings there? It certainly seemed so, what with all that stammering today when he talked to her. What a delightful thought! Such a man taking an interest in her!

But it would be most unbecoming to pursue the matter. Her mother had taught her that she must always maintain the proper distance. She was his housekeeper; he was her employer. To stray beyond those boundaries invited trouble. She must be sure to behave properly at all times. But in the secret privacy of her room, preparing for bed, warm and relaxed from her bath and the comfortable rituals of retiring, she could confide to herself.

The conspiracy between the marmosets and the basilisk in the garden that day was, of course, inexcusably naughty, and the incident itself had been frightfully embarrassing, but there had been in that moment of close physical contact an undeniable thrill.

"I think I am falling quite in love with him," she said to her image in the mirror with a girlish, self-indulgent giggle.

She was startled by a sudden commotion behind her. She turned to see the emerald lobster dancing about in circles, clacking its claws and waving its feelers wildly. Horrified, she leaped to her feet and rushed over, picking the lobster up by its carapace.

"Now, see here!" she commanded severely, "You had best not repeat a word of what you just heard, is that clear? Not a *word* of it to *anyone*! If you do, I swear, I shall throw you into a pot and make a bisque of you!"

The lobster regarded her fearfully with its crustacean eye stalks, nodding its feelers meekly. She set it back down on the floor and it crawled humbly to the door, pulled it open and scurried out.

"I've no blessed privacy at all!" she exclaimed, going to the door and shutting it again. With a huff, she turned down the lights and went to bed.

***

The next day, an unprecedented thing happened. Mr. Nesselrode did not show up for dinner.

The cats indicated that they did not see this as a problem at all, and would be quite willing to sample what she had intended to serve to their master. Heron, on the other hand, was very agitated, fluffing out her feathers and leaving the table clacking her beak. The Bishop climbed out of his teapot and was puzzled to see the chair at the head of the table vacant. Ms. Mare did not know quite what to do, but she suspected she knew the source of the problem.

"Bisque!" she declared hotly in the kitchen, slamming down the lid of a pot. "Bisque, I swear it!" The marmosets ran chittering into the living room. "What am I to do? He's hiding in his studio, I suppose. Such a nice dinner, and it will be spoiled!"

She stormed back into the dining room, balefully surveying the table, set with candles and napkins all in place, the Bishop waiting patiently on the edge of the teapot, leaning against his crook, the cats milling about and mewing impatiently. "Well!" she exclaimed, "At least you should have your dinner, my dears! This unfortunate business is hardly your fault!"

As she served the last of the cats, Heron appeared and tapped her firmly on the shoulder, regarding her soberly.

"What is it?" Ms. Mare asked, and Heron turned, clearly indicating that Ms. Mare should follow her. Wiping her hands on her apron, she muttered to herself, took off her apron and laid it over a chair, following the bustled, bespectacled bird. Heron conducted her up the front stairs to the door that went to the third floor.

"And now what?" Ms. Mare demanded. "I'm not allowed, as you well know! No doubt that is why he's taken refuge up there, although whether he intends to remain there until he starves, I'm sure I haven't a clue! Oh, that *wretched* lobster!"

Heron tossed her head impatiently and gave a quick peck at Ms. Mare's hand, then tapped the door with her beak.

"I'm to knock? Is that it? And do what? Inquire as to whether he intends to come down to dinner? I'm sure he knows very well it is dinner time, and has no intention of coming down!"

Heron squawked at her derisively and again pecked at the door.

"Oh, very well!" And Ms. Mare gave the door a stout rap. "Mr. Nesselrode, I would appreciate knowing if you intend to come down to dinner! Or shall I dump the whole lovely meal out the window for the basilisk?"

There was no answer, but just to satisfy Heron, Ms. Mare rapped again firmly. To her surprise, the door opened. Blinking up at her was a squat toad dressed in butler's livery. It bowed its broad head and stepped back, ushering her through the door with a sweeping gesture. Ms. Mare glanced back at Heron, and the ornithic matron nodded her bird head rapidly.

"All right, then," Ms. Mare said doubtfully, "I suppose."

She went through the door and up the stairs into the dimness above. She smelled dust, but also a strange subtle fragrance, like rosewood or patchouli. When she reached the top of the stairs she stopped, astonished by the sight.

It was like most attics, a repository for odd and assorted items, cluttered and piled high. But what an assortment! Wardrobes hung open trailing ruffled dresses and feather boas. There were sheet-shrouded chairs with open umbrellas, bookcases lined with jars filled with polished stones, tall brass vases, bird cages and music boxes; dress-maker's forms, a statue of a bearded man in a toga, a bird bath in the shape of a cupped hand, dusty gilded mirrors, yards and yards of all sorts of cloth, silk and brocade, corduroy and flannel hanging off of racks and draped over furniture; cardboard boxes and wooden crates, barrels and bags, all in no apparent order whatsoever.

The toad butler came puffing up the stairs behind her, and hopped up next to her. With another solicitous bow, he gestured, and led her through the labyrinth. She followed, gazing about herself in consternation. From all around came the sounds of chirps, squeals, squawks and whirring. Eyes gazed out at her, down at her, up at her. A peacock was perched on a trapeze. Half-seen rodent-like creatures dashed through the clutter. A winged fish flapped lazily from the top of a spiral staircase that ended in the air, made impassable by piles of shoes, clothing, blankets and hats on every one of its stairs. A bright pink grasshopper regarded her blankly from a wicker love seat upon which it was methodically chewing. With faint whinnies, a herd of tiny unicorns galloped out into the path in front of her, disappearing around the corner. Diffuse light came from a source or sources she couldn't identify. Sometimes the light seemed bluish, sometimes golden, sometimes a pale and eerie green. She remembered that somewhere in this inorganic jungle crawled the spider Arachne, and she shuddered.

Then the clutter opened up into an clear space, well lit by large, luminous globes that seemed to hover in the air near the ceiling. And there was Archimedes Nesselrode at an enormous table covered with piles of clay of every color, brushes, charcoals, pens, pots of pigment—an absolute riot of artistic paraphernalia. Around the table were at least a dozen easels, some with canvasses, some with pads of paper, covered with sketches, paintings, patterns, and designs.

As soon as he spied his visitors he jumped to his feet. "Ah," he said, "Ms. Mare. Thank you, Bufus, you may go now."

The toad bowed low and withdrew silently into the maze.

"My word!" she gasped. "This is where you work?"

He rubbed his hands together nervously. "Not what you expected?" There was the slightest quiver in his voice.

"Not really," she admitted.

"I do apologize for committing the mortal sin of missing the evening meal," he said, "But in light of the circumstances, I simply couldn't face it."

"That miserable crustacean!" Ms. Mare cried. "A mere momentary indiscretion, which should never have been repeated—!"

"Oh, you mustn't blame Lobster," he interrupted hastily. "He really couldn't help himself. He so rarely has an opportunity to be involved in something of importance, he was quite overcome by the drama of it."

"I am absolutely mortified," she said, feeling flushed with embarrassment, "I assure you, I know my place, and I would never presume—"

"That is what Heron assured me." He looked away, picking up a wire tool and poking compulsively at a lump of clay with it. "Heron convinced me that I was behaving quite foolishly, and that I had nothing to fear from you, and really—" he gave a nervous little half-laugh, "I couldn't very well hide from you up here indefinitely, now could I?"

Ms. Mare was having a very difficult time reconciling the wildly flamboyant artist she had read about at the library, who was involved in all those romantic scandals and outrageous behavior, with the painfully shy man who stood stammering and fidgeting before her. What possibly could have happened to cause such a radical change in a person? Whatever the answer, she was nonetheless faced with the task of putting him at ease again and repairing the damage done.

"Mr. Nesselrode, I promise you, whatever little fancies I may entertain in my private moments, they will not at all reflect on my behavior towards you. I shall practice the utmost discretion. I am quite appalled at the discomfort this has caused you, and apologize for it."

"Not at all, Ms. Mare," he said, forcing himself to put the tool down, turn and face her. He blinked and took a deep breath. "I am flattered and-and—" he managed a tentative smile, "glad to know that you find my company pleasant and perhaps, dare I say, appealing. In my present state I am, well, to be candid, not exactly an ideal companion. I don't know that I ever have been so, although there were those who insisted otherwise. Never mind. I am glad that we can come to an understanding."

"It is my greatest hope that we can," Ms. Mare said.

Relief relaxed the stiffness from his movements and expression. He nodded, as though considering the matter settled. "How awkward this incident has been for you!" he exclaimed, his voice regaining its customary confidence. "How uncomfortable to be at such a disadvantage! No, no, you are most gracious to make light of it, but I can fully appreciate how it must feel to have one's confidences revealed against one's wishes. It is only fair that I try to equalize things. A confidence for a confidence, you might say. So, I welcome you to my own inner sanctum. Come, sit down." He pulled a stool out from under the table.

"Please, Mr. Nesselrode, you needn't feel obligated."

"I insist," he said with a gesture towards the stool.

She needed no further prompting, surrendering to her curiosity. "It is a most fascinating place," she said, looking around her as she sat down.

"I have never invited another soul to come up here. I had never planned to. But now that you are here, I confess it is rather fun to share it with you." He picked up a piece of clay, idly rolling it around in his fingers. "I recall you expressed an interest in my methods. Under the circumstances," he glanced over at her with a shy smile, "I thought it appropriate to show you."

"Oh, yes," she replied, catching her breath.

He set the piece of clay down. It had assumed the shape of a perfect little horned caterpillar. A star-nosed mole with bat wings landed on the artist's shoulder and began nuzzling his neck. He stroked its chocolate brown fur. "It is really quite simple," he said. He reached under the table into a cardboard carton and pulled out an empty, sealed, perfectly clear Lucite cube. He set it on the table. Placing one hand on it, he consulted the star-nosed mole. "What do you think, Benjamin?" It squeaked. He nodded.

Vivian Mare watched him, fascinated. He took a deep breath, half-closing his eyes, letting his breath out slowly. His long, slim fingers caressed the sides of the cube, then tapped it lightly.

There was a dragonfly in the box, with green eyes and a scarlet body. It cocked its head and whirred its broad, black-spotted, iridescent wings.

"Dear God!" she gasped.

Archimedes Nesselrode laughed, a high, half-mad sound. "There! You don't know much more now than you did before, do you?"

She gazed at him in wonder, this strange, gentle genius. "There is no trick, is there?" she murmured. "It's you."

He nodded. "I create. That's what I do. It isn't a process that can be stolen, mass-produced, or mass-marketed. That is what those business people could never understand." He smiled ruefully. "But then, I could never understand business. What Frank Shekle and his like do? Utterly beyond my comprehension. So I suppose we're even."

"Oh, no, Mr. Nesselrode," Ms. Mare said softly. "Not hardly. Not even close." She picked up the cube very carefully. "But these are not like your other creations. Like Heron or the basilisk."

"Gracious, no," he agreed. "These have no substance. Open the cube and—" he snapped his fingers. "You might as well try to grasp the spectra of a prism." He sat on the edge of the table, folding his arms. "And yet people are fascinated by them. They'll pay all sorts of money to possess an empty cube filled only with illusions." It clearly bewildered him.

Vivian Mare held the cube, smiling, watching the dragonfly groom its head with one delicate foreleg. She thought of the salamander she had seen in the cube on Frank Shekle's desk the day she was hired. One assumed, of course, that there was some trick to it. The technological marvels with which one was surrounded nowadays were all utterly incomprehensible to anyone but an expert. One knew, of course, that it was not magic; they were all manufactured, programmed somehow. There was always a rational explanation.

And yet, for what she held in her hand there could be no other term, nor for the person who had created it. This was magic, inexplicable and wondrous.

"Thank you," she said quietly, "for sharing this with me."

"Thank *you*, Ms. Mare," he replied, "for being someone with whom I could safely share it."

CHAPTER SIX

Moonstruck

"Dearest Vivian," the letter began. "It is most fortunate that your recent missives arrived just as we were packing to leave, otherwise who knows how many weeks it would have taken to catch up with us? We had hoped to be in Belize longer, but you know how Esther is. She got it into her head that we must visit Wales before cold weather, and so off we go.

"I was intrigued by the news that you are presently in the employ of Mr. Archimedes Nesselrode. I congratulate you on finding what must be a most interesting situation! I related the news to the Galbraiths, and they were eager to know more. You see, they knew the family some years ago, and stayed with them while traveling in Greece. This was before I came into their employ. They tell me that the family has a very mysterious and romantic history. It seems the elder Nesselrode's grandfather was a very wealthy Russian count who sent his family and fortune out of the country just before the bloody Revolution. The eldest son married a mysterious Danish girl who was said to be breath-takingly beautiful, but who disappeared without a trace after delivering him a son. Thus the noble title has technically been passed on, even though the estates have long ago been confiscated and converted to the Socialist cause by the Soviet government. Certainly nobility isn't what it once was, but the old aristocracy in Europe still places a high value on it.

"Now, the present Count Nesselrode, Archimedes' father, married the daughter of a successful Greek art exporter named Praxiteles Kariotakis whose family has a very mysterious history of its own. The ancestral home was on the island of Lemnos in the Aegean Sea. There is an ancient temple sacred to Hephaestus on the island which the family has had restored at great expense for reasons which are left open to speculation. It is rumored that the temple was built on the site of an even older structure, consecrated to the ruling Goddess of a civilization even older than the Greeks. The Kariotakis family seems to have taken a very great interest in places of power sacred to bygone cultures; their home is filled with maps, pictures, models and histories of such places, from Chile to China. Many of the artifacts in their collection were brought back from sites sacred to Pre-Christian deities. The Galbraiths said that virtually everyone on Lemnos takes for granted that the family's continued wealth and success is due to traffic with the Devil.

"As far as anyone knows, your employer's parents were involved in nothing more sinister that the importation and appraisal of works of art. They moved to New York shortly after Archimedes' birth, and he was raised in the United States, thoroughly Americanized, if decidedly upper crust. The Nesselrodes were considered nothing short of respectable. It is my understanding that they left the country during the height of their son's fame. As you mentioned in your own account, they were scandalized by his antics, and it is rumored they completely disowned him, a rather serious matter considering he is the Count's only heir. I believe they are living in Switzerland, now.

"As for your Mr. Nesselrode, himself, I cannot add much to what you have already found out. From your description of him, it can be assumed he has grown out of that youthful desire to shock and outrage, and has settled down a bit. He sounds quite delightful. I hope you continue to find the position rewarding. You always were equal to a good challenge, and it sounds as if you have found yourself a whopper!

"Esther discovered some old witch selling potions in the market place, and swears it has all but cured the arthritis in her knees. As you know, Erasmus is much more a believer in modern medicine, and has been following doctor's orders faithfully. He has recovered completely from the surgery, and is looking forward to tramping around the Welsh countryside. It shall certainly be a test of the efficacy of Esther's witch's potion!

"We all send our love, and will write again with our new address when we know it. Best of luck,

"Your devoted mother."

Ms. Mare read the letter again. Heir to a title! The very notion brought her back to her childhood, to memories of elegant balls, of being taught how to curtsey properly, of how to address the various ranks of nobility, of how to dance—and dancing with older gentlemen whose eyes twinkled indulgently, humoring a young girl with stars in her eyes, gentlemen whose families had for generations owned castles, estates and villas.

Well, some of them, anyway. As her mother said, nobility wasn't what it once was, and many of the old titled families had come upon hard times. But still, it was a delightfully romantic notion.

"Count Nesselrode," she murmured.

***

Romantic notions aside, there were practical matters to consider.

"Mr. Nesselrode, I should like a dishwasher."

"Eh?" He looked up from his cutlet. "A dishwasher?"

"Yes. You know, an appliance which washes dishes."

"Hm. A dishwasher. What a splendid idea! By all means, get one." He returned to attacking his cutlet. He'd had more of an appetite lately. It was quite good to see.

"And a new stove," Ms. Mare continued. "I dislike cooking on an electric stove, and besides, one of the burners doesn't work."

"Really? How inconvenient. Well then, do see about it. That is," he paused frowning, "if I can afford it. I imagine I can. Still, perhaps you should check with Frank first."

"I shall do so."

Even though a certain critical threshold had been crossed with the exchange of profound confidences, their daily communications remained the same. They shared an unspoken understanding that polite, if cordial, formality was to be the status quo. He remained her employer, and she, his housekeeper. These were roles they each felt comfortable with. However, it must be admitted that Ms. Mare played her role with more devoted enthusiasm than she had in previous positions.

The following morning she called the office of Mr. Nesselrode's agent and manager. The secretary who answered the phone informed her that Mr. Shekle would get back to her, which he did within minutes.

"What's the problem, Miss Mare?" he asked, sounding as if he were bracing himself for the worst.

"*Ms.* Mare," she corrected him. "And there is no problem. I wish to purchase a dishwasher and a stove for the house, and have obtained approval from Mr. Nesselrode, providing he has sufficient funds to do so. He is concerned because of his creative dry spell of late. He instructed me to contact you about it."

Frank Shekle snorted. "Are you joking? He has sufficient funds to buy a whole damn restaurant. Hell, a *chain* of restaurants! At least at the moment. That dry spell better end soon, though."

"I see. He seems quite unaware of his financial status."

"You're telling me! I tried to explain it to him once. I gave up when I realized he had stopped listening to me and was completely absorbed in growing little flowers out of the tips of his fingers. God, I wish I knew how he did that!"

"I'm sure I don't know," Ms. Mare said coolly. "Thank you, Mr. Shekle, that's all I needed."

"Wait, wait. Are you sure there's nothing else?"

"Quite sure, yes. Ought there to be?"

"Well," Frank Shekle said slowly, "I'd guess that this job is rather different from others that you've had."

"Oh, quite different, yes indeed!" she agreed readily.

"And there aren't any problems?"

"None that I cannot handle," she assured him. "There is the matter of the appliances, of course. But that is easily remedied. I assume I am to send the bill to you?"

"Right. Make all the arrangements and have them contact my office about payment."

"Excellent."

"So, you're perfectly happy there?" Shekle persisted.

"Why, yes I am. Mr. Nesselrode is a most agreeable employer."

"I see. Well, I'm glad to hear that, Miss Mare."

"*Ms.* Mare," she corrected him sternly.

As Frank Shekle hung up the phone he muttered, "She's as crazy as he is!"

As Ms. Mare hung up the phone she sniffed, "Impertinent man! What would I possibly find to complain about in this position?" She smiled to herself as she called the appliance dealer. What indeed? Except for perhaps the refrigerator. It ought to be replaced as well. She didn't think she would ever really be able to get it clean again after the state in which she found it.

Later that morning she discovered that the winged snake had made a nest of the flower arrangements. It had uprooted most of the potted plants, to the distress of the striped emus whose own nests were disrupted in the process. It had then taken all the plant debris and added it to the flowers to make a very nice snuggery for itself in the woodbin by the fireplace.

Ms. Mare was, understandably, quite put out by this. She tried to shoo the snake off the mess so that she could clean it up, and it hissed at her.

"Well! Suit yourself, but I shall not set a place for you at the table if you are going to behave this way!"

The snake coiled itself defiantly and flicked its tongue at her. With a sniff, Ms. Mare turned her back. "I've got far too much else to deal with to waste my time with you!" She strode back towards the kitchen with a purposeful air, nearly tripping over the starfish.

She took meat out of the freezer and consulted her list of chores to decide what ought to be done today. The weather was fair, sunny and breezy, a good day to hang out laundry. Perhaps she might catch her employer out of bed. She could get it changed and air out the spread. A glance at the calendar discouraged her. The moon was nearly full. Very likely then he'd been up all night. He tended to do that around the time of the full moon. He wouldn't be out of bed until dinner time. She wondered if there would be strange doings on the lawn again.

It occurred to her that she had not seen the lobster in quite a long time. It no doubt still went in terror of being made into bisque. Poor thing, no real harm had come of its indiscretion.

"Should you happen to see Lobster," she commented to Heron as they hung out the wash in the sunshine, "do tell him that I am no longer annoyed with him."

Heron nodded her head agreeably and passed Ms. Mare a clothespin with her bill. The ornithic matron had warmed up to her, at least to a certain degree, and assisted her with the chores whenever she was able. Ms. Mare was glad for any help she could get. She hoped that the basilisk wouldn't knock the clothesline down again with her tail as she had last time they hung out wash. The beast had been dreadfully sorry afterward, hanging her head regretfully as Ms. Mare scolded her. The marmosets, for once, actually made themselves useful, helping them pick up the soiled wash and shake the dirt off of it. She would have expected them to run off with it and hang it in the trees. But they, too, seemed to be growing fond of her. Now, if only she could persuade the winged snake to be more cooperative.

Dinner was a chicken pie with a green salad; the cats had liver mashed with rice. Heron took her place at the table and the Bishop climbed out of the teapot to bless the meal. Mr. Nesselrode observed the lack of setting for the winged snake—who did not show up anyway—and Ms. Mare told him about the nest and the destruction of the household flora.

"I expect she may be laying eggs," Mr. Nesselrode suggested.

"She?" Ms. Mare echoed. "Laying eggs?"

"Just a guess," he said.

"Bless me! I hope they don't hatch! I've enough trouble with vases broken and pictures knocked off the wall!"

"Oh, I doubt they would. Poor thing. I suppose I ought to create a mate for her. She's been longing for a companion."

"Mr. Nesselrode, don't you think one winged snake is quite enough?"

He smiled at her. "I expect you're right." Their eyes met for a moment, and then Ms. Mare turned her attention firmly to her plate.

"I've called a man about doing some repairs to the house," she reported. "It really ought to be seen to before another winter."

"True," he sighed. "I've noticed the roof has begun to leak. Can't let that go on. Let me know when it can be arranged and I'll tell the basilisk to take a few days off and go down by the pond and nap in the shade, just while the workmen are here. Most of the others could come stay with me in the attic, but I have no idea what to do about the starfish. I don't believe it can climb stairs."

"Not to worry. The workmen wouldn't need to do anything inside. I can handle most of the interior work myself. I'm rather handy that way."

"You are a wonder, no doubt of it!" he declared, and took a forkful of pie. "Excellent dinner, as always." Then he said, "You've never married."

Ms. Mare froze, her water glass half-way to her lips. "No," she answered finally, taking a sip of water. "I never have."

"I can't help wondering why not."

She considered what to say, feeling a bit of warmth in her cheeks. "It would have interfered with my plans."

"And what *are* your plans, Ms. Mare?" He was smiling very slightly, his silver-blue eyes daring to hold her dark eyes while he waited for her answer.

She blinked and then cocked her head, gazing thoughtfully upwards. "I've been meaning to clean out the kitchen cabinets and give them a coat of paint. I believe I'll do that tomorrow."

"Excellent idea! But don't trouble yourself with the painting. Put the marmosets to work on it. They'd be delighted."

"The marmosets?" she exclaimed. "I should think not! They'd drip paint all over the counters!"

"Pish! So put a cloth down," Mr. Nesselrode replied. "You work too hard, Ms. Mare. You should have help."

It was time to clear away dinner, but she didn't like to do so until her employer indicated that he was finished. Tonight he seemed to want to linger and expressed a desire for a glass of brandy after dessert. Ms. Mare started to get up to fetch it.

"No, no, don't disturb yourself," he said, "Heron can fetch it. You wouldn't mind, would you, Heron?"

The bird regarded him over her spectacles, then obliged with a slight ruffle of her feathers.

"Thank you. You'll join me, won't you, Ms. Mare?"

"Well, it really isn't my habit—" she began to protest.

"Oh, but just this once, in honor of the full moon."

She hesitated, not sure what the moon had to do with it, then acquiesced. "I suppose. Just this once."

"Excellent!" He did seem to be in high spirits this evening. "By the way," he said as he took a sip of brandy, "May I assure Lobster that it's safe to come out of my studio?"

"Really, Mr. Nesselrode!" Ms. Mare exclaimed. "Surely you don't think I would do harm to any of your creations!"

"Lobster seems quite convinced of it," he said.

"Nonsense. It was just—" She felt an awkward flush of emotion, particularly since he was watching her in a very cryptic way. She was losing her perspective, falling under the spell of this inscrutable genie. With an effort, she shook it off. "Anyway," she continued briskly, "I have already asked Heron if she would kindly let the lobster know that I regretted the severity of my words. Didn't I, Heron?"

The bird nodded in solemn affirmation.

"Good, good." He sipped the last of his brandy. "I am looking forward to tonight. Though modern science would deny it, there is certainly something about the moon, particularly when it is full round and bright. Things happen."

"Yes, I expect they do," she replied, recalling what she had seen out her window during the last full moon. This was all very unsettling, and the brandy she had drunk was making it difficult to keep less appropriate feelings in check. In desperation, she said, "Shall I clear the table, Mr. Nesselrode?"

He set his glass down. "That would be fine." He rose to his feet, her cue to do the same. "Ms. Mare, the window in your room faces east, I believe."

"So it does," she said, stacking plates, cat dishes and cutlery neatly for its return to the kitchen. "I enjoy waking to the morning sun. It begins my day cheerfully."

"And the moon."

She looked up. Madam Beast leaped gracefully onto the master's shoulders and curled herself around his neck, rubbing her cheek against his ear. "The moon rises in the east," he said, reaching up to pet the cat.

"Quite," she agreed in a small voice.

She watched him, at a loss, as he left the room with the cat riding on his shoulders. She was certain now that she would not be able to sleep a wink that night.

However, after tossing a bit in her bed, watching the rectangle of pale light cast by the moon travel slowly across the floor with all the haste of the starfish, she fell into an uneasy sleep. Some time later, she segued from strange dreams into awareness of her bed and the room around her. She heard a soft squeak, and saw a fluttering shape pass overhead. It landed with a soft scratching on the post of her headboard, startling her. Then she recognized the little bat-winged mole, Benjamin.

"What are you doing here?" she asked him, sitting up in bed. The moonlight had narrowed to a thin strip across the floor near the window; the moon must have been quite high. She picked up her clock to look at it, and as she did, she heard a muffled pattering and soft whinnying. "Good lord, what is that?" She realized the door to her room was open and a herd of tiny unicorns came galloping across the floor. They stopped by the side of her bed, pawing the rug and rearing up on their hind legs, snorting and making a fuss, then they turned and raced back across the floor and out the door.

"What, am I to follow?" she asked. Benjamin squeaked and took off, flying silently across the room, also disappearing out the door. She realized with a shiver that this time she was being invited to join in the revelry. "Well, then, I expect I should go, shouldn't I?" she murmured.

She got out of bed, taking up her robe and reaching down to put on her slippers. As she passed the dressing table, she exclaimed, "Gracious,

I must be a sight!" She paused long enough to pick up her hairbrush and give her hair a cursory grooming. As she was pulling the brush through her hair she thought she heard music, but very different from what she had heard a month ago. It was faint and distant, like the delicately plucked notes of a music box. She put down her brush and crept to the door, her heart beating rapidly. The music had stopped. The house was quiet, but not completely silent. She could hear furtive scurrying, soft chitters, clicks and chirps, the creations of Archimedes Nesselrode stirring in the night. No laughter, no wild revelry. Tonight the mood was completely different.

As she peeked cautiously out the door into the hallway, she saw the winged snake fly by, its body undulating as its wings beat the air. As destructive as it could be in the house, it was a lovely thing to watch slithering through the air. She smiled with admiration as she followed it with her eyes down the hallway. Then she caught her breath.

There, standing in a pool of moonlight at the top of the stairs, was Archimedes Nesselrode. The snake flew to him, wrapping itself around his shoulders and slithering over his body. The softly tinkling melody began again, as if the music box had been wound and set to playing. It echoed ethereal through the hall.

He called to her. "Vivian."

It made her shiver to hear him address her by her first name. Just those spoken syllables cast a spell. All the rules of daytime were set aside. She walked towards him, her heart beating rapidly. The moonlight brought out yet softened the contours of his face, the cheekbones, the narrow, slightly crooked nose, the pointed chin. He wore a loose and flowing shirt that hung off his thin arms and over his hips, its collar low and open, showing the fine bones of his shoulders and upper chest. He held out a hand to her as the snake wriggled down to the floor and slithered away. She took his hand.

"Vivian," he said again softly, with unmistakable fondness.

She stepped into the moonlight with him, feeling the silver luminescence work its magic on her as well. She would look differently than she did in the harsh light of day. Her face, too, would be softened, her eyes made to sparkle. Pragmatic inhibitions melted away; she opened her mouth to answer, but found herself stymied. "I hardly know—" she said, her voice faltering.

"What to call me?" he guessed. "I know. My first name is atrocious. My mother was Greek."

"Your middle name—"

"Is not much better. Michelangelo." He laughed softly. "At the Academy, they took to calling me Michael. It persists among those out there who know me, but I've never really liked it."

She had known this kind of exotic rapture before, of being caught up in the enchantment of a strange and beautiful place. There was a freedom to it, liberating a part of herself that simply had no place in the ordinary world of strict responsibilities. But this was so much more personal than anything she had experienced before. In this patch of moonlight with his hand holding hers, she felt equal to something only dreamt of before. "I know what I shall call you," she said, reaching up to touch his cheek, unafraid to do so. In the moonlight, it was permitted. "I shall call you Angel. My Angel, for surely you are not of this world at all." The skin of his cheek was cool and smooth.

He laughed again, that high, half-mad sound. "Angel! Ah, Vivian, how marvelous! Your Angel I shall be. But you must understand, I can only be your Angel by moonlight. In the day, it must be as it always is. Can you accept that?"

"I accept you however you are," she replied. "Tell me what formula is required for the spell, and I shall repeat it faithfully." It was so easy; she seemed to know exactly what to say. *This time I know I am dreaming,* she thought regretfully. *But what a marvelous dream! What a lovely, precious dream!*

"Vivian! I *knew* you would be different!" he cried. "The others, out there, they frighten me. Terribly. I don't understand the rules of the game, I feel helpless. It is so very horrible! Here, I am at home. I am in control. I must be in control, do you see? Otherwise, I am overwhelmed, smothered, crushed!"

"I understand perfectly," she said with sympathy. "Have no fear, Angel. I am quite able to deal with that world out there, and everyone in it. It holds no terror for me! I shall be your shield against it. And I shall remain ever and always your devoted servant."

She could feel him trembling slightly. "Then perhaps," he whispered, "perhaps this will be all right." Shyly, timidly, he bent his head to kiss her. It was like a butterfly lighting, an exquisitely beautiful, fragile creature. One had to refrain from the urge to try to hold it, forcing oneself to be passive, gentle, to accept the blessing of its papery touch. His kiss was so light, so delicate, like the fine china bones of his body, so liable to damage by the heedless crush of passion.

And yet, she could sense something subtle beneath, deep and hidden, a low humming of force, a power that could animate a basilisk.

When he drew back, she promptly did the same. He gazed into her eyes. "That is all, I think," he said. "Enough for this night, this moon. The moonlight gives me courage, but only so much."

"It is enough for me, Angel," she said bravely, although in truth, she regretted having to let him go.

CHAPTER SEVEN

Repairs to the House

She woke up late, Heron tapping at her door, and she leaped out of bed. "I'm coming!" she called. "Do get the cats' food ready, would you please? I'll be there as quickly as I can!" She dressed hastily. Gracious, what dreams she'd had! No doubt the result of Mr. Nesselrode's strange talk and manner at dinner. Full moon, and who knows what sorts of doings in the night! She sat in front of the mirror, hurriedly brushing and braiding her hair. At least they hadn't been dancing outside her window again, waking her up, depriving her of a good night's sleep. Then again, something must have disturbed her so that she overslept....

Her hands slowed as the silver dream came back to her again. The moonlight, the haunting music, the shy confession of love. Angel. Her Angel. He had kissed her....

She sat, immobile, remembering. It had been so ethereal and yet so vivid. It *had* been a dream, hadn't it? Of course, it must have been. He would never... No, absolutely not. He had made it quite clear how things were to be between them, strictly professional, just as it should be. Certainly he would never do anything so improper.

She returned to braiding her hair furiously. This would never do! Not only was she harboring romantic thoughts about her employer, now she was dreaming about him as well! She must put it out of her mind. It would fade as all dreams did, dissolving into astringent reality. She had work to do. The cats needed their breakfast, and there were telephone calls to make, arrangements to be made, a shopping list—tomorrow was Thursday—how *could* she have slept so late?

He didn't show up until lunch, which was to be expected considering the phase of the moon. He seemed to be in a particularly nervous state, hovering in the kitchen doorway, stammering out his inquiry.

"Good day to you, Ms. Mare, ah, could I—would it be possible—that is, for lunch, might I have a fruit cup? My appetite, I'm not all that hungry, you see…"

It was disconcerting; his behavior surely had nothing to do with her. And yet, when their eyes met that impossibly romantic dream came back to her with unnerving vividness, and she felt a little shiver thrill its way over her skin.

"I do apologize, Mr. Nesselrode," she said briskly, clamping down with firm self-control, "but I'm afraid I don't have what I would need to make you a proper fruit cup. I could run to the store—"

"Oh no, no need of that," he said hastily.

"I shall be shopping tomorrow, so perhaps after that. May I offer you a little tuna salad instead? I could serve it with small squares of toast."

"Oh, that would be fine. But no toast. Might I have a bit of lettuce?"

"Lettuce, then."

"Torn up small, please?"

"Of course."

He smiled with shy warmth. "You are very good to me."

Again she was caught, for the space of a heartbeat, haunted by the ghosts of moonlit fantasies. She turned back to the counter, deliberately looking away from him, stern with herself. She said, "Just give me a moment to prepare it, Mr. Nesselrode. Why don't you go and sit at the table by the window and I shall bring it to you when it is ready?"

"Thank you, that would be fine."

She scolded herself as she opened the can of tuna, draining off the liquid into a dish for the cats. The grey Manx was prompt to respond to the can opener and staked his claim on the treat. The calico and the black one with white paws showed up while Ms. Mare was preparing the tray, and she was obliged to stop what she was doing to pour the tuna liquid off into separate bowls to accommodate them.

She brought the tray into the other room with a pot of peppermint tea, and informed him of the arrangements she had made for the work to be done to the house. As was usually the case, focusing his attention on mundane details served to calm him. The nervousness passed and he was his accustomed self again, pleased at the arrangements she had made, promising to see to the basilisk when the workmen arrived. She got him settled happily with his lunch by the window overlooking the back meadow which sloped down towards the pond, and she returned to surveying the larder and composing her shopping list. Soon the demands of her daily routine pushed the disturbing dream out of her mind.

At dinner her employer was in a splendid mood, particularly witty and charming. Later that evening she found the lobster in her bath tub. Things had pretty much returned to normal.

***

The workmen came to do the roof, throwing the routines of the household into an uproar. Ms. Mare harbored a deep distrust of workmen, convinced that the majority were incompetent crooks, so she watched them the first day like a hawk. The fellow in charge of the crew was a friendly chap with unkempt curly brown hair and a tooth missing in front. But he proved to be unexpectedly intelligent for all his rough appearance. His name was O'Rourke, and he had been recommended by the town librarian who knew him as a patron. Ms. Mare considered librarians to be among the most trustworthy of individuals, unconnected as they were from the twin demon realms of business and politics. Ms. Mare also considered an association with books to be excellent testimony as to a person's character. If Mr. O'Rourke was known to habituate the library, then he was likely to be a cut above the ordinary laborer. In spite of all this, Ms. Mare kept a close eye on him. His men—and one woman, Ms. Mare noted with approval—worked steadily and competently with a minimum of damage to the flower beds, and she was pleased with their progress. O'Rourke made a bid on the painting job which Ms. Mare said she would take under advisement.

The basilisk disliked being sent off to the pond, and grumped and pouted when called back in the evening. She felt a profound responsibility for the safety of the household and was highly distressed at having so many strangers about. She kept sniffing around the ladders and where the boots of the workmen had tramped down the grass. Ms. Mare worried that the beast would find it too much to bear, and might come slithering back at an inopportune moment, scaring off a crew which was proving to be worth the rather steep fee they were asking. Mr. Nesselrode assured her that the basilisk understood and would not shame herself.

The artist himself kept to his studio while the workmen were there, fearing that they were all peering in the windows for a chance to glimpse him. They *were*, of course, although with a reasonable amount of discretion. Archimedes Nesselrode had not put on a public appearance in years. What common person, no matter what his opinion of art in general, could resist the temptation of possibly catching sight of such a celebrity? Ms. Mare brought up his lunch and calmed his peevish queries as to how much longer this inconvenient state of affairs was going to go on.

"Next month I may have them paint the house," she said, "And that may take quite a bit longer."

"I'd rather you didn't."

"Now, now, it needs to be done," she reminded him as she spread his lunch out on the table, carefully pushing aside brushes and a scattering of pencils. "You agreed, you know."

"A prisoner in my own house!" he groused.

It was, at least, a productive imprisonment. He filled several crates with little Lucite cubes in which tiny fantasies swam, coiled, basked and drowsed. In his boredom he even concocted bubbling waterfalls, several roses that alternately bloomed and furled up into tight buds, and geometric figures which floated and changed color when the cube was jostled. He made trees which leafed out, budded and blossomed, then bore fruit which was eaten by tiny deer. He made underwater gardens and coral reefs where brilliantly colored fish swam in and out. He did seem exceptionally inspired. Ms. Mare called Frank Shekle two weeks in a row requesting a truck to pick up the crates. Mr. Shekle was delighted. The long drought was at last over, with a cloudburst.

When the work was done and the crew departed, Mr. Nesselrode spent an entire morning outside in the sun, riding the basilisk around the grounds. Both he and the basilisk were in much better spirits after that, although he came in with a dreadful sunburn on his face and hands.

On Monday she picked up the mail at the post office, then sat at the kitchen table making neat piles of it, deciding what required the attention of her employer, and what ought to go directly into the recycling. There was really very little to deal with; most of what was not junk was receipts and reports from the Agency of *Shekle and Kronor* on bills paid and business dispensed with, which Mr. Nesselrode would ignore.

Ms. Mare felt a growing concern with the extraordinary control that the Agency, Frank Shekle in particular, had over her employer. She supposed it was really none of her affair, but she could not help wondering if this arrangement were really wise. Could Frank Shekle be trusted? Of course, her employer did need someone to look after his affairs; he was completely incapable of making sure his bills were paid on time. But it did not seem prudent to invest so much responsibility in one person, especially when so much money was involved. No doubt the Agency made a handsome fee from their labors on behalf of the artist, but that was the problem with money. No matter how much one has, one can always use more, and even a basically decent person can succumb to temptation when there is no oversight.

She sat at the table frowning and tapping her finger on the supermarket flyer which sat on top of the pile of paper recycling. At the very least, as housekeeper, she ought to be in charge of all household expenses, including utilities. Mr. Nesselrode paid no attention to the accounts sent by the Agency. Perhaps Ms. Mare would obtain his permission to begin going over the receipts and keeping a file of them for herself. How long had it been, she wondered, since he had arranged for an independent audit of his accounts? Just to make sure everything was in order. Would it be presumptuous of her to speak to him about it? Or to suggest she make arrangements for it on his behalf? Normally she would never take such a responsibility onto her own shoulders, but Mr. Nesselrode was so desperately in need of looking after, and who but she could do the job properly?

She glanced at the calendar, and noticed the full moon was coming up again. That bit of astronomical trivia loomed large in her attention after her experiences of the previous two lunar cycles. First there had been that midnight frolic on the lawn with the dancing fox and the fantastical musicians. That had been real enough, she was quite sure. But then there had been that dream of waking and thinking she was being invited to join the revelry under the moon, only to walk out into the hallway and find her employer waiting for her, calling her by name, taking her in his arms. She still had not forgotten it; the details stayed with her, not fading as dreams usually did. She could recall clearly the echoing melody of the music box, and how he looked by moonlight, all silver and silk, the gentleness of his touch, the butterfly kiss. Her Angel—

That will be quite enough! she scolded herself, picking up the pile of junk mail and stuffing it into a paper bag to be taken to the recycling. It was all well and good to be devoted to her employer but she mustn't allow it to get out of hand. He had been very tolerant and understanding when it came out that she was a bit sweet on him. He had even taken her into his confidence, showing her his studio. He was fond of her in spite of the formal professionalism of their relationship. There was unquestionably a friendship growing between them. No doubt he appreciated having someone to talk to in whom he could trust. She definitely had a special place in the life of Archimedes Nesselrode as his only real companion, and it was a position of honor. She must at all times respect the gravity of that honor, and keep her feelings under firm control. She simply could not permit herself to go all calf-eyed, like some silly school girl.

***

At dinner on Thursday, her employer remarked quite casually, "The moon will be full again tonight."

Ms. Mare's hand froze, her fork full of tortellini. Her eyes blinked up and across the table to where he sat, stroking the calico cat who had settled herself next to his dish, sniffing it curiously to see if what the humans had been served was superior to her own fare.

"And the weather looks like it will be clear and quite mild," he continued, selecting a piece of lettuce from the green salad and spearing it with his fork. He liked the lettuce cut into small pieces to make it easier to eat daintily. Ms. Mare always obliged.

"It has been quite pleasant all week," Ms. Mare replied, carefully. Was she reading too much into his expression? Was there just the faintest glitter in his eyes?

The calico cat decided that she didn't care for the lemon pepper sauce on the tortellini and jumped lightly down from the table. Mr. Nesselrode said, "I'd been hoping the weather would stay pleasant. I do adore the night air, don't you Ms. Mare?"

"On occasion," she said carefully.

"A *special* occasion?" He laughed, high and wild, and she felt a little shiver. He did seem quite mad at times.

"I can't imagine what you mean," she said. If he would simply say what he planned then at least she could be ready for it, to humor him if necessary, or if it seemed preferable and would not offend him, to decline.

"Then it shall be a surprise!" he said, rising from the table. "Excuse me if you will, Ms. Mare, I have a great deal to do!" and he left the table with eyes full of mischief.

She felt distinctly ill at ease all the rest of the evening. Heron helped her with the dishes and the marmosets dried the silver and put it all away without dropping a single spoon, for which she praised them and offered them the reward of a cracker apiece. They took their crackers chittering with delight and scampered off.

"Do you have any idea what Mr. Nesselrode was referring to at dinner?" she asked of Heron as she wiped a pot and replaced it on its shelf. "About the moon and night air, I mean."

The bird shook her head and clacked her beak. It was really no use asking her anyway. Even if she knew, Heron wouldn't have spoken of it; she would merely have looked over her spectacles at Ms. Mare, prim and smug.

There was nothing to be done about it. So she went over her menu for the next day, saw to a couple other odds and ends, then went up to her room with a nice cup of tea. She had brought a book home from the library. The Galbraiths had taken it into their heads to winter in Australia this year, and the librarian had recommended Bill Bryson's *In a Sunburned Country.* "Humorous, full of factual information, and a very entertaining read," she had been told. Very well, perhaps it would get her mind off of her employer's cryptic allusions to the night's activities.

Before getting into bed, she stood for just a moment at the window, watching the great, orange orb of the moon rise above the trees. She remembered when she was a little girl seeing the moon rise like that over the mountains in a village in Austria. She had heard her mother and the Galbraiths talking with their host about the terrible fire bombings that had happened nearby during the War. When little Vivian went to bed, she looked out the window and saw the huge, ruddy light of the moon, and thought certainly it must be some terrible disaster in the distance, and she had run to her mother in alarm. Her mother laughed and reassured her, sitting with her by the window until the moon was high enough to be clearly recognizable.

"But, it didn't look at all like the moon," Vivian had insisted.

"The moon can play tricks on you," her mother had said. "There is nothing quite so marvelous or magical as the moon. No matter what part of the world you may be in, the moon is always with you, and always is just as mysterious!"

Ms. Mare wondered what her mother would think of Archimedes Nesselrode.

CHAPTER EIGHT

The Waltz

She did not recall putting out her light and falling asleep, but she must have done so. The book was closed and the light was out. The moonlight coming through the window had shrunk to a slim wedge, a sign that it must have been close to midnight. What had wakened her?

She heard a clacking. Lobster. It pushed her door open and came in, its claws raised. Then, with a soft beating of wings, the snake came in, swooping over her bed, undulating as if it were swimming through water.

It's like before, she thought. But I'm not dreaming, am I? Oh dear, I hardly know the difference anymore!

She heard very faintly in the far distance the sound of music. Not the music box. Nor the flute and drum of the midnight revelers. Strings? And something like a harpsichord. She got up, now thoroughly awake, and she put on her slippers and robe. She wished her robe were not so plain. Stopping by the dressing table, she brushed out her hair. She thought, I must look well for this, whatever it might be.

The unicorns came stamping in snorting impatiently, and then the winged fish that she had seen in the attic flapped leisurely through the room. She felt a moment's anxiety at the thought that Arachne might also be loose. But no, he had promised her.

When she emerged from her room she looked impulsively down the hallway to the landing, to the pool of moonlight where he had stood before, but he was not there. Of course not. That hadn't been real. This was going to be different. The music grew more distinct as she went down the stairs and through the living room, stepping carefully over the starfish. The sliding glass doors were open out onto the patio with its mossy, overgrown flagstones and rusted lawn furniture. But when she stepped through the door, the wrought iron table with its peeling paint was not there. Flambeaux flickered on either side of the path through the shrubs down to the lawn. There was a table and two chairs set with a white tablecloth, two glasses and a bottle. A candle flickered and dripped wax. She walked slowly towards it, the night air cool and filled with sweet damp fragrance. There, on the lawn, was the source of the music. A string quartet, consisting of a penguin, an ibis, an iguana and the familiar sea horse, all with nimble and dexterous fingers and playing their viols and violins exquisitely. The harpsichord was being played by the toad butler with solemn and rapturous concentration.

"My word!" she breathed.

There were candles and lanterns all around, hanging from the trees and planted in the ground. It was like a garden party at a villa in Italy she had been to once, except that the musicians were far different and there were no crowds in masques and gowns.

The music stopped and the toad rose from his seat before the keyboard. The sound of crickets filled the void left by the music. With great ceremony, the toad came over to her, bowed low and conducted her to the table. She sat down at the table looking around herself, quite amazed at it all. *Am I dreaming or not? This seems too impossible, yet I've never had dreams like this before!*

The toad stepped back and stood at attention. The ibis took up the violin and began playing a sweet, strange air. She recognized the melody of the music box from her previous dream. It added to the eerie sense of unreality hovering over it all.

"So glad you could come."

She looked up and saw him emerge out of the shadows to stand beside the table, dressed in a full, bloused silk shirt and cravat, dark pants and calf-high boots, a sash about his waist. The shirt was the color of moonlight and the pants shaped themselves to his slim hips. He bowed to her. "May I join you?"

"Why, of course," she said, now completely drawn into the situation with all its absurdity. She rose to give him a formal curtsey, as would befit a lady of her station to a gentleman of nobility. "Forgive me," she said, "If I'd known this was to be a formal occasion, I would have dressed for it."

"Why, my dear, I think your dress is quite perfect."

She began to protest modestly, looking down at her sorry chenille robe, and she caught herself with a gasp. She was wearing a dress of lace and what seemed to be light blue or lavender, the folds of which caught the light with a strange iridescence. "My word!" She touched her throat and could feel the coolness of a necklace of smooth stones hanging around her neck.

Archimedes Nesselrode laughed delightedly, and gestured to the toad, who took up the bottle of champagne and opened it.

"I know you to be a woman of discriminating tastes," he said as the toad poured, "so I hope that you approve of the vintage."

"I'm certain it shall be most adequate," she replied.

"You are too kind," he said, and took her hand. She never wore rings, since they were impractical with the daily chores she had to perform, but there on her finger was a silver filigree ring into which was set a star sapphire. On his own hand was a ring with the double eagle of the Russian monarchy set with a moonstone. "Do sit down," he said.

"Thank you," she said graciously, settling herself carefully, arranging the billows of her skirt around her and daintily crossing her ankles. She remembered how she had felt as a young girl being taken to elegant affairs by the Galbraiths, whose celebrity had gotten them into some very elevated circles. She had been taught refined manners, how to speak and how to dance, and she had felt like a princess among all those wealthy and aristocratic people. It all came back to her now, the magic of being a part of that privileged world, an illegitimate servant girl being allowed for a night to dance and dine among the elite, being introduced by the Galbraiths simply as "Miss Vivian Mare, the daughter of a dear friend of ours." Her mother never went to such affairs; she said they made her uncomfortable. But Vivian came home with her eyes full of stars, breathless with happiness, full of stories which her mother listened to gladly. The Galbraiths delighted in treating Vivian as if she were their own daughter, passing off the matter of her birth as nothing at all to be ashamed of.

"Gracious," Esther Galbraith used to say, "Every aristocratic family in Europe has had its share of children born on the wrong side of the sheets, including a goodly number of kings! You're a part of a time-honored and royal tradition, my dear."

The toad poured the champagne. Archimedes Nesselrode took up his glass and she did likewise. He raised it to toast. "To you, Vivian," he said.

"To you," she replied, hesitating, shyly, "Angel."

His smile broadened and his eyes sparkled. "To us, then!" He took a sip, his eyes closing ecstatically. "Ahh!"

She had tasted champagne of this quality before, at a wedding in New York. It was a quality which had defined the beverage for her ever since.

"Exceptional," she murmured, savoring the bubbling crispness on her tongue.

He nodded to the toad, who clicked his heels and bowed, then waddled back over to the rest of the musicians, returning to the harpsichord. They all resumed playing, another lilting air she did not recognize.

"You arranged all this?" she asked him.

He raised his glass to the moon, pale and round in the sky overhead. "The moon and the night obliged me," he replied. "The rest, yes, I had a hand in it."

"You are too modest," she said, taking another sip.

"Am I? Ah, but what would be the point of any of it, were you not the sort who could appreciate it?" He leaned his elbows on the table, gazing at her admiringly. "Ah, Vivian! You have done so much! And I have done so little!"

"I hardly think that's so!" she scoffed.

"Oh, but it's true! I have had such a coddled and cloistered life. My parents guarded me like a treasure."

"But surely, you traveled, and had opportunities to do a great many things. You were born into privilege. My access to privilege was only proximate."

"Oh, but you have *done* things!" he insisted. "You have ridden camels and yaks, and swum in the Dead Sea and run among the fireworks in the street during a Chinese New Year!"

"And nearly gotten trampled and scorched!" she replied. "My clothes were ruined and I was scared to death!"

"Oh, but don't you see? My parents would never have allowed me *near* such an event. I wasn't even allowed to ride any but the tamest pony, my mother went in such fear that I might be injured. I once got away from my nurse and climbed a tree in the park. Oh, it was so lovely up there! They shouted to me to get down, but I refused. I felt so free! I could see all the park, and the buildings all around, and the dogs running and the pigeons wheeling in great clouds. I wanted to fly. I thought that if only I had the courage, I could spread my arms and leap off into the air and follow the pigeons." He rose to his feet, reliving the memory. "I stood on the branch, believing I could make it happen! I just had to bend my mind to it. I would fly, far away from them, fly where I wanted to, above it all! Above the cathedral to thumb my nose at the gargoyles, above the smokestacks with their dirt and stink, far away, to the seashore, to play among the rocks and shoals, completely unsupervised! I threw out my arms, leaped into the air, and for just a moment, just a precious fleeting moment, I could fly!"

"And then what happened?" she asked him breathlessly.

He sat back down in the chair with a sigh. "I fell, of course. Broke my arm and my nose and sprained my ankle. My mother was hysterical. I was punished for being disobedient, but then they bought me all sorts of treats and took me to the country for a month."

"Where you were supervised every minute," she guessed sympathetically.

"Relentlessly," he affirmed with bitterness.

"My poor Angel!"

He grinned at her. "Ah, but I am grown, now, and able to do as I please. Would you care to dance, Vivian?"

"I'd be delighted," she said, draining the last delicious sip of champagne from her glass before getting up. He took her hand grandly, and the musicians took their cue to play a waltz.

"You dance marvelously well," she said as he led her lightly over the grass in elegant steps and turns.

"Of course. I had endless torturous lessons, when I would much rather have been mucking about with paints and clay. I was also taught to play the violin, which I was never anything but wretched at. Dancing, however, I came to enjoy, though I haven't done so in years."

"Nor have I," she cried laughing. "It feels wonderful!"

"Doesn't it?" he agreed. The musicians picked up the pace and the music grew far more full, as if suddenly a complete orchestra were playing. They changed key and suddenly they were playing the theme from the music box again. She tried to look past him to see what had happened, but the lights around them began to glow with an opalescence that obscured everything else. She closed her eyes for a moment, giddy with champagne and breathless with the dance, and she heard his high, wild laughter.

Opening her eyes, she stared with astonishment, for the lawn and the garden had quite disappeared. He was waltzing her down a hallway with a green marble floor, walls of pearl set with silver sconces, candles burning brilliantly in each. Along the walls between the sconces hung heavy velvet curtains of rich dark green, maroon, and midnight blue which billowed out to them as they whirled past. The ceiling was black onyx set with diamonds. Looking up at it while she spun made her dizzy. He laughed, and in his laughter was the rush of force she had sensed before, released and radiating like an invisible sun. It was wild and mad, and she felt giddy, almost afraid to let go of him for fear she would fly off and shatter some ice-thin wall and plunge away into surreality.

Then he swept her through a tinkling curtain of crystal beads, and they were outside again, but on a balcony overlooking a midnight garden of topiaries and fountains. The air was heavy with the scent of jasmine, and vines hung all around them. Above, the moon gazed down with a pale, inscrutable face.

"The moon," he said softly, holding her close to him, the night air cooling the perspiration on their skin, and stirring just slightly his long, silky hair. "The moon makes it possible, you see."

"You make it possible," she whispered in reply, raising her face up to his.

"Only by moonlight," he replied. He touched her hair, and it fell loose around her shoulders.

She closed her eyes, and this time it was not the butterfly which brushed her lips. It was much more.

***

The cats got her up the next morning, jumping on the bed, purring and rubbing against her face. They had learned who fed them and when, and they expected punctuality.

"Am I late again?" Ms. Mare mumbled irritably, reluctant to surrender her peaceful sleep. She sat up yawning, reflexively petting the grey Manx and then the marmalade tabby. "All right, all right. If you don't get out of the way I shan't be able to get up." She reached for her slippers and frowned. They felt damp. "Now, why on earth—?" She eyed the cats suspiciously. "You ungrateful wretches wouldn't be so vindictive as that, would you? Just because I'm a little late with your breakfast!" She picked up a slipper and sniffed it warily.

The marmalade tabby mewled, throwing herself against Ms. Mare's side, and the black cat with the white paws nearly knocked her water glass off the table. "Now, stop that!" Ms. Mare cried, reaching to catch the glass before it fell. She noticed her clock and saw the time. "Good heavens, it *is* late, isn't it? Why would I have overslept so?" Then she remembered the dream.

"Oh," she said, and sat, unable to move, the intoxicating memory of it washing over her. They had wandered through the midnight garden, through a hedge maze lit with glowing hummingbirds, to come out upon a riverbank where they sat beneath graceful willows and watched lotus blossoms floating gently downstream. They had talked, endlessly, about everything. It had been so beautiful that it nearly brought tears to her eyes. In the end he had confessed that he was growing tired, and he took her back to her room, kissing her tenderly good night.

"Dear me!" she said finally, "This really has got to stop. It can come to no good end." Yet she couldn't quite force herself to get moving, to face the day and abandon the rich, seductive, otherworldly enchantment of the images and sensations coming back to her. It had seemed so vivid, and yet it could not have been real. He could create all manner of strange beasts, certainly, but gardens, rivers, entire landscapes? It simply could not be. "But, that I could even *dream* such a thing!" she exclaimed aloud. "Working here is certainly having a disturbing effect on me!"

The cats, however, had no sympathy and annoyed her into accepting the inevitable duties that loomed before her. She dressed, trying to make haste, but finding herself helplessly distracted. Finally she made it downstairs to the kitchen. Heron was already there, clacking her bill impatiently.

"I know, I know," Ms. Mare responded peevishly to the implied criticism. "I've already been soundly scolded by the cats, thank you very much!" She got down their dishes. "What is the hurry, anyway? Don't tell me the Master is up already demanding his porridge? After a full moon? That would be a first!"

Heron shook her head and fluffed her feathers, obviously upset over something. She squawked and Ms. Mare turned around to frown at her. "Is he unwell?" Then she blinked in surprise. "My word, I've actually begun to understand you. This job is *definitely* becoming a trial on my nerves!"

Heron squawked furiously.

"You needn't take that tone with me!" Ms. Mare retorted, going to the refrigerator for the cats' food. "Now, what is the problem with Mr. Nesselrode?"

The bird ruffled her feathers again and bobbed her head in agitation. Ms. Mare's expression became concerned. "Dear me. A tray then? Toast and tea, perhaps. Do get the water going for me, would you?" She hastily finished spooning out meat and rice into the dishes, dropping a crunchy tartar control treat into each for their teeth's sake. The matronly bird filled the kettle and put it on to boil, then put two slices of toast in the toaster. Ms. Mare set the dishes down in the prescribed spots in the seething sea of mewing fur, making sure there was one cat face only per dish, thus increasing the odds that they would each get their tartar control treat. Then she prepared the tray. Heron fluttered about the kitchen, squawking impatiently.

"All right, here I come with it. Gracious! I hope he isn't too poorly off." Taking up the tray she stepped carefully through the pool of cats, pausing to note with relief that the winged snake had not molested the flowers and the marmosets had not broken into the cookie jar. As she passed the window she glanced out, then froze, looking again and staring at what she saw.

Out on the lawn were two chairs and the wrought iron table, a tablecloth spread over it, one side blown up by the breeze. The cloth was kept down by the weight of a champagne bottle.

"Good lord!" she breathed.

Heron squawked at her from the stairs, clacking her beak with fretful insistence.

"All right," Ms. Mare mumbled, tearing her eyes from the scene on the lawn with difficulty, "I'm coming. Where's the starfish? I don't want to trip."

She climbed the stairs, her head in a whirl, managing barely to recover her focus. She came to her employer's room and pushed the door open with her shoulder.

"Good morning, Mr. Nesselrode. Heron tells me you're not feeling well—"

She nearly dropped the tray at the sight of him. He looked ghastly. He was lying in bed, his face drawn and even more pale than usual. There were dark smudges under his eyes; his cheeks looked hollow and gaunt. His skin had a papery appearance that made it seem as though he had aged; indeed, there were faint lines around his eyes and mouth that had not been there before.

"Mr. Nesselrode!" she exclaimed, setting the tray down on top of the clutter that covered his dresser. She rushed over to the bed, sitting down on the edge of it. "Shall I call the doctor? Do you have a doctor? Shall I find one?"

"That won't be necessary," he reassured her, although the sound of his voice was less that reassuring. It was weak and hoarse. Speaking seemed to be an effort for him.

"But you look dreadful!" she protested, touching the back of her hand to his forehead to test for a temperature. He had none; quite the contrary, he felt unnaturally cold.

"Please don't be alarmed," he said, "I'll recover. I think."

Heron squawked reproachfully.

"I know," he sighed, "You're quite right." He looked at Ms. Mare with a weak smile. "I rather overdid it last night, you see. It took a great deal out of me. I hope you enjoyed it."

"I? Last night...?" she echoed. Her damp slippers. The table on the lawn with the bottle of champagne. The dream... "It was...real, then?" she whispered.

"Real? Well, yes, real enough." He sighed. "All gone now, of course. Fleeting substance, that's all I could give it." He sighed again. "Ah, but wasn't it grand?"

"It wasn't a dream!" she gasped.

"You thought it was? Yes, it was rather dreamlike, wasn't it?" He closed his eyes, smiling.

"And last month, in the hallway...!"

He opened his eyes. "Eh? Oh, that. Yes, that happened, too. That had to come first, you see. I had to find out for certain if you would be, ah, receptive. What Lobster told me led me to believe it might be possible...but one can't always rely on gossip."

"And... and you are ill this morning because of what you did last night?" she asked, trying to comprehend it all.

"I really did get carried away, I'm afraid. I wanted so much to impress you, and it was all going so well. We were having such fun! I created too much, and now I'm paying for it. But I have no regrets. None at all. I trust you don't, Ms. Mare?" he asked anxiously.

"Oh, no, none at all!" she assured him hastily. "It really happened," she breathed. The implications of it brought a rush of tenderness, and she reached out her hand to touch his cool, hollow cheek. "My Angel," she murmured.

Alarm clouded his eyes and he grimaced as if in pain. "You mustn't speak that way," he pleaded. "Only in moonlight. During the day it isn't right. During the day it becomes... frightening."

She nodded slowly. "I see. Yes, of course. Please do forgive me, Mr. Nesselrode. You must admit, this is an awful lot to have to absorb all at once."

Relief cleared his face. "Yes, quite a lot, true. I trust you can manage it, as you have managed so remarkably well with all the rest."

"I shall try," she assured him, unable to keep the tenderness from her voice. Then, taking a deep breath, she resumed her air of brisk efficiency, the housekeeper looking after her ailing employer. "Here now, let's get you sitting up so that you can have your breakfast. I'll help. That's it." He felt so light, delicate, as if his bones had become brittle and all the strength had left his muscles, almost like a doll, or a newborn babe, or a man frail with age. "Heron, would you move that pillow up please? Thank you. And that other one. Good. Now lie back. How is that?"

"Just fine, thank you," he said, settling back with a sigh. Heron fussed with his bedclothes while Ms. Mare got the tray.

"There now. Can you manage by yourself?" she asked him.

"I'll be all right," he said. "Heron will help me." He smiled at the bird, who fluffed her feathers, looking at him over her spectacles with stern fondness.

"If you want fresh tea, I'll gladly fetch it. This has gone a bit cool."

He picked up the cup, his hand trembling with the effort. "Oh no, it's fine."

"If you're sure. Heron, kindly let me know when he's done with his tray and I'll come and take it away."

The feathered matron bobbed her head in acknowledgment.

Downstairs, Ms. Mare went out to the wrought iron table to collect the tablecloth and the empty bottle. As she picked up the bottle she thought she could hear faint strains of music, soft and distant, a music box playing the waltz. She hugged the tablecloth and bottle against her, closing her eyes, again tasting the champagne, the scent of jasmine, the opalescent lights, the midnight garden, the dance.

She opened her eyes. "If I am going mad," she said to the bottle, "then I shall go gladly!"

CHAPTER NINE

Impossible Proposals

He did recover, but it was nearly two weeks before Archimedes Nesselrode was back on his feet again. During that period, Mr. Shekle called several times.

"Let me talk to him, please?"

"Mr. Nesselrode is not to be disturbed."

"It's important!"

"I'll take a message."

"Look, you're his *house*keeper, not *his* keeper!"

"I perform all my duties as assigned. Mr. Nesselrode is not to be disturbed. If it is important, I shall take a message."

Frank Shekle had no choice but to relent in the face of the immovable object.

"All right. Tell him this. That last batch of creations he released has been a sensation. Some of them were a real departure from his normal style."

"Yes. We were having the roof done, and he was bored."

"Okay, whatever. Anyway, even though it's not a medium they usually deal with—as if anyone even knows what the hell Nesselrode's medium actually is—the Rumpleminz Gallery of Art wants to do an exhibit of his works."

"Fine. I'm sure Mr. Nesselrode would be agreeable."

"No, no. You don't understand. This is a big deal. The Rumpleminz Gallery is one of the most exclusive, high brow outfits in New York. They do exhibits of fine arts. Big names. Usually dead. This is practically unprecedented. Claudia Van Maus is one of the sponsors. We've got collectors from all over the world loaning us some of his finest works for the exhibit. There's going to be a huge reception in Nesselrode's honor— all sorts of press and publicity lined up."

"How wonderful. I shall tell him. I'm sure he'll be delighted."

"Ms. Mare, you still don't get it. I don't want him to be delighted. I want him to be there."

"That's out of the question. Mr. Nesselrode doesn't make personal appearances. You know that, Mr. Shekle."

"I know, but this is an exception!"

"I'm afraid it won't be possible."

"Will you please let *him* decide that?"

"I shall inform Mr. Nesselrode. He shall return your call if he so chooses."

Frank Shekle had to be content with that.

Archimedes Nesselrode frowned over his lunch of cucumber and cream cheese sandwiches, which he was enjoying in the warm noonday sun out on the lawn. The blue sheep were grazing nearby, and the basilisk was napping under the elm. The marmalade tabby was stalking insects in the garden, and the black cat with white paws was stalking the marmalade tabby. Ms. Mare added a wedge of lime to her employer's glass and filled it with ice water.

"No," he said with a shake of his head, "I hate to disappoint Frank, not to mention all those others who are counting on this, but I simply can't do it."

"Shall I call Mr. Shekle for you, or do you wish to inform him of your decision yourself?" she asked him.

"Would you mind doing it, Ms. Mare?" he asked, looking up at her appealingly. "He'll weep and wail and gnash his teeth, and try so persuasively to talk me into it. I really couldn't stand it."

"I am quite immune to Mr. Shekle's weeping and wailing," she said firmly. "I shall take care of the matter this afternoon."

"Thank you!" he exclaimed gratefully.

"Not at all, Mr. Nesselrode. Now then, I have made appointments at the vet for all the cats. I shall be taking them by twos and threes until they have all been seen."

"Are you certain that is quite necessary? I just know they shall hate it and be furious at me for it. Particularly Madam Beast."

"You know it is for their own good," Ms. Mare replied. "They are not like your creations. We must look after their health. And yours," she added. "I really must insist that you allow me to schedule a dentist appointment for you."

He groaned. "I loathe going to the dentist!"

"No one enjoys it, Mr. Nesselrode," she said firmly, "But if one does not take care of one's teeth, it is most unpleasant in the long run. You should see a doctor as well."

"I shall agree only if they can make house calls!"

"No one does that anymore, least of all a dentist. I know how you dislike the idea of leaving the estate, but you must consider it, for your health's sake. It would be just a short trip and I shall drive you if you like."

He grumbled under his breath. She took it for grudging agreement.

"Now then," she inquired, "Will there be anything else?"

There wasn't, and she left him to take his lunch in the sunshine, mindful that he didn't stay out in it for too long. He was so prone to burns.

Back in the kitchen, Ms. Mare was scolded by Heron.

"I am simply looking after his health!" Ms. Mare replied to the stern bird. "I don't consider that meddling in his affairs."

Heron retorted with a fussy squawk.

"I beg your pardon! It is for his own good!" The two of them glared at one another for a moment, and then Ms. Mare relented, slightly. "All right," she said, "One thing at a time. I shall let the medical check-up go for now if you will help me persuade him to see a dentist. Dentists are, I expect, a bit less intimidating. At least one needn't disrobe."

That satisfied the bird.

At dinner, which was halibut baked with herbs, he brought up the business with the personal appearance again.

"Was Frank terribly disappointed?"

"He will survive, I'm sure," Ms. Mare replied.

"Still, I do feel badly. The Rumpleminz Gallery, after all. It is quite an honor. And it might be fun to put on a show. I haven't done it in years. I used to rather enjoy it."

"Well, it is of course entirely up to you," she said, eying him curiously. "If I may be so bold as to ask, why are you so averse to it now?"

He smiled at her sadly. "It simply got to be too much for me. It wasn't fun anymore. It became frightening."

"Frightening in what way?" she asked.

He hesitated, then answered carefully. "I find the world a very confusing place. When one doesn't understand what is going on, it is easy to become confused. To lose control. It can become quite dreadful."

"I see," she said, remembering what she had read. His fame and success had not suited his temperament. No doubt unscrupulous elements had attempted to exploit him. Something terrible had happened to him that drove him into seclusion. She wondered what it could have been.

"No, I really couldn't go out there again," he said firmly.

"As you wish," she said, masking her disappointment at his disinclination to reveal more. "Would you care for dessert?"

"Thank you, no. I've made a pig of myself on the fish. You really did a splendid job with the seasoning."

"Thank you, Mr. Nesselrode. It's good to see your appetite back."

He brought it up twice again the next day. He was clearly undecided. And it was preying on his mind.

On Tuesday, he didn't show up either for breakfast or lunch. She had planned on doing his room, but had to put it off. Never mind, there were always other projects to see to. At dinner he showed up as he sometimes did after a busy night, disheveled and still in his dressing gown. He complained that he couldn't find his other slipper, and he picked at dinner, eating and saying little.

"There is something bothering you, I think," Ms. Mare suggested.

He didn't answer. But at the end of the meal, he asked what the weather was to be that night.

"It is supposed to clear up and be quite chilly," she replied.

"No clouds?"

"I don't believe so," she said, "Although you know how weather predictions are."

"So the moon, it will be out, then?"

She paused. "Yes, I expect so. It is in its first quarter." She had become quite attentive to the cycles of the moon.

"That will have to do. Ms. Mare, could I impose on you to meet me in the hallway at the upstairs landing before you retire for bed?"

"I shall be there," she promised.

He wants to confide in me! she thought with excitement, no doubt about this trip to the city that Frank Shekle so dearly wants him to make. But it was a conversation that couldn't take place between an employer and his devoted housekeeper. It was one that needed to take place between intimate friends. Such an absurdly bifurcated relationship! But never mind, that's how it was.

In the time since the night of the waltz, she had scrupulously respected her employer's wishes and kept their everyday relations strictly formal. She kept the precious secret of what had happened between them safe and secure in her heart, taking it out every now and again in the privacy of her thoughts. She could delight in it behind closed eyes, going over every moment like the glittering jewels of a fabulous hidden treasure. The only way her feelings could be permitted to manifest themselves during the day was in her devotion to her duties and attentiveness to the needs of her employer. In this capacity she excelled as she had never excelled before. But tonight, moonlight would permit much more!

She went through her evening routine, glancing out the window now and again anxiously. To her relief, the moon was indeed out, even if not at its full strength. It stretched its light across the floor of her room as she put on her robe. Her door was pushed open by the winged snake, who regarded her questioningly. "Tell him I'm coming," she said, and the avian reptile withdrew. She buttoned her robe and followed, wondering momentarily how these creatures without hands managed to open her door.

He was waiting for her on the landing, silhouetted in the pale light from the tall window behind him. He was dressed simply, in his customary cotton shirt and khaki pants, but he greeted her warmly.

"Vivian!" He took her hands and drew her to him.

She kissed his cheek lightly. "My Angel." Then she looked into his pale eyes. "What is troubling you?"

They sat on the top stair at the edge of the pool of moonlight, the winged snake curled around them. She stroked its scaly head and soft feathered wings. She didn't mind snakes at all, at least when they weren't knocking pictures off the wall or making nests of the floral arrangements.

"I needed to speak with you," he said, taking her hand again, holding her rough, callused fingers with his smooth, slender ones. "There are things that can't be spoken of in daylight, that I can only talk about in moonlight."

"Tell me, Angel. I'll do my best to understand."

"I know you will," he said gratefully. "You are the only one who might understand. Besides Heron. She encouraged me to confide in you. I need to confide in you. I hope you don't mind."

"Not at all," she assured him. "I am honored."

"You see, I'd really love to go to New York, to attend that reception and put on a splendid show for them. I know Frank will arrange everything so it is easy for me. He knows how to accommodate me. It would be such fun! But there are people I am afraid of."

"Really? Who could possibly wish you harm?"

"Not harm, exactly. Or at least, they wouldn't see it that way. Oh, dear, it all seems so foolish! Yet, in truth, I'm terrified. Mortally terrified."

"Tell me, Angel. Who are these people and why are you so frightened of them?"

He huddled over, hugging his arms around himself, and she moved closer to him, putting her arm around his narrowed shoulders. "Start at the beginning," she encouraged him gently. "Or anywhere you like. I'm listening."

He spoke in a soft, fearful whisper. "Zarah Trebbiano."

"Your ex-fiancée?"

He shuddered. "That was *her* idea! Never mine! Dear God, how she pursued me! I fear she might pursue me still!" He looked at her beseechingly. "I know I must seem a contemptible coward, but unless you've met the woman, you can't understand. She is so powerful, overwhelming! She confused me, blinded me, I felt caught in a deluge. I didn't know where I was or what I was doing. She swept me up and took over. I couldn't say no to her! She was madly, obsessively in love with me."

"But you didn't return that love."

"I couldn't!" he pleaded. "No one understood. She is so beautiful, so..." He shuddered. "I mean, it was really quite flattering at the beginning. When I first started to be famous. It was fun to flirt with all those women, to feel like I was, well, *desirable.*" He laughed awkwardly, a self-conscious giggle. "It was marvelous, discovering that I had this talent that no one else possessed. I felt so powerful! I dared to do whatever I liked, things I had never been allowed to do before. The more outrageously I behaved, the more famous I became, and the more the women flocked around me. They all wanted to take me home with them. They all wanted to look after me. I thought it a wonderful game!

"But I'm not very good at games. I don't understand how to follow rules. I forget, I get distracted, I..." he shrugged. "Everyone was always getting so upset with me. I didn't do what I was supposed to. It's always been a problem for me, not being able to follow the rules. But when I became famous, they were willing to forgive me for it and accommodate me. Things got easier in a way. But things also got more difficult." He looked over at her apologetically. "I'm telling this badly."

"You tell me just as you need to. I can sort it out." She was glad she knew what she did of his history and background; it enabled her to pick through the confusion of details he was tossing at her and make sense of the story.

"You see, my parents, they didn't approve at all. My father shouted at me and my mother wept. But I didn't need to do what they told me to do anymore. I behaved atrociously, because I *could*. And so they washed their hands of me. At first I didn't care. I felt so powerful, so free! Then it all became too much."

"You had never been on your own before."

"Never! Everything had always been so easy for me. Everyone made it easy. So when things began to get difficult, I didn't know what to do. You see, I really am an idiot. Honestly."

"Not at all," she said firmly. "One cannot be brilliant at everything."

"I seem to be one extreme or the other," he sighed. "Either brilliant or utterly hopeless. When it comes to women, I am utterly hopeless."

"I find you charming and quite marvelous," she replied.

He smiled at her adoringly. "You don't frighten me," he said. "The others...." He returned to gazing anxiously straight ahead. "They began to frighten me after awhile. Things were getting so out of control. You see, I must be in control. If I get frightened or upset, well, unpleasant things happen. I expect it would be worse, now. It comes so easily to me. And there is no one so frightening and upsetting to me as Zarah Trebbiano!

"She came crashing grandly onto the scene and swept all the others away. She claimed me, and I didn't know how to say no. I *couldn't* say no. It was like staring into a dazzling light. The others I could always manage to evade. I couldn't evade her. She wanted me and she was determined to have me. She...." He shivered, hugging into himself again. "She trapped me, got me alone in her room. She refused to let me go until I complied with her wishes. It was horrible! Humiliating! I wanted to die!" He buried his face in his hands.

"My poor Angel!" she said softly, stroking his hair. He leaned against her, shivering.

"I had to get away. Frank was the only person I trusted. I begged him to help me. He found this house for me, and he arranged everything. But still, I couldn't work. Everything I created came out hideous, like some nightmare of Bosch's Hell!

"Then, I made Heron. She was the first creation that wasn't just a trifle. She came out of my heart, fashioned carefully from real things. I gave her substance. I spoke to her, made her to understand. Dear Heron! Then I made the basilisk, the same way. After that, things began to get better. Heron looked after me, and the basilisk kept everyone else away. Eventually, I was able to work again, to make beautiful things again. I was still so afraid of people! And yet, I was lonely."

"So you made the others."

He nodded. "It was all quite comforting. Secure. I was very happy. But, I'm really not awfully good at taking care of things. Living alone was sometimes a strain. So much to have to remember. So much to do." He looked at her with admiration. "I don't know how you manage it, to take care of everything, to remember everything. It amazes me."

"Oh, now *really*," she scoffed modestly.

"No, truly! I never realized how difficult it is to run a house until I tried to do it myself. I know I'm not very clever at such things and I did a terrible job. As I got more and more involved with my creations, and there got to be more cats, well, I knew I needed help. But I put it off for the longest time because I couldn't bear the thought of a stranger coming here.

"Then I got to thinking, it wouldn't be so bad. We always had servants when I was growing up. One could control servants. They remained in their place. If they did not, one dismissed them. So I thought, perhaps it would be all right if I hired a housekeeper. But just the right sort of housekeeper. I left it to Frank. Frank always knows what to do. He is remarkable! After all, he found you." He beamed at her.

"Not at first, I understand."

"No!" he laughed. "Not at first. There were several who came out here. If the basilisk didn't frighten them off, the state of the house did." He sighed. "Or me." He looked at her anxiously. "Vivian, do you really love me? I mean, not just because I'm famous and all that?"

"Oh, Angel!" she replied, "Can't you tell?"

"It seems so, but I am such a fool when it comes to these things. And it's so very complicated. During the day, in sunlight, it just seems silly. I wouldn't know what to do or how to act. But in the moonlight, oh! I want *so* much to be in love!" His expression was momentarily ecstatic. Then anxiety returned. "But love doesn't stay just love. It has a way of becoming something else. Something dangerous. You see, when their eyes become hungry, and they start to clutch at me... what they want would destroy me!" He shivered.

"I see," she said, but her expression clearly betrayed that she didn't, really.

He looked at her, at a loss for words, yet wanting to her to understand. The winged snake slithered up to rest her head on his shoulder and she nudged him gently. Taking a deep breath, he said, "It's just that, what they want, what goes beyond a kiss, an embrace, the ultimate consequences of what happens between a normal man and woman when they are attracted to one another, that physical communion would take from me a vital spark. That spark would be drawn into them for their own acts of creation, and I would lose my ability to create. There could be no greater disaster for me!"

Comprehension dawned in her and spread to illuminate all the implications of what he had said.

"My word!" she breathed. "But, how absolutely extraordinary! So you have never...?"

He shook his head violently. "Never! I cannot! It would be the end of me! Worse still, I cannot be sure of the consequences of such a communion to the other party. As I said, when I become upset, agitated, unpleasant things can happen. I have no idea what reaction that degree of agitation might trigger in me. It could be glorious, or, well, very dangerous."

As he spoke, she could sense for a fleeting moment, as she had before, an impression of invisible force, like the roar of a hidden furnace. It unsettled her, but as before, the impression passed, leaving only the benign presence of her gentle Angel.

She asked him, "How did you come to know this? To be so sure of it?"

"There isn't any way to explain. You must trust me that it is a fact, something about myself that I have come to understand, like my ability to create. Vivian," he pleaded, "knowing this, knowing what a freak I am, can you still love me?"

"My dear Angel," she said, holding his hand, "I would never do anything to harm you. I want to share with you only the things that bring us both joy and delight. I truly love you, Angel, with all my heart, as I have never loved anyone before. I accept you as you are without question."

"Oh, Vivian!" he whispered, hugging her tightly, "Don't ever leave me! Stay with me always!"

"I will, for always. I swear it."

The pool of moonlight behind them shifted and stretched as the moon fell towards the horizon, and they sat together until it was quite gone.

***

He tossed his napkin onto the table, and the calico cat took her cue to come investigate what was left on his plate. He pushed back his chair and rose to his feet, Madam Beast jumping into his arms. "A fine meal as always, Ms. Mare. I thank you. But now, I must go and prepare. There is a full moon tonight!" His silver-blue eyes glittered.

"So there is," Ms. Mare said, returning his smile. "So there is. I shall be seeing you later, then?"

"Oh, yes. Most certainly!"

She did not even bother to go to bed. She lingered in her bath, and took time with her cream. She sat before the mirror brushing her hair, feeling strangely different about herself. It made a difference, it truly did, to be in love.

On the wardrobe was a box which she took down and set on the bed. Never before in her life had she ever considered buying such things for herself. Delicate things. Satin things. Soft and lovely things. Before, sensible, plain cotton had always been good enough. Practical underclothes, practical sleepwear. But being in love made her want to feel softness and satin against her skin. She wanted lace and lovely, delicate colors. She indulged herself, and seeing what she had bought made her giggle. Such nonsense! But she put the things on and she felt a thrill. I am in love, she thought. Dear me! Who would ever have expected such a thing!

She looked at herself in the mirror, brushing her hair and arranging it just so. Feminine. Modest, of course. Soft and quite beautiful. The robe which replaced her plain and practical chenille was soft golden silk with a pattern of roses on it. Wickedly indulgent. No, it was just as it should be for a woman in love.

He may dress me in something quite extravagant, she thought, but no matter what, I shall look fine.

Then she heard it, the soft strains of music. The beautiful music of the waltz. The emerald lobster clacked its claws and hurried to the door to open it for her. She turned off her light, and the room became milky with the light of the moon streaming through her window. She waited for her eyes to adjust to the spectral illumination, and then went to the door. Taking a deep breath, she stepped out into the hallway.

There, in the pool of moonlight at the top of the stairs, was Archimedes Michelangelo Nesselrode. He was dressed elegantly, formally, perfectly, complete with a cane and flowing cape. He bowed to her. She stepped lightly over to him and curtseyed.

"Vivian," he said, taking her hand and kissing it. "You are lovely. It takes my breath quite away. But tonight, you must be lovelier still."

He stepped back and brushed the cane lightly along her body. She closed her eyes, feeling the change, the sense of weight as the rich fabrics formed themselves around her.

"Voilà!" he cried, and she opened her eyes to look at herself. It was soft, full, with folds and drapes of satin and ribbon, all in colors of moonlight. On her feet were silver slippers.

He bounced the cane off the floor and caught it, then waved it sharply around them. Crystal chandeliers blossomed from the ceilings and all the woodwork turned to gilt.

"Oh, Angel, you mustn't! You'll make yourself ill again!"

He laughed, high and wild. "What of it? It is worth it! Vivian, my love! Dance with me!"

He took her hand and swept her down the stairs and through the house. But it were as if the house had been turned into a palace. The music swelled around them, rich and full, and the air was scented with jasmine. He pulled her close to him. "I love you, Vivian."

"As I love you, my Angel." He spun her around and then abruptly turned to seat her on the soft cushions of what might have been the couch, but was now a velvet throne. The music fell to the gentle, tinkling melody of a music box. He took something from his pocket. "For you," he said.

It was a star sapphire ring in a silver filigree setting, precisely like the one she had worn the night of the waltz.

"Thank you, Angel," she said, slipping it onto her finger.

"It is quite real, not a creation. I ordered it made to my specifications, and had them bring it on a Thursday when you were out."

"Oh, my word! It is too lovely! Thank you so much!"

"You deserve all the riches of the world," he said. Then he dropped to his knee. "Vivian, will you marry me?"

Her breath caught in her throat. The music, the magic, the fantasy of it all, she almost went along with the story as it was meant to flow. The expected answer rose to her lips but froze there, unformed. Ms. Mare, even in moonlight, was inescapably sensible. Her heart sank. Her eyes fluttered downwards. With enormous difficulty, she forced herself to reply. "Angel, I'm sorry, I can't."

The music stopped. The lights grew dim. "Vivian!" he cried, pained, "You can't turn me down! I shall be devastated!"

"Angel," she said, taking his hands and pulling him up off his knee to sit beside her, "I do love you. And I'd happily spend the rest of my life with you—"

"Then isn't this right?" he pleaded. "When you love someone so much that you can't imagine life without them, so much that you feel your heart will burst if you don't do something, you propose marriage. Isn't that what is done?"

"You are so sweet and wonderful and incurably romantic, and yes, I expect that is just what one does in moonlight."

"I have it all planned," he said eagerly, "The Bishop can perform the ceremony, and Heron and Winged Snake can be witnesses—"

"Angel, oh my dear! But marriage is so much more than just what happens in moonlight. So very much more! It is a lawful contract, a matter for daytime, as well as a lovely romantic thing. There is so much to it that we should talk about, matters of money and responsibility. There are aspects of being married that, well, might prove awkward. I wouldn't be simply your housekeeper any more, not even in the daytime. Our roles would be different. And there is the marital bed, which you have given me to understand would have grave implications for you. You see, my Angel? It is no simple matter."

As she spoke, his shoulders began to slump and his head to hang. "You are, of course, quite right," he sighed heavily.

With a soft hush, all the illusions vanished. They sat together on the couch in the living room, she in her fine silk robe and he in a plain shirt with frayed cuffs and rather tattered pants. She looked down at her finger. The star sapphire ring still shimmered in the moonlight. She removed it regretfully.

"I forgot about Arachne," he said.

"I beg your pardon?" she asked uneasily.

"That was the first time I realized it. When you got so upset about Arachne. I discovered that you were not just a servant I could order about. I could not have things just as I wanted them. You had a mind of your own. But I realized that I could not do without you. It seems I did not learn my lesson then and you've had to bring me quite sharply to book."

"I'm sorry, Angel."

"I wish, sometimes, that you were not quite so sensible," he said sadly.

"But I must be," she said. "I must be sensible for both of us."

He nodded. "I never think of these things. All the daylight aspects."

"There are many. For instance, I am quite close to my mother. I know that if I got married, she would want to be there. And so would the Galbraiths. I expect Mr. Galbraith would want to give me away. He's been much like a father to me. So, as wonderfully romantic as your suggestion is, I couldn't agree to it. I'm sure Mother would be delighted for me to be married by a bishop, but not one that resides in a silver teapot."

He nodded with resignation. "Mothers are like that." He tilted his head, a sad smile on his face. "My mother would no doubt want a proper wedding for me. She would want everything just so. She always fussed. She called me her 'gift from the gods.' Sometimes I wonder if she meant that literally. I wonder if she's really my mother at all. We don't look a bit alike."

"Yet she was quite devoted to you wasn't she? Your estrangement must be hard on her."

"I expect she would have forgiven even my most outré behavior. But she is also devoted to my father. She would do anything for his sake. I suppose if I got properly married and settled down, she could arrange a reconciliation. As my father's only son and heir, I am of great significance to him. Even if I am far from the sort of son he would want. And not likely to produce any heirs." He glanced at her. "I don't suppose she would approve of you, I'm afraid."

"I am hardly the proper class or breeding," she acknowledged.

"They would have to accept it, as they would have to accept me!" But then he hung his head. "Oh, what's the use? It is all quite impossible."

"Angel," she said, "I'm content with our arrangement. Marriage isn't that important to me. My mother did without the whole thing and was perfectly happy. But if I am to be married, I want to be sure it is the right thing. I want to be married for the right reasons, in the proper way, and to the right man."

"And I am not the right man," he concluded unhappily. "No, no, I understand," he said, waving away her protests. "Never mind what my parents would think, it is I who am unworthy of you. I wouldn't know how to act like a husband during the day. I wouldn't have any idea what to say or do. It would be completely a moonlight marriage. And even then—no, it was a silly idea. A thoroughly foolish idea. My apologies, Vivian."

"It was a touching, beautiful, wonderful idea," she said, taking his hands in hers. "And I'm not turning you down, really."

"You aren't?" he brightened.

"Not completely. I just think we need to talk about it. Take our time about it. After all," she said carefully, "it is possible that as time goes by you may realize that perhaps ours is not a good match after all. Your feelings may cool towards me, and we shall be glad we did not act impulsively."

"Oh, no, Vivian!" he cried in horror. "Don't even *suggest* such a thing! Never in my life have I ever been so certain of anything!" Then he asked her with breathless apprehension, "You don't believe that your feelings towards me could change, do you?"

"I suppose it's possible," she admitted. "But I don't believe it really." She smiled at him. "No, I don't believe it at all. I can't imagine that I should ever stop loving you. I am, after all, a mature woman. I think I know my mind by now."

He nodded. "Then, it is possible, something might be worked out between us."

"We shall take it a step at a time," she said.

"And we shall see," he said with a decisive nod. "Yes, indeed, we shall see!"

CHAPTER TEN

The Decision

The next day he surprised her. Ms. Mare had just returned from shopping and Heron was assisting her in putting the groceries away.

"I believe I have changed my mind," Mr. Nesselrode announced. "I shall make the personal appearance that Frank requested."

Heron squawked and ruffled her feathers, dropping a box of fettuccine.

"No, no," he said holding up his hand, "My mind is made up."

"Are you quite sure, Mr. Nesselrode?" Ms. Mare asked with concern, picking up the fettuccine box and putting it on the counter.

"I am quite sure I am ready to go out there again," he said. "I don't think I will be as afraid of everything as I was before. That is, if you will come with me."

"Why, of course I will come with you," she said. "I shall help you in any way that I can. But I do wonder, does this have anything to do with what we spoke of last night?"

"A bit, perhaps," he admitted with an awkward smile. "I must learn to deal with things, after all. This is a first step." He nodded firmly.

Ms. Mare felt acutely aware of the limitations placed on her by the odd rules of their relationship. She could not speak or act as freely as she could have by moonlight. "Well," she said carefully, folding up the grocery bag, "I wouldn't want to be the cause of your doing anything you might regret."

"Good heavens, Ms. Mare! It's been ten years! I can't stay isolated here for the rest of my life now, can I? Surely this is for the best."

Heron clacked her beak skeptically.

"Oh, now it won't be like it was before," he replied to the maternal bird. "I shan't be living out there. Only visiting for a short while. And I'll have Ms. Mare with me to protect me."

The bird squawked a stern query.

"I'm certain she has forgotten all about me," he answered peevishly. "Heron, I can't go on hiding here like a miserable coward! I must take control of my life again!"

Heron objected with a fluff of her feathers.

"Yes, I know," he said more gently, reaching out to smooth her feathers, smiling at her with affection. "And that was just what I needed then. I couldn't have managed without you. But I've recovered now. I must move on with my life. I have certain hopes." He glanced at Ms. Mare with a shy smile. Heron looked over her spectacles at Ms. Mare with disapproval.

"I am sure I want only what is best for Mr. Nesselrode," Ms. Mare said, meeting the bird's cool gaze. "And I have no ambitions to disrupt the harmony of this household. This decision is entirely up to him, and we must go along with his wishes, mustn't we?"

Heron squawked darkly and sailed out of the room, her skirts rustling with agitation.

"It's only because she remembers," Mr. Nesselrode said apologetically. "She is so very protective of me. But I'm sure there is nothing to worry about. So long as you are with me, I'll have nothing to fear." It was a statement, but there was something faintly querulous behind it. Heron's objections had unsettled his resolve. Ms. Mare reassured him firmly.

"Mr. Nesselrode, if this is what you want to do, I shall do everything in my power to make it a success. And yes, I can't imagine that you would have anything to fear. There are ways of dealing with troublesome people."

"Yes, you'll see to it, won't you?" he said, looking enormously relieved. "You would know how. Nothing frightens you. It will be all right then, I know it."

"I don't see why not. If you want to go, then go. Have a wonderful time. Mr. Shekle and I will look after all the unpleasant details. Then you can come home again."

"It's settled," he said firmly, looking very pleased about it. "I shall call Frank myself to tell him. Oh, he will be so delighted!"

***

Frank Shekle was more than merely delighted. It was the answer to his prayers.

The event itself wasn't until November, but there were arrangements to be made. Archimedes Nesselrode had an appointment with Shekle, which he forgot. It was rescheduled. When the time came to go, he decided to forget again. This time, however, Ms. Mare knew about the appointment and insisted he must go.

"I don't want to go," he complained. "I know he's just going to talk about what I'm supposed to do, where I'm supposed to go and when, and who else will be there and all that. Wretchedly tedious, and I won't remember any of it anyway."

"Nevertheless, you are obliged to do it," she told him sternly. "I can accompany you if you like."

"I wish you would go in my stead." He looked at her beseechingly. "I'm just not ready to go out yet. Can you understand? Leaving this place, my sanctuary—"

"You must do it eventually. This will be a good trial run. Practice for you, to help you adjust to being out in the world again."

He looked mournful. "It's too soon. I'm not ready. Please, just one more full moon for me to prepare myself?" He took a deep breath. "I shall agree to go to the dentist if you will indulge me this one time."

She seized upon it. "Very well. But I shall hold you to this, Mr. Nesselrode!"

It actually made more sense this way. She at least would pay attention to the details and remember them. If she knew the arrangements and the agenda, she could make certain her employer followed them. Frank Shekle, however, did not at first see the logic of this. In fact, he did little to conceal his hostility when Ms. Mare showed up instead of his client.

"I believe my appointment was with Archimedes Nesselrode, not his housekeeper!" he snapped as she was shown into his office.

"He asked me to come in his place," she replied, removing her gloves and laying them across her purse as she sat down with a briskly business-like air. "You know how reluctant he is to leave the sanctuary of his home."

The office was just as she remembered it from her interview, decorated and furnished to give the best impression. This was an old firm with all the right connections and a reputation of generational excellence. It seemed more like the office of a banker than an agent, except for the prominence of works of art, a Wyeth on the wall and abstract sculptures making uncertain statements in various alcoves.

"I certainly hope he doesn't send you in his place on the day of the reception!" Shekle snapped.

"Don't be absurd, Mr. Shekle. I'd never agree to such a thing. This, however, is quite different. I understand you wished to discuss the schedule of events, and what would be expected of him."

"Of *him*, not of *you*!"

"Well, it may be all the same, since I shall be accompanying him." She regarded Shekle with a coolly challenging expression. His mouth tightened with anger.

"So that's how it is, eh?" he said. "It seems to me that you are going beyond your duties as housekeeper just a bit!"

"I was hired by Mr. Nesselrode, not by you," she replied crisply. "The terms and scope of my duties are between my employer and myself."

He leaned over to put his hands on the arms of her chair so that his face was only inches from hers. He spoke quietly but intensely. "Listen, Miss Mare—"

"*Ms.* Mare," she corrected him, but he plowed right over her, his voice rising in volume.

"—I am not going to allow some opportunistic gold digger to move in and exploit my client! He may not see what you're doing, but I do, and I hold the purse strings, is that clear? Back off from him!"

Ms. Mare leaned back slightly, cocked her head and replied, "How interesting of you to put it that way. I was just thinking of suggesting to Mr. Nesselrode that perhaps it might be wise to have an independent auditor look over his accounts to make certain that his lack of business savvy isn't being exploited by an unscrupulous agent and manager."

"Oh really?" Shekle said, straightened up and folding his arms across his chest. "Would that be to make certain he isn't being ripped off? Or to see how much he's really worth!"

Ms. Mare got to her feet. Standing up straight on her modest and sensible heels, she was the same height as Frank Shekle. She met him eye to eye. "It seems to me," she declared, "that this is completely unproductive. We clearly do not trust each other, yet we ought to be cooperating, since Mr. Nesselrode is counting on us to look after his needs. Considering that you have handled his business affairs for many years and give every impression of reliability, I am willing to give you the benefit of the doubt for the time being. Now, are you willing to hear me out concerning my own handling of Mr. Nesselrode's domestic affairs?"

Shekle regarded her suspiciously. "I'm listening," he said.

"I shall be perfectly direct. Mr. Nesselrode is terribly nervous about returning to the public eye. He refused to do so at first, as you know. It wasn't until I agreed to accompany him to this event that he was willing to change his mind. You see, he has come to depend on me because I have proven myself very capable and reliable in looking after him. Certainly you must be aware of a marked lack of self-sufficiency on his part."

"That's putting it mildly," Shekle muttered. "And it's just that vulnerability that makes me nervous when I see you starting to take over. I've seen this sort of thing before. I've been handling his business affairs, not to mention wet-nursing him through every minor crisis, for nearly fifteen years now, and I know him pretty well. It was just this sort of thing that led to his nervous collapse, predators and parasites trying to gain his confidence and suck him dry. It's my job to keep that from happening."

"And how did you manage to achieve this enviable position?"

"His father, the Count, knew my father, and knew the firm to be impeccably reliable and well-connected. He was in a position to know such things." He sighed. "And my father gave the account to me. Ever since, it's been suffering from mission creep."

Ms. Mare speculated to herself that perhaps Frank Shekle was a son unsuited to continue in the family profession, yet compelled to do so anyway. His speech and manners, though not grossly lacking, were still not quite up to the rarefied standards of such an exclusive firm. The Nesselrode account may have been passed off to him because no one else wanted it, and it kept the young man well-occupied. That Frank Shekle was intelligent and savvy she had no doubt. He might not have had the polish to deal with more sophisticated clients, but he was evidently very good at what he did for Archimedes Nesselrode. She decided to change her tack, and said, "I understand the Count has since disowned his son."

Shekle nodded. "The Count," he repeated with condescension. "As if the title really means anything anymore. But he still uses it. Old school, both of his parents. Very proper, never a breath of scandal. Can't understand how they managed to produce *him*. Nesselrode's freak show antics made the old man apoplectic." Frank eyed her. "You've been doing your homework."

"I discovered that my mother's employers were acquainted with the family," Ms. Mare explained with a shrug.

"Odd coincidence, that," he mused, his eyes narrowing.

"Not really. They traveled widely and in very privileged circles. Mr. Shekle, you will simply have to give me the benefit of the doubt that my intentions are honorable."

"Right," he commented dryly. "Keep talking."

"Now then, I agree that it would be very good for Mr. Nesselrode to attend this event which you are planning. From my perspective, it would be good for him to get out, to see people again, to begin to interact socially in the world again. As charming as I find the world he has built in his isolation, I do not think that it is healthy for him to live exclusively in that world. And he has said himself that he would love to, as he expressed it, 'put on a show' for the public. Therefore, I am quite willing to go along with him, to provide whatever emotional support he finds in my presence, so that he can achieve this end. Are we understanding each other so far, Mr. Shekle?"

"So far," he said, leaning against the desk. "Go on."

"Good. Now, am I correct in assuming that interest in this event would suffer enormously if he were to change his mind about attending?"

"Oh, his work can stand on its own," Shekle said. "And we've put together an excellent representational exhibit of some of his finest pieces. People would still come. The show wouldn't fold if he didn't put in an appearance. But you're absolutely right. When I announced that Archimedes Nesselrode had agreed to come out of seclusion to attend the opening of the exhibit and the reception following, interest in the event shot up astronomically. Passes are already sold out. The press are fighting tooth and claw for an opportunity to get access. The bidding for an interview is hotter than the auction for the Ruby Slippers. This will be *the* Arts event of the year, maybe the decade, especially if Nesselrode comes on anything like he used to."

"So, from your perspective, his attendance at this event is very much to his own financial and professional benefit."

"Absolutely."

"Not to mention your own."

Shekle smiled coolly. "That's how it works." He eyed her speculatively, then said, "I'll be candid with you. He needs to milk this event for all it's worth. I wouldn't say he's exactly in trouble financially, but these ten years of isolation and spotty production haven't done him any good. If he intends to keep that chimera farm of his going, he's got to get back to work supporting it."

"I see," Ms. Mare said. "Then it is in the best interest of all concerned for the two of us to put aside our hostilities and work together to make this a success for him."

Frank Shekle's cool smile broadened into a grin. "By God, you're either my worst nightmare or the best thing I could have hoped to find for that fruitcake!"

Ms. Mare answered him primly. "If you are the sort of man who is discomfited by a strong, independent, self-assured woman, then I expect I am indeed your worst nightmare. If, however, you recognize that I am precisely the sort of woman our Mr. Nesselrode needs to look after him, then we shall get along very well. And I take exception to your referring to that brilliant, extraordinary man as a 'fruitcake.'"

Shekle laughed heartily. "Very well then, *Ms.* Mare! So we call a truce. For now, anyway. But I'll still be keeping an eye on you, just in case."

"And, after all this is over, I should like to have a look at Mr. Nesselrode's financial records, once I've had an opportunity to retain the services of a skilled and trustworthy accountant."

"Fair enough. Well then, let me get out the tentative schedule and show you what we have worked up."

She listened carefully as he went over it all. It seemed a bit intense, an awful lot of stress in a short period of time, particularly having to endure an assault by the press and possibly an interview. She said as much.

"I'd hate to see him refuse the interview," Shekle said. "It could be worth a good piece of change for him. And really, it's just the sort of circus he used to love. It'd wear him out, I'll grant you, but he didn't mind."

Ms. Mare nodded thoughtfully. "I'll have to talk to him about it. Would you be willing to cut back a bit on the schedule if he requests it?"

Shekel shrugged. "It's negotiable to a certain degree. But let me know as soon as possible. A lot of other people are going to have to be told and things reshuffled."

"Certainly." Ms. Mare paused, then approached her next concern. "Now, Mr. Nesselrode has expressed a good deal of anxiety regarding certain individuals from whom he wishes to be protected. Naturally I assume bodyguards will be provided."

"You'd better believe it! There will be plenty of security."

"I wonder if it is possible to screen who will be allowed to attend the opening and particularly the reception."

Shekle regarded her soberly. "*Certain individuals.* It wouldn't be one individual in particular, would it?"

Ms. Mare met his gaze. "Yes, to be direct, it would."

He leaned back in the chair. "So, he told you about *her*, did he?"

"I assume from the significance assigned to that pronoun that you are referring to Zarah Trebbiano."

He sighed. "He still hasn't gotten over that."

"From the way he spoke of it to me, I doubt that he ever will."

Shekle got up from the chair and went over to the window, speaking with his back to her, half to himself. "Amazing. Any other man on the face of the earth—myself included—would have given his left testicle to have been in Nesselrode's position with Zarah Trebbiano!"

"Mr. Shekle, please. I am a woman of the world, and quite conversant in most forms of slang, but I ask that you kindly show a bit of respect in your choice of colloquialisms."

"My apologies," he said agreeably. "It's just that I've never been able to figure that whole thing out. For that matter, I've never been able to figure out what it is about Nesselrode that women find so damned appealing. If I knew, I'd bottle it!"

"It's nothing you could exploit, Mr. Shekle, any more than you could exploit the secret of his creations. It is all in who and what he is, a beautiful mystery that none of us can ever fathom. We can only wonder at it, cherish it, and protect it from harm." She realized she had waxed far more poetic than she meant to, and she regretted it.

"Well, well," Shekle said, regarding her with curious interest. "So, you're hung up on him, too, aren't you? It isn't his money. It's him."

"It's really none of your affair, Mr. Shekle," she said stiffly, furious at herself for being at this sudden disadvantage.

"Son of a gun. And he's taken to you, too, hasn't he? He's confided in you. He told you about Zarah Trebbiano. He trusts you. Wants you with him." He laughed. "I'll be damned! You've become his mistress, haven't you?"

"That is an exceedingly inappropriate thing to say!" she exclaimed indignantly. "Besides, I'll thank you to remember of whom we are speaking! Mr. Nesselrode is hardly the type to take a *mistress*!"

"No," Shekle agreed, "You're right. He's got the mind of a child. He doesn't need a mistress so much as he needs a nanny. And you fit the bill nicely."

"That will be quite enough!" She rose ominously to her feet, ready to storm from the office. "I'll have you know that Archimedes Nesselrode is a deeply sensitive and intelligent man who knows precisely what he wants and needs! I'll remind you that I am here to discuss how we may accommodate those wants and needs while allowing him to perform in the capacity required by his profession! Now, are you going to confine yourself to pertinent subjects, or shall I leave and inform my employer that the entire thing is off?"

"Take it easy, Ms. Mare!" he said, grinning. "It's your own private business, and I'll leave it alone. Look, I'm delighted to have you on board. I've had custody of that sweet, brilliant lunatic ever since the Count washed his hands of him, and it's been a pain in the backside. I appreciate all the help I can get. Please, sit down."

She returned to her chair and sat stiffly. Shekle leaned back against his desk. "Has he confided in you about the secret of his creations?"

"As much as there is to confide," she replied. "And I could not explain it to you even if I were so inclined."

"But you've watched him work."

"I have," she retorted, "and I can tell you, there is no secret process that anyone could steal!"

"Ms. Mare, even if there were, I would just as soon it remained secret. I would lose exclusive rights to market this marvel if it got out, remember?" He cocked his head, regarding her thoughtfully. "There really is no secret process, no rational explanation at all for what he can do, is there?"

"No, there isn't," Ms. Mare said quietly. "He has the ability to conjure something from nothing, to give form to his imagination. And he has the power to shape and animate inanimate substance with only his whim. It truly is nothing else but magical."

"Incredible," Shekle murmured. "You know, I envy you in a way." He chuckled. "On the other hand, I don't think I could stand living in that kind of bedlam! You must have nerves of steel!"

"I was raised to keep my head in unusual situations," she replied modestly.

"And you two are an item. Go figure!"

Her eyes flashed at him warningly.

"All right, all right!" he said, holding up his hands, "None of my business. All I really care about is that he shows up at the opening and does what he's supposed to do and enjoys himself doing it, and if you can help in that capacity I'm all for it." He smiled, picking a pen up from the desk and tapping it against a thumbnail. "I'll admit something to you, Ms Mare. Never mind that he's my golden goose. I've gotten rather fond of Nesselrode over the years. And what he does amazes me. I sure would hate to see anything happen to him. It would be nothing short of a tragedy."

"And Zarah Trebbiano?" she asked. "You may be skeptical, but the danger to him from her is quite real. He goes in mortal terror of her."

Shekle shrugged. "Zarah Trebbiano has been married twice and divorced since that whole business with Nesselrode, and I have no idea if she gives a damn about him anymore. I'm not even sure she's in the country right now. She's an international celebrity, as big a name in her own right as he is. But if she decides she wants to crash the reception there's not a whole lot we can do to keep her out."

CHAPTER ELEVEN

Out There

The worst part was getting him through the gate for the first time.

Having fulfilled her part of the agreement, Ms. Mare saw to it that her employer fulfilled his. After careful research, she settled on a dental practice that seemed suitable. Dr. Meyers assured her that the utmost discretion would be employed. All the arrangements were made. On the day of the appointment, Mr. Nesselrode hid in his studio.

Bufus loyally refused to participate in the search, but Heron, recognizing the practical necessity of the situation and the fact that the artist had, after all, agreed to this, assisted Ms. Mare in ferreting him out.

"Mr. Nesselrode, *really*!" she scolded him when he emerged sheepishly from the wardrobe.

"This is all dreadfully upsetting!" he replied defensively, brushing the cobwebs from his shoulder.

"Nevertheless! Now, go and get a clean shirt on and comb your hair. Heron, would you kindly see to it that Mr. Nesselrode is made presentable and conduct him to the car as soon as possible? We are going to be late!"

The bespectacled matron nodded her head curtly and herded her master downstairs, responding to his fussy complaints with firm squawks. Ms. Mare swatted dust from her skirt and went to get out the Daimler.

As she drove towards the gate, he shrank into the seat, his fist to his mouth, a finger clenched between his teeth, his eyes wide with anxiety.

"Mr. Nesselrode, please pull yourself together. Honestly, I don't know what you think is going to happen!" She parked the car to open the gate, momentarily concerned that he might bolt back to the house the minute her back was turned. But he remained pressed deeply into the seat, pale and staring. He squeezed his eyes shut as she drove through, remaining immobile as she stopped and went to close the gate again behind them.

"There, it's done," she said, getting back into the Daimler and fastening the seat belt. "Do relax! Everything is going to be fine!"

He uttered a small, fearful bleat as she put the car into gear.

The drive to the dental practice was rather long, and her employer was not able to maintain his state of nervous tension indefinitely. After ten or fifteen minutes he began to look around himself, and soon became absorbed in the scenes outside the window. The anxiety evaporated, and he was commenting excitedly on what he saw.

"Look at that!" he pointed to a riding ring beyond a long white fence, "I've always wanted to ride a horse."

"You've ridden a basilisk," Ms. Mare replied, "which is more than most people can boast."

"The trees are so lovely this time of year. Oh, look at that one! So intensely red! The way the sunlight strikes those yellow ones— extraordinary!"

"Those are beeches, I believe. Watch on your side, I seem to recall that there is a very nice view coming up."

"Oh! Marvelous! Are those geese in the sky?"

"Canada geese, yes. Migrating."

"Look, Benjamin, geese!"

"Benjamin?" Ms. Mare exclaimed, her head snapping over towards her employer. The little bat-winged mole was perched on the back of his hand looking out the window with his creator.

"I brought him with me for company," Mr. Nesselrode explained.

"Gracious! Well, he shall have to stay in the car when we go into the dentist's."

"Oh no! He must come with me. He'll behave himself, won't you, Benjamin?"

The star-nosed rodent gave a little squeak of assent.

"Very well, but he must stay in your pocket at all times!"

As they approached the city he eagerly took in everything they passed, the buildings, the vehicles, the people, obviously having a wonderful time.

"I'd forgotten," he murmured. "It really feels quite safe, being in the car. I can see everything, but it cannot touch me."

Oh, dear, Ms. Mare thought. Will it be a bother then, getting him out of the car when we arrive?

She parked at the curb in front of the great glass doors to the professional building which was their destination. "Come along, now," she said briskly, opening the door for him. He hesitated a moment, and then emerged with a brave smile.

"It's quite the adventure, isn't it?" he said, only a bit of a quiver in his voice. People passed them on the sidewalk, largely oblivious. One elderly man was more interested in the Daimler than its occupants, eying it as he walked by, and nodding his approval.

The lack of overt attention to him emboldened the artist. He looked around himself and up at the efficient concrete and metal façade of the tall building with its opaque squares of window. "This is where we are going?"

"That's right. Come this way, Mr. Nesselrode." As per the arrangement, there was a young woman waiting in the lobby to conduct her employer upstairs to the dental office.

"Hello," she said cheerfully as Ms. Mare guided the artist in. "Ms. Mare? Mr. Nesselrode? I'm Sheila. It's a pleasure to have you with us!"

"Are you the dentist?" he asked, his eyes sweeping the lobby, glancing uneasily at a small group of professionals in suits. Their conversation had paused and they were looking curiously in his direction.

"Oh, no!" Sheila laughed. "I'm the receptionist. I've come to greet you. If you'll come this way, I'll show you where the office is."

"Go ahead, Mr. Nesselrode," Ms. Mare said. "I'll go and park the car and I'll be right with you."

He frowned in momentary uncertainty and then rallied. "Very well. Are we to ride in an elevator?" he asked Sheila as they walked away. "Bless me, it's been years since I've ridden in an elevator. Years since I've done much of anything."

Assured that he was in capable hands, Ms. Mare went and parked the Daimler.

All went smoothly until Benjamin, unable to restrain his curiosity any longer, emerged from the artist's pocket and poked his star-nose out from under the paper bib. The hygienist uttered a small shriek and leaped back, scattering an entire tray of dental instruments across the linoleum. At the sound of this commotion, Ms. Mare dropped her magazine and rushed from the waiting room to see what was the matter. She found Mr. Nesselrode surrounded by uniformed hygienists and other bibbed patients with cotton-balls distorting their mouths, all emitting gasps of amazement and delight."It's so cute!"

"Is it real?"

"May I touch it?"

"It won't bite, will it?"

Far from quaking in terror from this onslaught, Archimedes Nesselrode was cheerfully obliging their inquiries, showing off Benjamin and allowing them to, timid fingers extended, stroke the creature's soft dark fur and leathery wings. Debbie, the unfortunate hygienist who had suffered the initial shock, hung back a bit. It seemed her feelings towards rodents were akin to Ms. Mare's towards spiders. Despite all Mr. Nesselrode's assurances that the little creation was harmless, very friendly, and no, not a mouse, nor a bat nor a mole, but simply Benjamin, she declined to make his acquaintance, and asked if she might be relieved by one of the other staff. There was no trouble finding a substitute, aside from settling on which one of the eager volunteers would be chosen. Dr. Meyers dealt with the issue by taking over the task herself.

The remainder of the appointment went well, without further incident. Remarkably, it proved that the artist's teeth were in perfect condition in spite of long neglect, although they did require an extensive cleaning. He bore this unpleasant necessity gamely enough, Benjamin observing the whole procedure from his perch on top of the light, clinging to it with his little clawed feet when the dentist adjusted it to better illuminate her work.

"There, now," she said when the job was finished, switching off the light and unclipping the bib from around Nesselrode's neck, "So far, you've been lucky. But I promise you, if you ignore your teeth, they *will* go away. Regular brushing, flossing and check-ups from now on. And Benjamin," she said, smiling up at the winged creation, "is welcome to come with you."

"I'll be sure not to schedule you with Debbie," Sheila said with a grin.

Mr. Nesselrode was in excellent spirits as they returned down the elevator.

"I did well, didn't I?"

"You did splendidly, Mr. Nesselrode," Ms. Mare assured him, enormously relieved for that fact.

"It was really quite fun! They liked Benjamin. Except for that one poor girl. She was dreadfully upset! Aren't people odd? Imagine, getting upset over you," he spoke fondly to the little mole's head peeking out of his pocket.

"Well, one must take into consideration—"

The elevator doors opened. "Oh, dear," Ms. Mare murmured. Waiting for them in the lobby was a small crowd of people whose shoulder bags, notepads and ready cameras identified them indisputably as The Press. Hovering ineffectually in front of them was a lone security guard, looking overwhelmed and mortified. "I am so sorry," he started, "I tried—"

But he was swept away by the irresistible tide. Cameras flashed and a barrage of questions washed over them. Ms. Mare took her employer's arm, ready to rush the mob and get him to the door and away to safety. But, to her surprise, the artist seemed in no great panic. His initial expression of stunned dismay melted.

"Gracious!" he exclaimed, "What a reception! Is all this fuss really in my honor?"

He grinned broadly at the response to this, nodding to the cacophony of queries about the rumors of his first public appearance in ten years and his unprecedented emergence for this mundane errand.

"But, of course! The Rumpleminz Gallery, how could I refuse? And I am looking forward to seeing some of my old creations again. It should be a most pleasant reunion." He struck obliging poses and swept through the crowd without the need of Ms. Mare running interference, completely at ease. "Naturally I had to visit the dentist before my return to public life. Must be sure my smile passes muster. The dentist assures me my teeth are perfectly sound. I can confidently recommend this practice. Mostly painless, although I did receive a stern lecture for the neglect to my dental health. Benjamin gave them a bit of a shock, but in the end it was quite all right. They even invited him back, didn't they Benjamin? Smile for the camera." The bat-winged mole obligingly perched on the artist's shoulder and lifted his star-nosed face to grimace in the best he had to offer for a smile.

"I'll just go fetch the car, shall I?" Ms. Mare murmured. Frank Shekle had been right. As unsuited as Archimedes Nesselrode may have been to some aspects of fame and fortune, in this kind of situation he swam like a duck.

***

November came with remarkable speed.

The moon waxed full during the first week of the month, and they met in its light at the top of the stairs. Mr. Nesselrode saved his strength, refraining from invoking any overly elaborate scenes, but could not resist turning their customary meeting spot at the top of the stairs into the willow-curtained riverbank from the night of the waltz.

"It surprised me how easy it was," he said as they sat on the grass watching the silvery rippling of the river. "Talking to those people at the dentist's office, and then those reporters, it all came back to me."

"And you are not anxious about your coming public appearance?"

"Not at all," he said. "In fact, it is almost a relief."

Ms. Mare plucked a tiny white flower growing in the grass. "I can see where it might be. In returning to the world, you are finally closing the book on what sent you into seclusion in the first place."

"Do you think that is it?" he asked, rolling onto his back and looking up at her.

"I suspect so. As long as you continued to hide, you were perpetuating the fear inflicted on you. You are now taking steps to stop that fear from ruling you any longer."

"What a brilliant insight!" he exclaimed, sitting up. "You are so very wise, Vivian!"

"Nonsense. I merely pay attention to things." She twirled the little flower between her fingers, smiling as she watched it dance. Did he control all of it? Each motion of the created things? Creatures of substance, like Heron and those naughty marmosets were, sometimes all-too-willfully, independent. But what of things like this, the fantasies that he spun out of his whims? She was about to ask him when he spoke.

"Have you ever been afraid, Vivian?"

"Gracious, yes! Many times."

"I can't imagine you afraid. Not of anything."

"Only an utter fool has no fear, Angel," she said. "One must simply learn of what to be justifiably afraid." She tossed the flower into the river to float serenely away in the currents, and she turned to look at him. Gentle Angel, as blithely serene as the river, trusting in her completely. She suddenly felt a shudder of fear for him; this adventure before them might well hold unknown dangers. She and Mr. Shekle would protect him as best they could, but what if something happened that they could not anticipate? The world was filled with such a number of things, joys and terrors. How vulnerable he was! Perhaps taking him out there was a mistake.

But then, she thought, would I not be as guilty as his mother was? Stifling him and rendering him miserable with walls and swaddling? What happiness he knew when he climbed the tree that day! Even that simple trip to the dentist was a treat for him, getting out and seeing the ordinary scenery of a car ride. And how well he did when he faced the public! He truly enjoyed it. No, it will not do to keep him like a creation in a Lucite cube. He must be encouraged to live and grow in freedom, for all its risks.

***

When it came time to leave, Mr. Nesselrode was eager, bags packed and one foot out the door. There was no fuss passing through the gate this time. He had his nose to the window the entire trip. They arrived at their hotel amidst a fanfare of excitement, cameras, shouting reporters and gawking spectators. Mr. Nesselrode beamed happily at his public as he was whisked away into the lobby and quickly to the elevator to escape to the privacy of their suite. He made the transition from timid recluse to celebrity with the ease of a veteran performer returning to the stage.

Now at last Ms. Mare had a moment to relax. Her employer was in the next room, busily at work with his preparations. His afternoon was full, talking on the telephone, meeting with various people, taking delivery of shoes and clothing and what-not. He was presently engrossed in the task of costuming himself which was, evidently, a most serious and involved business; one which did not require the services of his housekeeper.

While she waited, Ms. Mare checked her bag to be sure she had everything. Two clean handkerchiefs—she always brought a spare, and had a tissue tucked in the pocket of her skirt—her wallet and change purse, envelope with instructions and papers, hair brush, all the little sundries one might need in an emergency, and oh! the letter from her mother.

It had arrived in yesterday's mail, which she had picked up in haste in the course of performing a host of other errands. With all the excitement of Mr. Nesselrode's grand return to the world, she had quite forgotten it. Well, now she had a little spare time while her employer fussed with his habiliments. She settled in a comfy chair by the window and took the letter from its envelope.

"Dear Vivian,

"The news of the exhibit and all the fanfare surrounding its opening has reached us. How exciting it must be for you! All this talk of Archimedes Nesselrode inspired the Galbraiths to stop in Greece for a fortnight on our way to Sydney, in hopes of paying a visit to the Kariotakis family. Unfortunately, we found out when we made inquiries that the matriarch of the household had just passed away suddenly and the family was in mourning and not receiving visitors. The Galbraiths sent their condolences and we made arrangements to stay in Crete. You may wish to relate the news of his maternal grandmother's passing to your employer, since, being estranged from his family, he might not have heard about it.

"Now, I simply must tell you about the most remarkable coincidence which has occurred as a result of our little detour. Or perhaps it isn't coincidence at all; one sometimes wonders if there isn't some puckish unseen spirit that nudges events in our lives into place. You see, yesterday Esther ran into old Calantha, who used to work in the Kariotakis household. We're staying in a villa owned by some dear friends of the Galbraiths, just outside the village where Calantha grew up. She had to return here last year to look after her mother, who is still alive, impossible as it seems; Calantha herself looks to be half the age of the earth!

"Anyway, they got to talking, and Esther mentioned that my daughter was in the employ of Archimedes Nesselrode, and well, the most incredible story came out! Mind you, take it with a grain of salt, since this is only servants' gossip, and the gossip of extremely superstitious servants on top of that. But I simply can't help repeating it, it is so fascinating.

"When Count Nesselrode married Iphigeneia Kariotakis, they stayed at the family's estate on Lemnos for some time before moving to New York. That is, in fact, where the Galbraiths met them. The couple was quite happy, devoted to each other, but the years began to pass without the anticipated occurrence of a child. Iphigeneia was quite distraught, because she knew how much it meant to the Count to have an heir. In the end, she finally did become pregnant and gave birth, supposedly to Archimedes.

"The reason I say 'supposedly' is because the servants tell a very different story. In the spring of that year strange lights were seen at the old temple the Kariotakis family had restored on their estate on the island. Music was heard in the dead of night, and there were sounds of comings and goings in the house at hours when everyone ought to be asleep. It was shortly after this that Iphigeneia announced that she was going to become a mother at last, and the servants whispered that she had gone to the ancient temple and performed certain rites in order to overcome her infertility. In the early winter, the baby came. Calantha recalls a strange brief storm that night, which lasted barely an hour, but which brought with it high winds and a profusion of thunder and lightning. Before and after, the night was perfectly clear and calm.

"There was great joy in the house with the birth of the baby, but the chamber maids whispered that there were none of the signs or residue of labor and delivery, and that the Countess had never really been pregnant at all. The newborn infant had been somehow smuggled into the house during the night, and presented as the Countess's own child.

"Common speculation is that a great charade was performed in order that an illegitimate child fathered by the Count by some unknown mistress could be passed off as a legitimate heir, and Iphigeneia went along with it in order to please the husband she adored. But Calantha declares she believes something even more fantastic. Based upon what she has seen and overheard through the years, including the odd occurrences in the year of the birth itself, she has concluded that the child is not from an earthly mother at all. She believes that the Kariotakis family used their dark powers to induce the cooperation of a pagan spirit to act as surrogate mother. She is convinced that the Count went to the Temple that night in the spring, and lay with a nymph, or perhaps even an ancient goddess who was delighted with the worshipful attention after so many centuries of Christian neglect. At the proper time, the baby was delivered to the Countess to be raised as her son.

"Of course, one can hardly imagine someone like the Count being involved in such antics! He is really rather a stuffy old gent, not at all given to cavorting with goddesses at midnight in secluded Greek temples. Erasmus found the tale quite a laugh when Esther repeated it to him. No doubt the elder Nesselrode would be absolutely horrified to learn that such scandals were being whispered about him behind his back! The story about the mistress is plausible, I suppose, but only barely. He was quite a dashing and handsome man in his youth, most attractive to the ladies, but always very proper. He was reputed to have always been scrupulously faithful to his wife. But Iphigenia's infertility and his desire for an heir may have forced him to resort to extreme measures.

"Well, my dear, you may take that story as you choose. Perhaps it explains some of your Mr. Nesselrode's peculiarities! At any rate, I am delighted with your continued satisfaction in his employ and intrigued by your hints of a growing friendship. I'm sure I don't need to remind you of the hazards of becoming too intimately involved with one's employer.

"I wish you well, and hope this upcoming event is a fabulous success. Keep me posted. I shall write to you with our new address as soon as we are settled.

"love as always,

"your Mother."

Ms. Mare put the letter down. "Bless us!" she murmured, and picked it up to read it again.

CHAPTER TWELVE

Exhibition

Archimedes Nesselrode stood gazing in the mirror at his own reflection as if mesmerized by it. It was not so much vanity as an honest delight in what he saw. He had frosted his eyelids with silver blue and outlined his eyes with a fine line of burnt umber. He had reddened his lips subtly. His reddish-brown hair was parted precisely in the middle and combed smooth on either side of his face. His fingernails were painted silver. He wore a bloused silk shirt of powder blue that brought out the color of his eyes. His clothing was, in fact, very much like what he had worn on the night of the waltz, with midnight blue pants and a sapphire blue sash around his waist. In addition, a cascade of gold and silver chains hung over his chest; nested in the middle was an elaborately wrought pendant with a milk-white stone. His height was elevated another few inches by thick-soled black boots with steep heels.

Ms. Mare was watching him from the communicating door of the suite of rooms they occupied, still in a bit of shock from her mother's letter. She kept reminding herself that Calantha's tale was nothing but silly gossip, hardly something to be taken seriously. And yet, there had to be some sort of explanation for his creative powers, hadn't there? He was certainly no ordinary man. On the other hand, he didn't exactly seem the sort of heroic figure one would expect out of a union with a divinity. One would think the son of a goddess would have his wits more solidly about him.

He looked up and saw her watching him, and cried out, "Wait! Not yet!"

The artist leaped for the pile of suitcases with surprising grace, considering the platforms his feet were perched upon. How on earth had he managed to learn to walk on such things? He generally wore moccasins or sneakers at home.

Rummaging in the luggage, he finally exclaimed, "Ah! Yes, here we are. Oh, my poor dear! You can come out now." To her astonishment, she saw a pair of wings stretch and flex, and the winged snake slithered up his arms and around his neck, arranging herself to best advantage.

"Now!" he cried, striding into the middle of the room. "Now, what do you think?"

She wasn't quite sure what she thought. The effect was certainly theatrical, a degree or two more conservative than the excesses of his youth. The way the snake was coiled around him, her head draped over his shoulder, her wings looked almost as if they sprouted from the artist's own back. He grinned at her, his expression canny and devilish. She realized she was seeing the public persona of Archimedes Nesselrode in full flush. Yes, there it was, that aura of otherworldly superiority, the mystique of the artist who could perform acts which defied explanation. He looked very different from the man she was accustomed to, and it wasn't just the effect of the make-up and clothing. He looked larger than life, and it wasn't just the absurd boots. It was a kind of divinity. She felt a little shiver.

"Mr. Nesselrode," she said finally, "you are quite magnificent."

"Oh, Ms. Mare!" he said with a little giggle, catching his lower lip between his teeth. Then he turned his head to address the snake. "It is good to know I haven't lost my touch." He returned to the mirror again. "I haven't put make-up on in years. Do you think I did a good job? Not too much, but enough for effect?"

"It is perfect," she assured him.

"And the clothes, I think the style becomes me, don't you agree?" He turned, posing, inspecting himself.

"Absolutely."

"And Donati knows just what colors suit me best. He remembered me, and had all the records of my size and preferences all right there! Do you know, my shape hasn't changed a bit since the last time he fitted me?"

"You have kept yourself very well."

"I have, haven't I? Oh, I *do* look marvelous!"

"Mr. Nesselrode, you are behaving quite immodestly!" she scolded him. "Very much like a peacock!"

"Am I? Oh, but I must look absolutely right! There will be cameras and ever so many people, you know." He reached up to stroke the snake's scaly head. "And you shall see to it that they don't get too close to me, won't you, my precious?"

The snake obliged him by hissing with reptilian menace and dropping her jaw to expose her wicked fangs.

"Most effective," Ms. Mare said, and the artist laughed, high and loon-like. She felt a smile tug at the corners of her mouth. She could see her dear, eccentric Mr. Nesselrode showing through the cracks of the grand disguise.

She checked her watch. "Mr. Shekle should be here any moment with the car."

"Good!" He clapped his hands with delight. "Oh, this will be such fun! I am *so* glad you persuaded me to do it!"

"Now, Mr. Nesselrode, I believe you persuaded yourself."

"Ah, but I never would have done it if I didn't have you with me. Promise you'll stay by me every moment."

"Every moment," she assured him. "Unless, of course, you need to go to the Gents'. It wouldn't be quite proper for me to accompany you there."

He laughed. "Oh, my, no!" He went to the window to look out. "Is the car here yet?"

"Mr. Shekle will call for us when it is time," she said, and surreptitiously walked past the mirror to check her own appearance. Simple, conservative, no-nonsense. Dark grey skirt and jacket with a mauve blouse, good solid shoes, no make-up, her hair pulled back, wound and pinned securely to the back of her head. She would blend into the background nicely, allowing all the thunder to go to him. She would not be noticed, and therefore would be able to move freely and remain close by without interfering.

"Ms. Mare," he called to her with a gesture.

"What is it?" She joined him at the window.

He pointed up into the sky. "Look!" There, pale and small, diminished by the blazing robust illumination of the city lights, was a horned crescent moon, hovering in the sky between the towering buildings that surrounded them.

"I think," he said softly, "one final touch." He covered his left hand with his right, taking a deep breath and half-closing his eyes. He let his breath out slowly, then drew his right hand away. On his finger was the moonstone ring with the double eagle crest.

"I think I am entitled to wear this," he said. "I had a great-however-many-great aunt who was a Romanov."

"I don't think there are many left of the family to dispute your claim," she said, standing close to him, wondering if the horned moon gave her leave to call him Angel. Then she took a deep breath and said, "I'm sorry to have to mention this, but speaking of relatives, I've just had a letter from my mother."

He frowned. "Nothing wrong, I hope."

"Oh, she and the Galbraiths are fine," Ms. Mare reassured him. "But you see, the Galbraiths knew your mother's family in Greece, and they have been in touch with them recently. It seems your grandmother has passed away. They thought you might not have heard."

He sighed. "Indeed, not. Well, it's a small matter to me, no disrespect intended. I didn't know her well, the frightful old spider. I only met her once or twice. My father disliked going back there, and disliked my going there too, for some reason. So my mother generally visited on her own. I hardly know any of my cousins or uncles or what-not."

"Then the news doesn't sadden you."

"Only in the vaguest way." He smiled at her, his silver-blue eyes bright. "Everything that truly matters to me is here." He took her hand and pressed his gently over it, taking a deep breath and gradually releasing it again. His fingers slid down to curl under her fingertips, and there, on her finger was the star sapphire ring. "Oh, my!" she gasped.

"Not the real one, of course," he said. "I am not entitled to ask you to wear that yet. But seeing this on your finger will give me courage."

"Thank you," she breathed, holding out her hand to see the shifting stellar beauty at the stone's heart. To think this fabulous being who commanded mastery over the very fabric of the world should need courage; and to think he sought that courage from her! "My dear Angel," she said softly, looking up at him.

He brought her hand to his lips and kissed it tenderly. "Someday, Vivian, I—"

There was a sharp rap at the door, and they both jumped. He cringed away from it, blinking in bewilderment.

"It's Mr. Shekle," she explained, gently drawing him back into vicinal reality. "It's time to go."

"Oh, yes," he said, slowly readjusting. Then he grinned, fully back into the professional persona. "Do let me get it!"

Frank Shekle whistled with amazement when he saw his client. "Jesus, Nesselrode! Where'd you get the snake?"

"Oh, she's mine. Isn't she lovely?"

"What's that, wings? Holy shit. Oh, hello, Ms. Mare. Pardon me."

"Not at all," she said graciously.

"Yow," Shekle said again. "You look fabulous, Nesselrode. We've got... Is that snake real?"

"Of course she's real. Aren't you, my precious?"

"But you said... it isn't a prop?"

The winged snake slithered down her master's arm and began to demonstrate just how real she was by coiling around Mr. Shekle's body.

"Jesus Christ! Call it off, Nesselrode!"

"That will be enough, my lovely," he cooed, and the snake flapped her wings and uncoiled herself, rising up over their heads and then resettling on her master's shoulders.

Shekle stared, then laughed out loud. "Wow!" he exclaimed. "I just hope Claudia Van Maus isn't afraid of snakes! Well, come on, the limo is waiting, and so is the world." Shekle was clearly delighted that his prize client had lost nothing of his theatrical flair.

Archimedes Nesselrode paused, turning, his eyes twinkling with excitement. "Ms. Mare?" he said, and she joined him, keeping an appropriate distance to his side and slightly back. She knew her place, both in moonlight and the spotlight.

***

It was a carnival, the crowds and the noise, for all its being a posh affair at the Rumpleminz Gallery. Ms. Mare was a little worried at first, but Frank Shekle had been right; Archimedes Nesselrode, in spite of his fear of The World Out There, didn't mind this scene one bit. He knew exactly what was expected of him, and he was absolutely in control. He led them like a piper, a magician performing tricks, his audience enthralled. He posed for the cameras with photogenic perfection and answered awkward questions with witty non sequiturs. His reputation as a half-mad eccentric freed him from any pretense at serious conversation and he made no effort to recall anyone's name. Yet he was charming, good-natured, and accommodating to the press, all of which thrilled Frank Shekle.

Ms. Mare watched, a few feet away at all times, yet playing the role of a non-entity. There was security all over the place, the most obvious being the two burly gentlemen who shadowed the artist. Both were built like stevedores, one red-headed, fair-skinned and freckled, the other dark with short, spiked hair. She could not help but think of them as Shamus and Bruno even though she was told their names.

Shekle made sure all the security people knew who Ms. Mare was, and made sure no one would interfere with her, but he also deliberately avoided introducing her to anyone. She did not wish to become an object of interest herself, subject to the harassment of having to answer questions or make conversation. Her full attention must be on her employer. Occasionally she would see Nesselrode look around, just the faintest trace of anxiety on his face, and she would make sure he saw her. As soon as he did, the anxiety vanished, and he resumed his performance. She minded the time and watched for signals from Shekle or the other people in charge of managing this event. She would then slip inconspicuously up to her employer and catch his attention, speaking to him quietly, making sure he kept to the schedule. She guided him where he needed to go when necessary, prompted him to speak to the people he was supposed to speak to and pose where he was supposed to pose. Archimedes Nesselrode sailed through it all grandly, with his winged snake about his shoulders and his weird, high laughter rising from time to time above the sounds of the crowds.

While minding her responsibilities to her employer, Ms. Mare also took advantage of this opportunity to see some of his celebrated works, the "trifles" he sold to amuse the public and support himself. They ranged in size from paperweight to dining-room table. There was a mobile from which were suspended an assortment of cubed insects, brightly colored and intricately patterned, some sporting delicate, feathered antennae, some spreading pearlescent wings and humming. There was a family of tiny monkeys which chased each other around a tree a foot and a half tall. There was a three dimensional labyrinth through which energetic, multihued caterpillars crawled. She had found the grinning golden-winged griffin that she had seen in the magazine photograph of ten years ago; it was on loan from the collection of a Hollywood celebrity. The still image did not do it justice. The mythic beast, brought to life by the artist's genius, moved about, sometimes sitting and preening its feathers, sometimes lashing its lion's tail and crouching, glaring with menace, sometimes reclining with sociable ease, watching passers-by.

It was nearly time to go. The artist was engaged in conversation with a small group of nominal colleagues. He had irreverently perched himself on top of one of his own cubed creations, a plumed and crested fish with iridescent scales and large, sleepy lavender eyes, who lazily floated in a watery medium tinted to match. From time to time little silver eels appeared to swim about her in peaceful orbits. The effect of the creation and its movements was one of serene beauty.

Reclining on the cubed fish, Archimedes Nesselrode was having the closest thing to a serious conversation that he'd had so far that evening.

"Would you say, then, that these creations of yours have some measure of consciousness?" The question was posed by a woman with tepidly red, sadly overworked hair, whose plumpness ought to have warned her away from the provocative style of dress she was wearing. Her feet bulged out of her shoes, the leather of which struggled to contain them.

"Why, of course," the artist replied. "How else would they be able to respond and react?" He sat up. "Like this," and pointed a few feet away towards a great, Buddha-like gorilla seated on a cushion within his cube, surrounded by gently waving palm fronds. The fat, placid ape occasionally produced a banana from beneath the cushion, leisurely peeled and ate it, stuffing the peel beneath the cushion when he was finished. The artist made a face at him, sticking out his tongue, and the ape mugged back grotesquely, then laughed with delight, pulling out another banana and chuckling to himself as he ate it.

"Then, they are alive?" the woman persisted.

"They certainly are lively," Nesselrode replied with a broad gesture, leaning back down on his elbow again.

"So how can you justify imprisoning these poor creatures in cubes for display? Is this not the cruelty of a zoo?" This came from the woman's companion, a middle-aged man whose round head and uniformly short bristle of salt and pepper beard and hair gave him the appearance of a puffer fish. He was dressed in black with white suspenders, the latter certainly necessary to keep his pants up.

"My dear fellow," the artist answered, "They are all quite satisfied with their lot."

"How can you be sure of that?" the woman demanded.

"Why, because that is how I made them. They are safe in their cubes, they have no memory of yesterday and never worry about tomorrow, and they spend their every waking moment doing exactly what it pleases them to do. Is that not an enviable state of being?"

Standing beside this rotund couple was a tall, gaunt young man with dark shaggy hair. His vest and jacket were of some faded, brownish material that hung nearly down to his knees. He had thus far contributed little to the conversation, mostly standing with his hands clasped, and gazing at the artist through his glasses, awe-stricken. Suddenly, he spoke: "Do you think of yourself as being like God?"

"Gracious, no!" Nesselrode exclaimed. "I do a much better job! All of *my* creations are happy!"

Frank Shekle appeared in the doorway opposite, caught Ms. Mare's attention and pointed to his wrist. She nodded.

"I'm very sorry to interrupt," she said, "But I'm afraid Mr. Nesselrode needs to be on his way."

"Is it time for the reception?" he asked eagerly, sitting up. "Capital! I am starving!" He leaped off the cube and landed without the slightest wobble, pausing to allow Winged Snake to slither off the cube and resume her place on his shoulders.

When they reached the relative privacy of the limousine, Ms. Mare asked him quietly, "How are you feeling, Mr. Nesselrode?"

His eyes sparkled. "Simply splendid, Ms. Mare!" He stretched out his legs and folded his hands behind his head, forcing Bruno and Shamus to dodge his elbows. "It's been marvelous seeing them all again!"

"Your adoring public?" Frank said with a grin.

"Heavens, no!" Nesselrode replied, "Much as I do enjoy entertaining an audience. No, I meant my creations. It's good to see that they are all well, still charming and delightful, still enjoying themselves. I was reasonably certain, but then I couldn't be absolutely positive about the perpetuity of what I'd made."

"What do you mean?" Frank asked, frowning.

"Well, nothing like them has ever existed before, has it?" Nesselrode answered. "It's all a grand experiment."

"You don't think they could just, like, evaporate or something someday," Frank asked him uneasily.

"Who knows?" the artist replied. "They have no substance. How long can a fancy endure? How long can a dream persist? For all I know, some day I, myself, might simply deliquesce like a bubble on a summer breeze!"

"Let us hope not!" Ms. Mare declared.

"Frank," he said, "would it be possible for me to have an opportunity for a bit of a touch-up before I make my entrance at the reception? I feel somewhat disheveled."

Shekle pulled out his cell, making a quick call. "No problem," he said finally, clapping the device shut and pocketing it. "We'll go around back first and there'll be a man there to show you where to go. Rand and Duggin, you'll go with him and keep an eye on him. Ms. Mare, you'll make sure he makes it to the reception, all right? I've got to go right in. There's someone I need to see."

"Certainly," she replied. She would be glad of the chance to smooth her stockings and make sure her hair was all in place.

When they parted briefly in the hallway, she felt a passing anxiety. She didn't like having him out of her sight, but he had the two bodyguards with him. She went to the ladies' room and took care of personal maintenance as quickly as possible, returning to the hallway to wait impatiently. She did not relax until he reappeared, chatting amiably with the young men flanking him.

"Back to the Circus Maximus!" he sang. "Lead on!"

This time, at least, it was a bit more low key. The guests were all there by invitation, and the members of the press were of the tamer sort, all from terribly high-brow publications or nationally syndicated programs. Mr. Nesselrode toned down his theatrics accordingly. It had been a bit much for the poor winged snake, who was now drowsing on her master's shoulder, her wings folded shut.

They also had an opportunity to sit down, for which Ms. Mare was grateful, and for which she imagined her employer must also be grateful. Surely his ankles were aching by now from those boots; even if he once was accustomed to such footwear he must be out of practice. Yet he seemed to be showing no signs of fatigue. Mr. Shekle sat down next to her for a moment, grinning from ear to ear.

"Man, this could not have gone more smoothly!" he exclaimed.

"You're pleased, then?"

"Ms. Mare, you have no idea! We'll talk afterwards. *He* might have no appreciation of it all, but you might."

"Why, thank you, Mr. Shekle, I would indeed." It seemed her efforts tonight had won her the eternal gratitude of Frank Shekle, not to mention his trust and a sense of comradeship. At the moment, she was watching her employer at the buffet, conversing with an expensively coiffed matron dressed somewhat ostentatiously in scarlet and diamonds. The snake woke up and lifted her head, and the matron uttered a little shriek. The artist laughed.

"You were absolutely right," Ms. Mare said. "He's like a duck in water."

"I've seen it all before," Shekle said. "He'll probably spend the next three days in bed, but all he'll talk about is how much fun it was. He's nothing but a flaming ham."

Ms. Mare smiled fondly. "He is, really, isn't he?"

"That's why I couldn't understand why he'd give it all up, just like that, and go into hiding for ten years."

"Well, there were reasons, as you well know," she replied in a low voice.

"And speaking of which," Shekle said cheerfully, looking around the room, "So far, so good. I'd heard rumors, but—"

"You'd heard rumors?" Ms. Mare demanded sharply. "About *her*? What did you hear?"

"Oh, nothing much. Anyway, I didn't want to say anything. I was afraid it might spook the poor fellow."

"Mr. Shekle, what did you hear?"

He waved his hand dismissively. "What does it matter? We've only got about another hour to go, and it'll be all over. You and Nesselrode can return to your hotel and in the morning you can both go back to the chimera farm. No problems at all." He patted her hand, cutting off any further protests. "I've gotta go. I'll check in with you before you leave, okay?"

An hour, Ms. Mare thought nervously. A great deal can happen in an hour.

It was really perfectly timed. No one had left yet, but there was the general sense that everything important had happened and everyone was beginning to glance at their watch. They were on their feet, eyes toward the door, when it opened with a grand commotion.

"No, no, but of course I must go in! Don't be absurd. Renard, see to this silly little man." And there she was.

No photograph, no matter how skillfully posed and taken, could capture the presence of Zarah Trebbiano. She had the face of a goddess, but a goddess not to be messed with. A Hera, not an Aphrodite. She had thick black hair that fell in shining curls around her shoulders, arching black brows and flashing gypsy eyes. She was tall, long-legged, with ample hips, a slim waist and an operatic chest. Her gown was emerald green, black and gold, and its design sang the praises of her abundant assets. She was awesome.

No wonder Mr. Shekle expressed a willingness to sacrifice a vital part of his anatomy to become romantically entangled with that woman, Ms. Mare thought.

Having made her entrance, she then began greeting people she knew, which seemed to include nearly everyone present. Ms. Mare realized in a moment of panic that she had lost track of her employer. Bobbing about, she caught sight of him at last and nearly collided with Frank Shekle in her haste to reach him.

"We've got to get him out of here!" she hissed to Shekle.

"My thought exactly," he replied. "There's an exit over by those curtains. We can slip out without too much of a fuss."

"Excellent. Mr. Nesselrode?" she spoke to him, touching his arm. "This way if you would, please."

"Eh?" he murmured, but he wasn't paying attention. His eyes were focused on a spot in the crowd where a flash of green and gold could be glimpsed. The winged snake, now very much awake, was writhing on his shoulders in a state of alarm.

"Come on, Nesselrode," Shekle said a bit more forcefully. "Let's get going. This way."

"What?" He glanced at them distractedly. "No, I can't go now. She's here. I saw her come in."

"You don't want her to see you, do you?" Ms. Mare asked him urgently.

"She already has. It's only a matter of time, now." He reached up to pet the snake. "Calm yourself, precious. There's nothing to be afraid of." He grinned at the two of them. "What on earth could there be to be afraid of?" He tapped a finger against his chin—the finger that wore the moonstone ring—and he winked at Ms. Mare. He was still very much in character, riding high on the intoxication of his evening's success. He was fearless.

Ms. Mare and Frank Shekle stayed with him as he allowed the currents of the crowd to carry him towards the inevitable. Ms. Mare could hear the rich tones of Zarah Trebbiano's voice, slightly accented, as she grew closer. There was a tension in the crowd among those who understood the significance of her arrival here, an eager anticipation of what might prove to be a dramatic confrontation. When the artist and the singer drew close to each other, the crowd parted between them, as if to hurry the encounter.

She must have known he was standing there, yet she did not turn around at first, continuing her conversation with a tall bearded man in a tuxedo, who was quite obviously distracted by the sight of the artist standing behind her, a smirk on his face.

"Well, bless my spotted soul!" exclaimed Archimedes Nesselrode, "It's—no, wait, don't tell me—Maria Callas!"

Zarah turned around, her eyes bright and color in her cheeks. "Hah! You scamp! So there you are! Ah, Michel, did you think that you could come to New York and I would not come to see you?" She pronounced his name "Mikkel," and the way she said it implied all the intimacy of old lovers.

"I'd rather hoped so, yes," he replied blithely.

She spun the possible ambiguity of his answer into her favor. "Well, now I am here. Forgive me, I could not come sooner. I am in rehearsal for La Traviata. Marconi is directing, and such a tyrant he is!"

"Really?" he purred. "Well, I'm sure you are equal to it."

She laughed, a lovely melodic sound. "Dear Michel! What has it been? Years and years! But you look marvelous. And all of New York talks of nothing but you and your creations. We have both been blessed with great success, eh? But come, they have no more need of you here. We must go and have a drink somewhere, just you and I."

"I'd as soon be alone in a room with a Bengal tiger," he replied pleasantly.

"Oh, you are too cruel! Come, come. There is so much we must catch up on after all this time." She got a little too close and the winged snake reacted protectively, hissing menacingly and coiling herself to strike.

"Such a bizarre pet!" the singer exclaimed, drawing back. "Is it not tame?"

"Not really. I'd advise you to keep your distance."

"An excellent bodyguard! Oh, Michel, you have lost none of your originality and charm!"

"I expect you haven't changed much, either," he replied. "I fear I must disappoint you, Zarah. I'm really quite fatigued after all this excitement. I must return to my hotel room." He glanced at Ms. Mare and Frank Shekle. "Shall we go?"

"I shall call upon you later, then," she said as they started to leave.

"I shall be asleep," he answered pointedly.

"I shall wake you with a kiss!" she called gaily after him.

"I shouldn't advise it," he called back. "My snake guards me tirelessly, and her bite is rather nasty." He began to walk more quickly towards the door, still smiling aloofly, but he said quietly aside to Shekle, "I do hope the car is ready and waiting."

Shekle pulled out his cell. "I'll make sure of it."

Once in the privacy of the car, Archimedes Nesselrode collapsed against the seat with a groan, shutting his eyes tight. "Bless me in Latin!" he exclaimed. "I can't believe I just did that."

"You were magnificent, Mr. Nesselrode!" Ms. Mare praised him.

"Was I?" he asked, grinning at her, opening one eye.

"Absolutely!" Shekle enthused. "I've got to hand it to you, Nesselrode! You handled that beautifully! You handled *everything* beautifully! I've never seen you in such fine form! And I was afraid you'd be out of practice."

"Like riding a unicycle," he said, stroking the snake's head affectionately. "It *was* fun, wasn't it, my precious? But, my stars, I am *exhausted*!"

"Never mind, Mr. Nesselrode," Ms. Mare assured him, "It's all over. We shall go back to the hotel and you can rest, then in the morning we shall go home."

"I'd like that," he said, closing his eyes again. "Very much."

CHAPTER THIRTEEN

Lunacy

Before retiring, Ms. Mare had her customary bath, although she missed the comfortable familiarity of her tub at home. She did not care for the contours of the hotel tub, for all its pretensions of luxury. But she had packed her creams, and felt quite relaxed when she had completed her ablutions.

She heard low mutterings from the room next door, and she went to check on her employer. She found him wrapped in his dressing gown, ensconced on the couch before the television, a novelty which he didn't have at home. Winged Snake was curled up on the cushion next to him fast asleep.

"Still awake, Mr. Nesselrode?" she asked. "I should think you'd be done in after such a day."

"I'll retire presently," he said. "But I've gotten pulled in by this movie. It's about a young woman who works at a quite ordinary job as a secretary, but in her spare time she takes photographs. Remarkable, beautiful photographs, but she is too shy to share them with anyone. She is fearless behind the camera, but terribly timid on her own. I like her. She reminds me of myself."

"You are hardly timid around people, Mr. Nesselrode," Ms. Mare pointed out. "You were positively outrageous today."

"Oh, but that is different! I was merely performing. That's hardly how I truly am." He turned to look at her with a gentle smile. "I think you understand that."

She returned his smile with as much affection as she dared betray in ordinary light. With his fancy clothing and platform boots put away and the make-up scrubbed off his face, he looked very much like his old familiar self, dependent and dear to her. "Yes," she said fondly, "I expect that I do."

He turned his attention back to the television. "I have ordered some cookies and a pot of tea from Room Service," he said. "I will have my snack and finish the movie, and then I will retire."

"Very well. I shall see you in the morning, then."

She left him to his entertainment, returning to her own rooms. She made certain the communicating door was properly shut. Then she settled into bed and quite quickly fell asleep.

She had the enviable ability to sleep soundly in nearly any sort of circumstance, and found the bed very comfortable. Yet her dreams were uneasy, and the sound of a door closing penetrated her consciousness. When the snake landed on her bed, she thought for a moment that she was in Brazil, and an anaconda had dropped from the ceiling, through the mosquito netting and onto her legs. It was a most unpleasant way to awaken. She sat up quite suddenly, glancing about for a weapon, and realized it was only Mr. Nesselrode's harmless creation.

"What is it?" she demanded irritably. Her irritation quickly turned into alarm at the sight of the winged snake's writhing agitation. It implied that something was amiss in the next room. Ms. Mare leaned forward, fully alert. "Is Mr. Nesselrode all right?"

The reptile's anxious side-to-side waving indicated that he was not.

"I must go to him at once," she said, throwing off the covers and jumping out of bed. The snake flapped her wings, rising off the bed and flying over to block the way to the door.

"Why shouldn't I go?" Ms. Mare demanded.

The snake lowered herself to the floor and coiled herself up in front of the door. Ms. Mare cocked her head. She could hear voices in the next room. It was certainly not the television. "Who is in there with him?" she asked, and the snake writhed with distress.

Listening carefully, she could make out the distinctive accented voice of Zarah Trebbiano. "Good Lord!" Ms. Mare breathed. "But, he doesn't want me to interfere?"

The reptile bobbed her head in affirmation.

"And he sent you out of the room?" Winged Snake hung her head mournfully. Ms. Mare stood undecided for a moment. If her employer wished to handle the matter privately, then she certainly should respect his wishes. He had been quite able to deal with the woman at the reception. Perhaps he knew what he was doing. Yet every instinct warned her that her employer was in mortal danger, no matter how self-confident he might be.

"I must know what is going on." She pressed her ear to the crack in the door. The snake hovered close by, flicking her tongue nervously.

His voice was saying, "...two marriages since then."

"Disasters, both of them," Madam Trebbiano replied. "A futile attempt to replace you in my heart. It cannot be done, Michel! For me there can be no one but you!"

"It is impossible, Zarah. I can't return your love."

"Oh, but there has been no one else for you, has there? Yes, yes, I have made inquiries, and I know you have lived alone in absolute solitude since you left me."

"That's not strictly true."

"I have heard of the creatures you surround yourself with, Michel. The rumors of your magic enchant me even more. But they hardly count. There has been no love in your life since you left me. Can you deny it?"

"I can," he declared. "I am very much in love with someone at this very moment!"

Ms. Mare felt a smile warm her face and she glanced down at the star sapphire ring, which had not yet faded, and which she could not bear to remove at bedtime. "Go away, you conceited harpy!" Ms. Mare whispered to her rival beyond the door. The snake hissed in concurrence.

"Bah!" Madam Trebbiano exclaimed scornfully. "I do not believe it! I should have heard of it if this were true! No, you are lying to me, Michel, and to yourself as well. In your heart you know it, if you will but admit it. You love me! Yes, you do! Do not deny it!"

He began to protest, but she cut him off, her voice sweet and imploring. "Oh, Michel, I made so many mistakes, but I am older now, and so much wiser. It will be different this time, I promise you! I know, I was too passionate before. I frightened you with my great passion. But I understand now, I must be gentle. You are a fragile treasure, an orchid, Michel, my sweet prince, my angel—"

"You mustn't call me that!" he cried out in horror.

"Oh, but that is what you are, blessed with a divine face and body, with a holy gift of creation. What mortal man could ever capture my heart as you have?"

"Zarah, I must ask you to leave!" There was panic in his voice now.

Her voice was musk and honey. "That is not what you want. Not really. The desire is in you, I know it is. Let me give it wing! I shall be gentle, I promise, so very gentle this time—"

"Zarah, don't—please—!"

There was an ominous silence. Ms. Mare pressed her fist to her mouth in unbearable anxiety. It was all she could do to keep from grabbing the doorknob and yanking open the door, putting a stop to whatever blasphemy was taking place in the next room. The snake began writhing hysterically.

"Zarah—Zarah, stop! You don't understand, it would be the end of me!"

"It would be the making of you! Your fears are phantoms, Michel, they keep you from becoming a man. Let me free you, release you, so that you may become all that you were intended to be!"

"Please don't—!" His protests were smothered. There came a soft moan and a sigh.

"Yes, my love! Give in to your desires!"

I can't stand any more of this! Ms. Mare thought and reached for the doorknob. The snake curled her tail around Ms. Mare's wrist in restraint. For all her anguish, the reptile still insisted on obeying her master's orders. Ms. Mare leaned against the door, her eyes squeezed shut.

Then she heard his voice again, shaky, out of breath. "Not here, Zarah. I can't—not with my-my assistant in the next room."

"Why not?" the woman replied huskily. "She is asleep."

"She might wake up. Please, anywhere else. Your place."

"That would have its advantages," she agreed. "We shall go."

"You go ahead. Give me an hour to dress and prepare. I'll be there."

"Oh, no, Michel! I stay with you."

"I'll come to you, I promise. I give you my word. Half an hour, then. Enough time for me to pack a few things. In case we decide to go off somewhere together. And I should leave a note."

"I do not trust you, Michel. I shall wait for you."

"Zarah, please, I'll do whatever you want, I swear to you. I won't fight you. Just give me a little time to prepare, I beg of you. When I come to you, I'll be ready. I'll be all yours. Here, I'll give you my ring. It's a priceless family heirloom. There. I'll have to come to you now, won't I?"

She hesitated before answering, and when she did her voice was cool. "Yes, you will come. You must. I shall see to it." There was silence again, and a half-stifled moan.

"All right!" he gasped. "Give me a few minutes. Just a few minutes. Please!"

"Very well. I am staying at La Montaigne. Suite 1411. I shall be waiting for you. If you disappoint me, I shall make you regret it bitterly. I promise you that!"

"I'll be there, Zarah, I swear I will."

After a moment or two Ms. Mare heard the door open then close.

She waited. Why didn't he call to her? Surely it had been a ruse; he did not really intend to go to that woman, did he? Her heart pounding, she leaned against the door, straining to hear any sound. She looked at Winged Snake, but the reptile seemed to be waiting as anxiously as she.

Then it came, a soft, wretched, pain-wracked sob.

"Vivian!"

She felt a flush of relief. Now she could act! She pulled the door open with a slam and rushed into the other room, the winged snake flying with her. She found him sitting on the edge of the bed, his dressing gown clutched around his shivering body, his eyes squeezed shut. She sat on the bed next to him, putting her arms around him. "I'm here, Angel. I'm here. It's all right." The snake landed on the bed and slithered up his arm to rub her head against his cheek, her wings spread around him shelteringly.

He looked up at Ms. Mare, miserable and guilty. "You heard me call?"

"Of course. I came immediately."

"Then, you were awake?"

"Winged Snake got me up when you sent her into my room."

"So, you heard? Everything?"

"Nearly, yes. I would have come in immediately, but Snake said I shouldn't."

He winced, grimacing with shame. "I was a fool! An idiot to try to deal with her alone! She said she only wanted to talk—swore that was all she wanted! I was an utter ass to believe her!" He covered his face with his hands. "I should have known better! Without you or Snake I was helpless! Oh, Vivian, can you forgive me?"

"Don't be absurd," she soothed him, "There is nothing to forgive. That woman is a fiend. But you managed to get rid of her very cleverly before any real damage was done."

"Oh, no, I'm not rid of her. She'll be back! She has tasted blood and she wants more! She wants *me*!"

"Then we must leave immediately," Ms. Mare said firmly. "We will pack and go before she can return."

"Yes, yes, we must." He clutched her. "Oh, Vivian! The worst of it is, a part of me wants to go to her! Even though I know it will be the ruin of me. Once she has me, once she possesses me body and soul, I know I shall never be able to create again. Then she'll tire of me and toss me aside like the rind of a fruit sucked of its juice. Yet, even knowing that, a part of me doesn't care! I would willingly sacrifice myself, burnt to a crisp on her altar!" He was shaking violently, half-mad with self-loathing.

"I won't let that happen, Angel," Ms. Mare said. "We won't let it happen, will we, Snake?" The avian reptile coiled herself around him protectively.

"I hate this!" he cried. "It is so confusing, so frightening! I want to go home! Please, I want to go home!"

"We shall go home, Angel. I'll take you. It's going to be all right. I'm here to protect you even if she comes back."

"I can't move. I feel sick. She is a monster, a demon, she poisons me with the venom of her lips, her touch, her words! I nearly gave in to her!"

"Angel, calm yourself, please! We'll get you home. It will be all right, but you must get a hold of yourself." She had to shake him out of this hysteria. There would be time later, in moonlight, to comfort him with tenderness. Right now they needed to act, quickly and efficiently, to get him to safety. Ms. Mare assumed the appropriate role.

She stood up and spoke to him firmly. "Mr. Nesselrode, we must get busy. I shall go into my room and dress, and pack my things. You must do the same. Snake, kindly assist him as best you can. As soon as I am ready, I will return and assist you myself. Now, don't fuss, I'll leave the door open between our rooms. You shan't be alone. But really, Mr. Nesselrode, the first thing we must do is get properly dressed. Surely you can see that."

It worked. He took a deep breath and nodded. "Yes. Yes, of course. You're quite right, Ms. Mare. I shall see to it. Right away."

Ms. Mare returned to her room, dressing quickly and throwing things into her suitcase in a distressingly haphazard manner. Never mind, she told herself, it can all be sorted out and ironed later. She hesitated about taking the time to do her hair properly, but decided that appearance was as important as haste. She must inspire confidence and calm in her employer, and that meant looking her normal, neat self. She listened, and could hear him moving about in his room, talking to Winged Snake. Had it been half an hour yet? Would the woman begin to suspect the truth and come back for him? Well, they'd just have to deal with it if she did. Madam Trebbiano would discover that she had no easy mark in Vivian Mare!

She came back into his room smartly dressed and groomed, and was relieved to see that he had managed to get proper clothing on himself. But that was about as far as he had gotten. He was wandering back and forth with things in his hands, talking to himself, distracted and distraught. Damn that woman! She had picked a fine time to attack, when he was already exhausted and not at all himself. No doubt she had planned it that way.

"Come, now, Mr. Nesselrode, this will never do. Into a suitcase with those. That's it. It can all be sorted out when we get home. Snake, would you kindly fetch the things from the closet?" She picked up the telephone to call for a porter. The desk clerk was taken by surprise. "Yes, I'm quite aware of what time it is," Ms. Mare said briskly, "Mr. Nesselrode wishes to check out now. Please have his car brought around and send someone up for his luggage."

Her employer was looking at her with gratitude and wonder. "You do know how to take care of things," he marveled.

"Naturally, that is why I was hired. Now, we must finish getting you packed. The porter will be here any moment. Thank you, Snake. Get the things from the bathroom, Mr. Nesselrode. Never mind if you forget something. We can replace it later."

It took longer than she would have liked for the porter to arrive, but at least it gave them ample time to get everything assembled. The snake refused to go back into her suitcase, insisting on remaining coiled protectively around her master. Under the circumstances, Ms. Mare was not going to argue.

She settled matters with the desk clerk and tipped the porter handsomely for his trouble. Her employer stood in the lobby, absently petting the snake, an expression of vague unease on his face. But he seemed reassured by Ms. Mare's attitude of confident control.

"All right, Mr. Nesselrode, let's be off," she said, and he followed her obediently out to the curb.

It was at that point that their luck failed them.

"So, you run away again, eh, Michel? You are a coward and a liar!"

He froze as if he had been shot, his hand on the door handle of the car. Madam Trebbiano had come out of the shadows, waiting for exactly that moment to attack.

"Get in the car, Mr. Nesselrode," Ms. Mare said firmly, "I shall handle this." She knew she probably would have been better off if she had simply gotten him in the car and driven off without a word to the woman, but she was so mad she couldn't help herself. There were a few things she just had to say.

"Oh, yes, get into the car, Michel!" the singer mocked. "Do as your woman servant says! Spineless worm! That is all you are! Gutless and spineless!"

"That will be enough!" Ms. Mare snapped in an imperiously commanding tone that any school mistress would have envied. "You will leave immediately and do not *dare* attempt to contact Mr. Nesselrode again in any way! He does not desire your revolting, obscene attentions, so take them elsewhere!"

"Call off your dog, Michel," Madam Trebbiano said with contempt, "her yapping annoys me."

"You are a crude, ill-bred woman who ought to be ashamed of herself, but is too arrogant to realize it! Now, good night to you!" Ms. Mare turned on her heel to go. Her employer had still not moved. He looked like a rabbit who knows the fox has seen him and there is no place to run.

"Ill-bred?" the singer cried. "This from an illegitimate brat of the serving class! Oh, yes, I know who you are! You're the housekeeper, aren't you? Do you think to improve your position by coddling your master? A bit of advice to you—don't attempt to bed him! He is a passionless, impotent fish!"

"How dare you?" Ms. Mare cried in outrage.

"Can't you say anything, Michel? No, you pathetic, sniveling poseur! You are a fraud! I shall make sure all the world knows it! I should never have wasted my time with you! You are not a man at all!"

"That will be enough!" Ms. Mare commanded, uncomfortably aware that they were beginning to attract a crowd. "Mr. Nesselrode, get into the car. We are leaving!"

"Go on, Michel! Run with your tail between your legs! That's all you've got down there! Go home with your faithful dog! Perhaps you can reward her with a few limp-wristed caresses! Or do you prefer little boys?"

"Zarah, shut up!"

The transformation of Archimedes Nesselrode from rabbit to wild-eyed fury was sudden and astonishing. He spun around to face her and his voice rose into a screech. "Shut up! Shut up! *Shut up!*"

Madam Trebbiano was shocked speechless, taking a step away from him. Ms. Mare was frozen, her mouth open. She had seen him annoyed, fretful, peevish and irritated. She had never seen this. His eyes blazed with madness, but not the gentle, harmless madness she was accustomed to. His face was twisted horribly and malignantly. The winged snake flew up into the air with alarm and darted over to Ms. Mare, coiling about her legs and cringing, afraid of her own master.

"You summon great passion in me, Zarah! Oh, yes! You inspire me with wild emotion!" He laughed, but it was a fearful, maniacal sound. "You are fascinated by my magic, eh? I'll give you a demonstration! See what I create in your honor!" He held out his hands. To Ms. Mare's horror they were dripping with scorpions. If there was any creature which inspired greater loathing in her than spiders, it was scorpions.

Madam Trebbiano's expression showed much the same sentiment. She was grimacing in revulsion. Archimedes Nesselrode, quite monstrously insane, walked towards her. "Embrace me, Zarah! I'm all yours!"

"Get away from me!" she cried, backing away. But she found her retreat blocked. They were no longer standing on a city sidewalk. Archimedes Nesselrode had conjured a chamber of horror.

The stone walls that enclosed them slanted at bizarre angles and intersected with unbearable asymmetry. The seams where the stone blocks met were cracked and seeping with fungoid slime. From the slime bubbled shapeless things which crawled and dripped to the crazily tilting floor. The ceiling was thickly hung with sticky webs which seethed with black legs and bloated bodies.

"Gifts for you, Zarah!" he shrieked, his voice cracked and shaking, "From the bottom of my heart!" He threw the scorpions at her, and began to laugh hideously. He became swathed in robes of black and scarlet, and from beneath the folds of the robe erupted monstrosities, deformed and hideous. Like writhing hunks of severed flesh, embedded with eyes, oozing like open wounds, they flopped and crawled around him. Zarah Trebbiano screamed and clawed helplessly at the venomous creatures that clung to her, stinging her repeatedly.

Stunned with horror, Vivian Mare stared, unable to believe that her timid, sweet employer could have so suddenly mutated into this terrible monster. It took an act of strongest will power to break the paralyzing spell.

"Snake, for pity's sake, let go of me!"

Yet even when she had finally managed to extricate herself from the reptile's terrified grip, she hesitated, unsure what to do. The spectacle of the mad, malevolent artist frightened her. She had to put an end to this abomination somehow. Ms. Mare took a deep breath.

"Stop this at once!"

Archimedes Nesselrode turned to face her, his eyes wild. "Zarah wanted to stir my passions!" he cried. "She has succeeded!" And he began laughing again. From the hanging sleeves of his raised arms came a parade of horrors, lipless mouths stretched tight with rictus, teeth bared, embedded in corded, raw flesh, propelling themselves by means of bloody sinews that whipped and coiled. The teeth snapped and slavered as they fell and rolled on the ground, gory sinews spasming.

He would not harm me, she told herself, ignoring the snake's panicked misgivings about her creator. Fighting down revulsion, she forced herself to walk into the writhing, biting pandemonium of malevolent mutations. They squelched beneath her shoes, or squirmed as if she were treading on rats. She took his arm sharply and shouted.

"Mr. Nesselrode, that is enough!"

He blinked at her, startled.

The illusions melted around them, and they were once again on a city sidewalk, standing next to the Daimler, surrounded by a shocked and baffled crowd. But to Ms. Mare's dismay, the scorpions had not vanished with the rest of it. The anguished singer's screams and struggles continued.

Ms. Mare pulled open the door of the car, pushing the deranged artist into the back seat. He made no effort to resist, but began laughing again. Ms. Mare looked back at the stricken woman, helpless. They're only phantasms, she told herself frantically, they have no real substance, they can't really harm her. But the screams were very real. The madman continued to laugh and the woman to shriek as Ms. Mare ran for the driver's side of the car, pulled open the door and got in. She could feel the stares of the crowd on her, but no one made any effort to stop her. As she was slamming the car into gear, the winged snake landed with a heavy thud on the hood.

"All right! Hurry up! Get in!" she cried, rolling down the window. The frightened reptile quickly slithered in down over her lap and coiled herself up tightly on the floor. Ms. Mare pulled away from the curb, narrowly missing another car, her heart pounding.

The screams faded and the hideous laughter in the back seat subsided.

She drove, aimlessly at first, just wanting to get away. Finally she began peering at street signs, her badly shaken faculties taking up the problem of where she should go. She had to get out of the city and on the road to home. But she didn't know New York well enough to manage it without checking a map. She was already looking for a place to pull over when she heard a coughing and gagging in the back seat.

"Ms. Mare, stop the car, quickly!"

She obeyed, pulling over to the curb in front of a garage which was closed for the night. She turned around in time to see him throw himself against the door, opening it and leaning out, violently sick.

Ms. Mare watched the heaving of his body, biting her lip, slowly coming out of shock. When he was done, collapsing back into the seat and pulling the door shut, she handed him a clean handkerchief to wipe his mouth. He accepted it wordlessly, his hand trembling. She pulled into the garage lot, parking in front of the first bay and turning off the lights.

She did not know what to do with him. After what had just happened she was more than a little afraid of him. She turned around to look.

He was sitting, staring straight ahead, unseeing, his hands gripping his knees. "What have I done?" he whispered.

"It's over now," she said, hoping that it was true, searching his expression for confirmation that the terrible madness had indeed fully passed.

"Oh, my god!" he cried, "What have I done?" He covered his face with his hands and began sobbing. "What have I done? *What have I done?*"

"It's all right," she said. "It's over," but even as she spoke to comfort him, she felt a sense of revulsion, the terrible images coming back to her with the echoes of that hideous laughter. It horrified her to realize that his power to create could be twisted so, that he was capable of such murderous malice. The provocation had been extreme, but his retaliation had gone far beyond. Her idealized perception of her gentle, harmless Angel was forever shattered.

He began shivering violently. "I should never have come back out here again! It is all too much for me! It sickens me, poisons me, confuses me so horribly. Oh, Vivian, help me, I'm falling to pieces!"

She watched him indecisively, torn between the impulse to try to console him and horror at the monstrous way he had behaved. His helplessness, a quality that had inspired her protective instincts before, repulsed her now. Even his own creation had no wish to be near him; Snake huddled on the floor, shocked senseless. He took his hands from his face and hugged his arms around himself. His pale eyes turned towards her, frightened. "You saw what I did. You find me repellent."

"Nonsense," she said firmly, "Not at all." But her reluctance to get near him betrayed her.

"No, it's true!" he sobbed, "I am a monster!" He threw himself back against the seat, his face twisted in self-loathing, his eyes squeezed shut. "A monster! A horrible monster! I ought to be destroyed!"

The agony of his remorse broke the spell of her indecision. She got out of the car and got into the back seat next to him. "Angel—"

"I am no angel!" he cried, wrapping himself into a ball of pain. "You saw what I can do!"

She put her arms around him. "I saw," she said quietly. "The episode was regrettable, but it is over. You acted in self defense after being fearfully provoked."

"Why wouldn't she leave me alone?" he moaned. "Why do they do this to me? I should never have come back out here! I should never have taken the risk!"

"I would never have encouraged you to come, had I realized," she said. "But what's done is done. I am going to take you home, but first I must know a few things."

"I can't go home! I can't go anywhere! I am a freak, a vile, pernicious mutant! I ought to be destroyed!"

"Enough of that!" she said sharply. "You must pull yourself together. Like it or not, you are who you are, and mostly you are very good, and what you do is very wonderful."

"But what I did to Zarah—!"

"Was unfortunate," she interrupted firmly, "and we must deal with it. Now, do get control of yourself! Sit up. Wait a minute, I think I have another clean handkerchief. Yes, here it is. Now, collect yourself."

He responded to her clear, disciplined tone. Obediently, he sat up and blew his nose, wiped his eyes and made an effort to compose himself.

"Good. Now, it's important; you must tell me. Will Zarah Trebbiano be all right?"

"I-I'm not sure," he whispered.

"Tell me what you know, then. What about the scorpions?"

"Very poisonous," he whispered, "but very insubstantial. They and their venom will go away. I don't know how long they will last. I don't know if it is long enough to-to k-kill her."

"Is there anything you can do? Can you make them go away?"

He shook his head. "I can't un-create things."

"Then there is nothing to be done about it," she concluded firmly. "It is out of our hands. She was not alone, so presumably medical help has been called for her. They will simply have to do what they can for her until the venom disappears on its own."

"I didn't want to kill her, not really, I just wanted—she made me feel so—they tear me up inside and it all comes out horrors! I can't stand it! Oh, why did I come back out here?" He began to weep again. Compassion softened her, bringing tears to her own eyes. The poor creature. He couldn't help what he was. And mostly he was very beautiful. She loved that beauty. For a moment she held him, that fragile, imperfect being with the wonderful, terrible power, and let him weep.

At last, her practical sensibilities reasserted themselves. She sat up, giving him a gentle shake.

"Now, Mr. Nesselrode, listen to me. It is all over. Do you hear? All over. We are going to go home. Snake? It's all right, you can come out, now."

The winged snake poked her head timidly over the top of the front seat.

"Your master is very ill. I must drive. Comfort him as best you can, please."

The snake slithered over to him, spreading her wings over him and rubbing against his cheek. He sniffled miserably, but reached up to stroke her scaly head. Ms. Mare got out of the back seat and returned to sit behind the wheel.

"Ms. Mare," he said softly.

"Yes?"

"Thank you."

"Not at all, Mr. Nesselrode," she replied, and started the car. When she checked the back seat again, he was asleep, his knees pulled up and his head pillowed on the winged snake's coils.

CHAPTER FOURTEEN

Fallout

They arrived home just at daybreak. The basilisk greeted them joyfully, bounding across the lawn to the car. Her master called out the window to her, "I'm home! Oh, you beautiful creature!" and Ms. Mare stopped the car so that he could pet the guardian dragon's broad, rough snout. The basilisk rumbled happily in her throat. She chased the car, prancing clumsily like a great, scaly dog, all the way to the house.

Ms. Mare parked the car and got out, helping her employer to the door. He was weak and dizzy, leaning against her as they walked. The winged snake flew in with them.

"Heron?" she called as soon as they were in the door. "Heron!"

The ornithic matron came fluttering into the kitchen, clacking her beak.

"Heron, kindly take your master up to his room and put him to bed. He's had a dreadful experience and needs looking after. I must unload the car and see to things."

Heron squawked, all upset and gravely concerned, supporting her master with a surprisingly strong wing and ushering him towards the stairs. "It was *her* again," Mr. Nesselrode said softly, and Heron clucked sympathetically.

"I expect he will be thirsty," Ms. Mare called after them. "See to it that the marmosets bring him a nice glass of water. And tell them to mind that they don't spill! I'll bring tea as soon as I'm able." No doubt the retching and the weeping had left him dehydrated. Tea and soup, she thought. That will be just the thing.

Knowing he was in good hands, so to speak, Ms. Mare took the time to unload the car and put it away. That done, she put on tea water and some soup to heat, and took her own luggage up to her room, dropping it on the floor. There would be time enough to unpack later. What had been squashed and jumbled would simply have to stay that way for a little while longer.

When she brought up his tray, she found her employer comfortably settled in bed, Heron fussing over him. Although he looked pale and ill, he also looked content. Five out of seven cats including Madam Beast had come to greet him, competing for attention and purring resonantly. His room was filled with creatures, all milling about, cooing and bleating, chattering and singing, welcoming him home. Even the Bishop had left his silver tea pot to come up and stand at the foot of the bed, reciting a solemn blessing in Latin. Benjamin the bat-winged, star-nosed mole landed on the tray and nearly spilled the soup. "Careful, now!" Ms. Mare scolded.

"Oh, that looks splendid!" Mr. Nesselrode said eagerly as she set the tray across his lap.

"There, now. Is there anything else I can get you?" she asked him.

"No, I can't think of a thing." He looked around himself happily. "I have *everything*!"

***

Later that morning the telephone rang. Ms. Mare had finally gotten things in order and had an opportunity to make herself a cup of tea, but fell asleep in a chair without drinking it. The ringing of the phone roused her. She had been expecting it, and braced herself as she answered.

"Ms. Mare!" Frank Shekle cried. "Thank god you're there! Is he all right?"

"Quite all right, now that he is home," she replied.

"Jesus! What the hell happened last night?"

Ms. Mare took a deep breath. "Before I tell you a thing, I must know, is Madam Trebbiano all right?"

"Yes, by some miracle. A few hours ago she was in the hospital, damn close to dead from multiple scorpion stings. *Scorpion* stings! The police tell me they've got witnesses who say Nesselrode threw them at her. Now, I'll ask you again, what the hell happened?!"

Ms. Mare related the events of the previous night with a certain discretion, leaving out details that were none of Shekle's business while communicating the essentials. He listened, with an occasional bit of muttered profanity. When she was done he groaned.

"This is going to be ugly," he predicted grimly.

***

It was ugly, indeed. As soon as Zarah Trebbiano recovered, she retaliated with the vengeful fury of Hell. Her lawyers descended on Frank Shekle informing him that Madam Trebbiano intended to sue Mr.

Archimedes Nesselrode for everything he was worth or ever would be worth. She was also pressing charges for assault and attempted homicide. There was some doubt and confusion on the part of the police, who had eye witness reports and the medical evidence of her symptoms in the hospital, but not a shred of physical evidence. Though the entire block had been combed painstakingly for days, not a single scorpion, part of a scorpion, or scat of a scorpion was found.

A police detective and his assistant came to the house to question Mr. Nesselrode, who answered their questions with simple apologetic honesty, but the story was so fantastic that they left even more confused than when they came. How does somebody—even an artistic genius—*make* a scorpion in the palm of his hand? Especially one which conveniently vanishes a short while later? They questioned him persistently about how he accomplished this particular feat of legerdemain, but he couldn't really enlighten them. It was all utterly baffling, and unlikely to ever make it to court, at least as a criminal case.

However, Madam Trebbiano had more than sufficient resources to bring it to court as a civil case, and she intended to do so. Since Archimedes Nesselrode absolutely refused to leave his house, Frank Shekle was forced to make the trip out there to talk to him about the matter. It was the first time Frank Shekle had been to the Nesselrode household since Ms. Mare took over, and he was pleasantly surprised at the improvement. The place really looked nice. Neat as a pin with new curtains, everything scrubbed, and a fresh coat of paint on the house. He glanced around nervously for the basilisk as he parked his car, and braced himself for the parade of singularities as he came into the house. But it wasn't too bad. Ms. Mare had apparently tamed that crew as well. There was that huge, unnatural star fish which Nesselrode was using as a footstool, and that stern, bespectacled heron perched next to his chair. But it was just an ordinary housecat that purred on the artist's lap. Ms. Mare brought them coffee, brewed especially for the occasion, and she had made little orange cakes.

"Well, then," Shekle said, after taking a sip of coffee, a bite of cake, and complimenting Ms. Mare on both, "This is where we stand. Madam Trebbiano is bringing suit against you for all her hospital bills and for lost revenue due to her inability to work, as well as compensation to the opera company for its estimated losses due to the loss of her services while she was ill, plus a whopping enormous sum for pain and suffering, and to top it off, punitive damages twice that."

Archimedes Nesselrode, appearing quite unconcerned, shrugged. "We must pay it, of course."

Frank Shekle winced. He should have expected this. There the blithe idiot sat, in a comfortable chair with his feet up on a starfish, flanked by his devoted housekeeper and his devoted...heron, absolutely oblivious to the financially suicidal gravity of what he'd just proposed. Ms. Mare, at least, would have the sense to grasp the realities of the situation and might be able to get through to him.

"Look, Nesselrode, we can't do that."

"Why not?" he asked. "I'm guilty, after all. I did do a dreadful thing to her and she is entitled to compensation."

"Now, Mr. Nesselrode," Ms. Mare interrupted, "I must insist that you were severely provoked, and what you did was, in part at least, self-defense. She brought it on herself."

"I really wasn't myself, either," he admitted. "I was terribly tired and overwrought. But still, if it will satisfy her and make her go away, I'd just as soon pay."

"Let me try to make this clear," Shekle explained patiently. "You can't possibly give her the settlement she is asking for. It would bankrupt you."

"Can't I just sell a few more things?" he asked.

"Excuse me," Ms. Mare said sensibly, "May I ask exactly what the figures are?"

Mr. Shekle took a legal pad out of the briefcase open on the table next to him and consulted it. He told her. She gasped. "Good Lord! That *is* rather excessive."

"Exactly," Shekle concurred.

"Can't we negotiate with her?" Ms. Mare asked. "Try to get her to settle for something more reasonable out of court?"

"Our lawyers have already pitched that. She refused."

"It's not a matter of money for her, obviously."

"No, I'd say not."

"What then?" Mr. Nesselrode asked, puzzled. "What does she want, if not money?"

Shekle took a sip of coffee. "I'd say revenge."

"Revenge?" The artist looked genuinely baffled. "But, you said she is all right now. She's recovered completely."

"That's not the point," Shekle said.

"Well, then, what is?" he asked.

Ms. Mare patted his shoulder gently. "You wouldn't understand, Mr. Nesselrode. Never mind." Then she said to Shekle, "What chance does her case have in court?"

"Our lawyers think not much. There were never any criminal charges because there was no evidence. Because nothing can be proven, she's got only the testimony of eyewitnesses, who also reported some pretty far-out things besides the scorpion business which the police have dismissed as some kind of mass-hallucination. And the testimony of her doctors, who claim her symptoms were genuine, but can't explain why they all just went away. If Nesselrode refuses to deny any wrongdoing, it might be enough to get some kind of settlement, but probably a lot less than what she's asking."

"Then, we must simply call her bluff and go to court," Ms. Mare concluded.

Shekle took a deep breath. "Ms. Mare, think about it. A trial involving two major celebrities for a whopping huge settlement, with all the elements the tabloids love: Sex, scandal, mystery, assault, pain and suffering, and more sex, implied or otherwise. You can be sure Zarah Trebbiano is going to get nasty, because she is out to humiliate her former lover—"

"I am not!" Mr. Nesselrode objected. "I never was!"

"Prove it in court. She's likely to claim anything in order to make you look as bad as possible."

"Oh, dear," Ms. Mare murmured, realizing the implications all too clearly.

"I can't prove it in court. How could I?" the artist asked plaintively. "Why does she want to do this to me?"

Heron squawked with disgust, then spread her wing across the artist's shoulders. She clucked soothingly like a mother hen.

"Mr. Nesselrode will have to appear in court, then, won't he?" Ms. Mare said. "He will be subjected to public degradation. Oh, that odious woman! No, there must be another way. We can't have that."

"We're working on it," Shekle said, "But right now, it's looking like you get your choice of which tine of Hell's pitchfork you get speared on."

***

On Thursday, Ms. Mare went out to run her errands as usual. She checked her shopping list carefully, went over in her mind what stops she needed to make and worked out the most efficient order in which to make them. She checked her purse to be sure she had the letter for her mother that she intended to post. On her way out the door she paused for a moment to check to make sure her hat was on straight and her hair was properly in place.

As she got into the Daimler she looked around to be sure there were no unauthorized riders. The marmosets had once hidden themselves in the back seat, and had escaped when she opened the door at the post office. They had climbed up into an oak tree and had refused to come down, chittering and cavorting about in the branches, pelting acorns at passers-by. A most frustrating and regrettable incident, which had attracted an embarrassing amount of attention. Nothing short of bribery would get them down, and it took the offer of an entire box of crackers. Ms. Mare was extremely put out, as it threw her entire schedule for the day into disorder.

But today all was as it should be, the basilisk escorted her down to the gate as usual and watched her leave sadly. The poor creature seemed convinced that Ms. Mare might never be coming back, in spite of having gone through this every Thursday since the housekeeper's arrival, and always seeing her safely return in a few hours.

It was a pleasant day, cool but cloudless, and Ms. Mare was in good spirits, foreseeing nothing that would interfere with the swift completion of her rounds. If the market had fresh fish, she would prepare a nice filet for supper, perhaps with some greens, lightly steamed, with slivered almonds. If not, then just a fluffy omelet. Her employer's appetite had not be good lately, and he would not touch anything too heavy.

It was at the market that Ms. Mare began to notice something odd. She was accustomed to the occasional surreptitious stare thinking that it was to be expected, after all. She served in an extremely unusual household. The curious noted her passing, and sometimes whispered about her employer. She ignored it. The butcher and clerks at the market were always polite, and the librarian often asked after her employer in a friendly, conversational way. Mr. Nesselrode did not patronize the library, but did order books through the mail, and when he was done with them, could be persuaded to donate them to the library's collection. It cast him in a favorable light.

But as she stood at the fish monger's counter, inspecting the catch of the day, Ms. Mare became uncomfortably aware that she seemed to be evoking more attention than was usual. People were stopping and peering around corners, and murmuring to one another. The man behind the counter was no less polite than he normally was, but she received the distinct impression that he was watching her more closely than he might ordinarily have done. It was not until she had finished selecting her purchases and made her way to the check-out that she noticed the papers for sale on the racks. She caught her breath.

The reputable papers sported their customary headlines focused on the political machinations of the government and disasters abroad. But the tabloids flashed lurid headlines and shocking photographs.

Dear god, Ms. Mare thought, *it has begun!*

She hurriedly paid for her purchases and left the market.

At the post office and the pharmacy she kept her face a stern mask of brisk efficiency. But she was uncomfortably aware of the attention her presence drew, and the hushed whispers of: "That's her!"

That is *she*, Ms. Mare reflexively corrected them silently.

At the library, she was greeted with the usual friendliness, but there was a certain restraint, an awkwardness, as if the librarian didn't know quite what to say to her. She supposed she understood. Would asking after Mr. Nesselrode under these circumstances be calling attention to the gossip on everyone's lips? Or would the omission of a customary pleasantry serve to accomplish the very same thing? Did the cordial relationship the librarian had cultivated with this most regular and reliable patron constitute sufficient grounds to make sympathetic inquiries? Or was the subject best left alone?

Ms. Mare returned her book and borrowed magazines and did not linger at the desk, discouraging conversation. There was nothing she could say that could even begin to explain what had happened or how she felt about it. There was no point discussing it.

She was relieved that there was no one in the periodicals reading room. If there had been, she would have left, preferring not to be seen looking at the newspapers, calling yet more attention to herself. The tabloids were not to be taken seriously, although she knew all too many people would devour those glaring misrepresentations hungrily. But she had to know what the reputable press was saying. At least they had the sense to confine the story to the section where it was appropriate. But there it was sensationally highlighted.

As she read it, her heart sank. What would her mother and the Galbraiths think? She thought of the letter she had just mailed, with its glossed-over reference to "a bit of unpleasantness" spoiling what was otherwise a triumphant occasion. She'd have to write another letter to follow that one, and try to remedy what damage the papers might have done.

A stout man with eyebrows that bushed out over his glasses came into the room, picking up a magazine on photography. Ms. Mare folded up the newspaper and put it away, quietly leaving.

They were waiting for her on the sidewalk.

***

There was little conversation at dinner that night. Mr. Nesselrode picked listlessly at his meal. Ms. Mare was still shaken by the day's events, particularly her disturbing encounter with the reporters outside the library. She was unaccustomed to being the center of public attentions. It was simply wrong; she was merely the servant in the household, not the object of the spotlight. Oh, certainly she had dealt with the press in the past. There were always the rudely enterprising individuals who pestered the domestic staff for inside information about a noteworthy employer. Ms. Mare had always maintained a strict rule of loyalty and enforced it in those under her, cultivating a reputation of being monumentally unhelpful to the press.

This had been different. The quality of the questions had been different. The persistence and the offensiveness of the interrogators had been different. Of course she braved it all, unflappable as rock. She strode to the Daimler looking neither to the right nor left, firmly repelling their attempts to overwhelm her and rattle her into letting something slip. She knew their game; asking the most outrageous things in order to provoke a response from her. She gave them nothing.

But it still unsettled her. And her discomfort stayed with her, all during the afternoon and while she was preparing dinner. How long would this unwelcome notoriety persist? Would she face this each time she went out? Perhaps she ought to begin ordering things delivered. There were some excellent services. Just until this horrid business blew over. She needn't subject herself to this.

But to think they could do this to her, sending her into hiding, depriving her of her liberty to come and go as she pleased. It made her angry. They had no right! Yet, there was no law against it. It was an all-too-common practice. She simply had to show them that she would not be intimidated by them.

"Ms. Mare?"

She looked up, startled out of contemplating her dissatisfaction with the sole on her plate, which had not come out nearly as well as she had hoped, and the greens were too limp, having been overcooked. Her preoccupations with the day's unpleasantness had spoiled dinner. This would not do.

"Yes, Mr. Nesselrode?"

He rose from his chair, depositing his napkin on the table. "If you would please come up when you have cleared?"

"Of course," she said.

It was Heron who conducted her upstairs when the dishes were washed and put away. They stopped outside Mr. Nesselrode's bedroom door.

"Really, Heron?" Ms. Mare frowned. "I don't think this is quite proper, do you?"

The bird fluffed her feathers in agreement, but nevertheless, this was what her master wished.

"Very well, then." Ms. Mare opened the door hesitantly.

Her employer had torn apart his bed and reconstructed it on the floor in front of the window, using pillows and quilts borrowed from all over the house. Furniture had been dragged over and upended to make a sort of fort, as if to defend him against the onslaught of the world. He was ensconced in the midst of it, this sanctuary within a sanctuary, with several cats and assorted creations, gazing up at the gibbous moon. Ms. Mare regarded the untidy assemblage with dismay. I hope I won't be expected to put this all back in order in the morning, she thought.

"Ah!" he cried, getting up, "Ms. Mare!" He gestured to the pillow next to him. "Please sit."

She came over, doing as she was bid, sitting straight and proper as he settled back down again. She waited, but he took his time to begin. Finally he said, "I am seeing it now. My isolation here, it isn't just to protect me from them. It is to protect them from me."

"Now, Mr. Nesselrode, I hardly think one solitary incident—"

"I nearly killed someone," he said. "I think I would have, if you had not stopped me."

It was true, and the memory chilled her. He sensed the cold.

"Ms. Mare," he said, and fixed her with his strange, silver-blue eyes, "Vivian, do you still love me? Please be honest with me."

She considered her answer carefully. "Yes," she said. "I have a better, deeper understanding of you now, but my commitment remains the same."

"And your feelings?"

"Are different, as my understanding is different. That is the nature of love, Angel. It endures and adjusts."

He closed his eyes, sighing deeply with relief. "Then we can talk." The artist looked around himself at his creations. "Would you all mind leaving us alone, now? We need a bit of privacy. The cats may stay."

There were a few chirps and clacks of protest, cut short by Heron, who took the responsibility of herding them all out. They politely closed the door behind themselves.

He lay back against the cushions, and she allowed herself to relax a bit. A cat purred behind her head, perched on the raised-up end of a mattress. It was a wonderfully comforting nest, small and secure. Yet he hadn't populated it with illusions. Everything here was real. He had even dismissed his creations.

"I am trying to understand it all," he said. "It isn't easy for me. I am such an idiot when it comes to people."

"I wouldn't say that," she replied. "You handled everyone marvelously at the exhibition."

"Oh, that." He waved his hand. "It's all fun, and people enjoy it. I make a creation of myself. I know all about *that*." He sighed. "It's all the rest. It can't all be just a lovely game all the time."

She smiled at him sadly. "You're quite right, Angel."

"But it's the way things are, and I must try to understand it. And I must take responsibility for who I am, and what I have done. I can't just run and hide and expect you and Frank to make everything all right."

"Things will sort themselves out eventually," she said.

"Vivian," he said, sitting up, "this could happen again. I am dangerous."

"Nonsense!"

"Please, don't try to deny it. You were there. You saw."

"Yes," she said quietly. "I did."

He stared out the window, his expression hardened in an unaccustomed way. It was a hardness she didn't like. "If I gave in to her, or to someone else..." he glanced sideways at her, "to you perhaps, I would no longer be a danger."

She gasped. "No, Angel!"

"I would be an ordinary man. I could be a husband, provide the heir my father so desires. It would solve a great number of problems. And I could never harm anyone again as I did Zarah."

"And you would be miserable!" she cried. "Not only that, but think of the beauty you would no longer be able to create! The magic, the joy you bring to others!"

"Is it worth it?" he asked. "Are those little delights worth the possible horror I might be capable of?"

"Yes!" she said without hesitation. "How much poorer a place this world would be without your magic! How many people have looked at your jovial ape and laughed along with him? Stared in awe at your winged griffin? Felt their hearts lifted by your wondrous flowers and dragonflies, fish and fauns, floating and living in perpetual contentment within those cubes? And Heron, Winged Snake, Benjamin and the basilisk, and even those wretched marmosets... would you take away their existence? Trade it all in because of one dreadful woman and the flash of violence she wrung out of you?"

"But I cannot bear the thought that I might harm someone!"

"You will not! I will see to it." She took his hand. "I know so much more about you now, and I know your weaknesses. I can protect you from situations that might be dangerous."

"But the risk—"

"Oh, Angel, don't you see? There is so much goodness in you, so much kindness, and this extraordinary gift that you possess! It is worth the risk. It is beyond all price!"

He looked at her closely, searchingly. "You are practical, sensible. I can trust your judgment." It was as much question as statement.

"Of course, you can," she said firmly.

He collapsed back against the pillows as if exhausted from some Herculean effort. "Then I need not do it," he breathed.

He opened his eyes, gazing upwards. "I cannot tell you what it was like, the madness, the terrible thrill of power. I confess, it was exhilarating, letting go and lashing out, knowing I could torment my tormentor with agonies a thousand times worse!"

She recalled with a shudder how he had transformed himself into exultant malevolence, and the hideous way he had laughed. But then, no one can truly know what extremes one might be capable of when pushed beyond one's limit. Archimedes Nesselrode had the power to make manifest the extremes of his nature. Thank heaven his nature was mostly extremely gentle!

She reminded him, "Whatever satisfaction you may have derived from it you paid for tenfold in remorse when you recovered from your madness."

"That may be true," he replied, "But what a horror to discover that I could take such pleasure in causing suffering to another!" He looked over at her. "You see, when I discovered I had the ability to create, it was an epiphany. Before that, I had no idea what to do with my wayward, coddled, pointless existence. I was useless. My creations gave meaning to my life. Surely to give them up would be the end of me. That conviction kept me from surrendering to the temptations of women like Zarah. But now I have you, and I can imagine salvaging a life out of the wreckage. It would not be so bad, knowing I had your love. And so, to put the darker side of it out of my reach forever, I could consider the sacrifice."

"I don't know which would be more selfish," she said with a faint smile. "For me to possess you for my own, taking your power but making you mine, or to urge you to remain as you are, with me as your protector, enjoying the benefits of your gifts, yet knowing you would always be out of my reach."

"I should love you either way, Vivian," he said.

She smiled at him. "I know."

"But you believe I should not give up my ability to create, even considering its possible consequences?"

"Absolutely not!"

He nodded with obvious relief. "Going to Zarah's bed might have diffused her anger. If you had said you thought it was the right thing to do I would have gone. But if you judge it to be not worth the sacrifice—?"

"Certainly not!" she said quickly and firmly.

He grinned at her. "I must confess I'm not disappointed. If I were to make that choice, I'd rather lose myself to you."

She felt herself blushing at the thought, particularly ensconced as she was with him in his bedroom in this cozy nest of cushions and quilts. He was a frightfully attractive man. Had it fallen to her, she would have found the task a most agreeable one.

Madam Beast found her way down to his lap and settled herself. "As it is," he went on, idly stroking the cat's thick fur, "we are left with the same dilemma as before. What are we to do about this lawsuit business?"

She laid her hand on his arm. "I'm afraid I haven't an answer. But whatever we do, we shall face it together."

"That helps," he said. He put his hand over hers. She felt acutely aware of the touch of those fingers, which could conjure such incredible extravagances. Yet they felt quite ordinary, mere flesh and bone. He said, "If we give her what she wants, Frank says that it will bankrupt me. I would lose everything, wouldn't I?"

"I'm afraid so. You would have to sell the house and everything you have."

"Oh, no. I couldn't do that. My creations, what would become of them?"

"You'd have to sell them, too."

"Out of the question! Oh, but you said it wasn't money that she really wanted, anyway."

"No, it isn't," she said gently. "I'm sorry, and I'm afraid it's very ugly, but you must accept it."

"She wants to hurt me. To ruin me."

"Yes, I'm afraid she does."

"Why?" he protested, sitting up, and Madam Beast jumped from his lap. "She says she loves me, and yet she would do this to me!"

Vivian leaned over, gently brushing the hair from his face. "I suspect she must have a great deal of pain in her heart. People who are cruel often have experienced cruelty themselves."

"But, I would think if someone were hurt, they would see how awful it is, and they wouldn't want to do that to anyone else." He sighed. "But that isn't how it is, is it?"

"No, Angel," she said. "I fear it is much more often just the opposite."

"So, we have to go to court," he said, dropping back down onto the cushions. "That means questions and people, and her saying horrible things which aren't true, and me having to face it all. I can't just be silly and play it all for fun. I have to try to answer their questions, even though it's frightening and confusing and I haven't any idea what to say."

"I will be with you. And Mr. Shekle will be with you, and you'll have lawyers to defend you." But in her heart she knew he was right. It would be agonizing. That wretched woman would make sure of it.

"And she'll say horrid things about you. She'll make it all seem ugly and obscene."

Her heart sank. That was likely to be true, too. She had already seen the beginning of it, the agents of the press leaping upon her. She would be publicly humiliated, her completely blameless—not to mention private—relationship with her employer turned into something sordid, the subject of malicious, derisive snickers.

She told herself fiercely, It doesn't matter what people think!

But it did matter, to her mother, and the Galbraiths, and it mattered what they thought of her. They wouldn't understand. They would be ashamed. Their Vivian, caught up in such a scandal!

"No, I cannot allow it!" he cried, sitting up. "There has got to be some way to stop what she's doing, to turn away her anger. I can't allow her to do this to us!"

"I'm afraid we have no choice," she said. "We must fight her, and do our best to endure what comes of it."

He shook his head. "This is all because of me. Because I was so foolish and cowardly. And yet when I fought back, it only made things horribly worse. There's got to be another way. I've got to be brave and I've got to be clever. It's up to me."

She sat up next to him, rubbing his shoulders gently. "It's not your fault, Angel. You mustn't take this all on yourself."

He turned to her. "I love you, Vivian. I'll not have you hurt. And I won't have my house and my creations threatened. I'll think of something. I *must*!"

"Oh, Angel," she said softly. His face bathed in moonlight looked so resolute, so beautiful and unearthly, that she almost could believe in his power to make a miracle. But lawsuits and scandals were things of harsh daylight. What power could her Angel have over them? She should never have encouraged him to leave. It was bloody awful out there, no place for a creature like him. She should have kept him here, safe and secure in his own mad, marvelous little world.

Ms. Mare, unaccustomed to the feeling, wanted to weep.

CHAPTER FIFTEEN

The Dove

Archimedes Nesselrode was up well before dawn to be certain he wouldn't be caught by his very prompt and efficient housekeeper. Heron, ever alert, accosted him in the kitchen with querulous squawks.

"I have a mission," he said firmly. "I've planned it all out."

The bird protested, listing all her objections. He held up a hand to silence her.

"My mind is made up. You'll not dissuade me."

Heron shook her head. What would Ms. Mare say?

"Whatever she says, tell her not she's not to worry. I know precisely what I am doing."

The matronly bird was skeptical, and highly apprehensive, but she acknowledged her beloved master's orders with a compliant bob of her beaked head.

He made sure he had everything he needed; he could be so forgetful sometimes. He took the key to the Daimler from the hook in the kitchen (how clever of Ms. Mare to think of keeping it on a hook, so it could never be mislaid!) and went out to the garage. He stood looking at the Daimler, the box under his arm, maps clutched to his chest, the keys dangling from his fingers.

It had been years since he had driven away from home on his own. He knew he could do it, of course; in his youth he had driven all over the place on his own, absolutely fearlessly. In those days he had been afraid of nothing, exhilarated by his new freedom from his mother's obsessive protection. But she had been right, hadn't she? At least in part. What had she known about him that she never would tell him?

He had learned much since then, to be afraid of the world, and to be afraid of himself.

"Today, I must be brave," he said aloud, and got into the car.

He had kept in practice over the years, driving down to the gate on delivery days. It had been safer to meet the delivery people at the gate than to have them come up to the house and risk an incident with the basilisk. He had taught her not to be quite so aggressive in her guard duties, but she did have the instinct. She couldn't help it; he had made her that way.

Basilisk came out of the bushes at the sound of the car passing and followed him down to the gate. She seemed puzzled when he opened the gate, but there was no one there waiting.

"I'm going out for awhile," he told her, but that baffled her even more. This was something that simply never happened.

"It is happening today," he said. "I have an important errand I must run."

Basilisk cocked her head, gazing at him with her lovely ruby-red eyes. Why wasn't Ms. Mare with him?

"I must do this alone," he explained. "Don't fret. I should be back before nightfall. At least, I hope so."

With a low, anxious rumble, the beast watched him drive through the gate, her tail lashing uneasily.

"It will be all right!" he said to her as he got out to close the gate behind him. "I know what I am doing!"

Do I really? he questioned himself as he got back in and drove away from the gate.

He had thought about it very carefully. Of course there were risks; terrible risks. But neither Frank nor Ms. Mare had a better solution. It was up to him. That was only right, after all. He had been the cause of it. He must take responsibility for the situation.

It had come to him all on his own. He hadn't dared to discuss it with practical Ms. Mare in the daylight, nor with dear Vivian by moonlight. She would forbid it, he had no doubt. But there really wasn't any other way. Usually he wasn't very clever at these sorts of things, understanding people and dealing with them. But he knew what he was good at, what always seemed to work. There was much about Zarah that frightened and confused him. But there were parts he understood, and he must go with what he knew.

It ought to work. It had a good chance of working. He had only to keep his head about him and not lose his nerve.

He felt quite cheerful as he drove along the highway, humming to himself. The weather was clear, the sun rose in the sky, reflecting off the snow. He didn't do well in bright sunlight. It hurt his eyes. He reached over and opened the glove compartment, groping around until he found the dark glasses he kept in there. Yes, that was better. He glanced at the box on the seat beside him. Such a lovely little thing. He hated to let her go. Still, it was for a good cause.

As forgetful as he was for details, and as upset as he had been at the time, he remembered clearly the address Zarah had given him. La Montaigne, suite 1411. Of course, she might not be there. But wherever she was, he would find her. He was quite sure that if she heard he was looking for her she would make the time to see him.

There was a place by a river where one could pull off the road and park. He took advantage of this to stop a moment and consult the maps. He unfolded each, studying them, scowling. Blasted confusing things, maps. Why did they include so many unnecessary details? A map ought to tell one where one wanted to go, and never mind all the rest.

A flock of ducks landing on the river distracted him, and he began watching them, and the water, and the way the wind stirred the trees along the bank, and there was a heron! Oh, what a delightful and interesting spot this was! He could spend hours watching everything, observing all the details, absorbing the inspiration of it.

He very nearly did. Quite suddenly he remembered that he had a very important mission, and he must be off. Throwing the maps unfolded into the back seat, he returned to driving. If he watched the signs and tried to recall which direction Ms. Mare had driven that day, he could probably find his way back to the city.

He hummed to himself and thought up ideas for new trifles to pass the time. So many little towns, so many little houses. So many people, all with lives very different from his own. It amazed him.

He turned on the radio and listened to it for awhile. He had hidden himself from the world for so many years, yet it was remarkable how little the news had changed. They talked about all the things they always seemed to talk about: money and politics, what the president was doing—at least it was a different president now—terrible things going on in other countries—different countries from last time—and people he had never heard of. They talked about it all with such seriousness, as if it were terribly important—well, some of it was, he supposed. War was a horrid business and he could not for the life of him understand why anyone would want to get involved in it. But the rest of it seemed to be of such little consequence. He recalled the last time he had listened to the news, before his retirement into seclusion. All those matters of grave importance discussed and debated so seriously then; all were forgotten, now irrelevant, replaced by new things to be concerned about.

He listened to a man talking about investments, and how to manage money. What a dreadfully dull business it all was! How could anyone endure it? Particularly when the world was filled with such marvelous things to think about instead. He changed the station. A woman sang achingly about a lover that was gone. How sad, he thought. It is so wonderful to be in love. Well, it can be, he corrected himself. It all depends. How strange it is that such a glorious feeling can have clinging to it such a complicated host of dreadful attendants! Again he thought of Zarah and shuddered.

He changed the station. The music was violent and pounding, and a man sang brutally about what he was going to do to his woman. He turned the radio off hastily. Things like that made him want to go back to his house and hide in the attic. It made the world seem like a very nasty place filled with ugliness.

Yet, he reminded himself, people do love my little trifles. They see beauty and they are charmed by it. I perform for them, and they are charmed by me. They aren't all bad. I must remember that. They are not all bad. Neither is Zarah.

But thinking about her eroded his courage. So he thought about Vivian instead. He loved thinking about Vivian. What an astonishing thing that within stern, strong, proper Ms. Mare there was Vivian. Ms. Mare was an awesome woman with all the shrewd capabilities he lacked. How he admired her! What a comfort to him she was! He had known almost from the very first day that she was absolutely right. Just what he needed. But then he had discovered Vivian, who was tender, who was lovely, who was clever and witty, who danced and laughed and thought he was marvelous!

So many women had thought him marvelous. Lovely, laughing, charming women. They all wanted to take him home and look after him. But then, with that first playful kiss came the look of hunger in their eyes. They desired him, to devour the bright essence inside him. They are not evil, he reminded himself. They really had no idea that their love would destroy him. He bore them no ill-will. Still, he feared them.

But Vivian! Dear, kind, understanding Vivian! There was no hunger in her eyes. She was complete, whole and satisfied. He could safely hold her, kiss her, be wildly in love with her, and there was no danger at all. Best of all, Vivian could become in a twinkling Ms. Mare again when the situation required it, ready to take charge and protect him in ways that Heron and Basilisk could never do. Except that now, she was in danger. Everything precious to him was in danger. It was time to repay the love, devotion and joy they all had given to him.

"Today I will be brave," he said aloud again.

The City was frantic with confusion and he had no idea where he was or where he was going. So much traffic, all in a hurry, with a wild collage of signs and lights which he couldn't make sense of. He was slow, uncertain, blocking the way of those who knew where they were going and were impatient to get there. He didn't want to inconvenience anyone, but how could he find his destination? He spied a standing taxi. Taxi drivers always knew where everything was. So he pulled over next to the cab and rolled down his window.

"Excuse me, can you tell me how to get to La Montaigne?"

"You're in the wrong neighborhood, Jack," the driver said. "You want Goddard Street, uptown."

That was not much help to him. "Which way do I go?" The cars behind him were honking their horns at him to get moving. Even the taxi driver seemed annoyed with his helplessness. He hated being a bother to people, but he must have help. Money often worked wonderfully to improve people's attitudes. Surely if the taxi driver were trying to earn his living, he would respond favorably to an offer of payment. The artist dug his wallet out of his back pocket and opened it, taking out the first bill he saw. He had no idea what sort of remuneration would be appropriate.

Evidently it was quite sufficient. The driver's eyes lit up. "Hold on, Jack, let me turn around. For that kind of dough I'll lead you to the place!"

Pleased, Mr. Nesselrode waited for the traffic to allow him to get in behind the taxi, and he followed him. City driving was dreadful, and once or twice he lost sight of his guide. He worried: the man had his money; would he simply disappear with it? Sometimes people out here could be so dishonest. But the taxi waited for him each time to catch up, and finally the driver waved his arm out the window to indicate they had arrived. The artist pulled over to the curb in front of the portico and parked, getting out and calling, "Thank you!" to the departing taxi.

Now then, didn't places like this generally have a valet or something? Sure enough, he had barely had the thought before he was accosted by a tall uniformed man who politely questioned his presence there. Mr. Nesselrode tried to recall what it was one said in such circumstances.

"I have business with Madam Trebbiano in number 1411. Could you please have someone take care of my car for me?"

"One moment please, if you would, sir," the man said, taking a device out of his pocket and speaking into it. It was a device similar to what Frank had used. Evidently they were quite common now. After a few moments' exchange with a voice from the device that Mr. Nesselrode could not make out at all, the man looked up at him. "Your name, sir?"

"Archimedes Nesselrode."

The man arched his eyebrow slightly, and repeated this information into his device. After a moment he clapped it shut and returned it to his pocket. "Go right on in, sir. I'll have your car brought around to the garage."

"Thank you," the artist said. He got his little box from the front seat of the car. Did one tip? He ought to make the offer, just to be safe. Evidently one did tip, and his choice of bill was more than appropriate. The man seemed very nearly as pleased as the taxi driver had been. Very good, so far at least. He had arrived.

In the elevator he again felt a twinge of nervousness. Standing there with the box in his hands, the reality of what he was about to do began to seep in. Perhaps this was a dreadful mistake. What made him so sure he was doing the right thing? What a disaster it had been when he had tried to cope with her alone before! All the possible consequences began to dance before him, each one more horrible than the last.

The elevator door opened. He found he couldn't move. The door slid shut again.

What if it all went terribly wrong? He was such a fool. What business did he have trying to take this on himself? Alone, with no one to protect him, or to stop him if he lost control. He should leave, quickly, while he still could, without seeing her at all.

But then, nothing would be accomplished. They would all be in the same awful mess and he would have done nothing to try to solve it. Besides, he had been announced. He was expected. He would seem an even greater fool and coward if he backed out now. He had to go through with this.

"I shall be brave. I must be!"

He took a deep breath, pressed the button to open the elevator, and he stepped out. He walked along the corridor looking for number 1411. This was the right thing to do. It was the necessary thing to do. He was doing this for them, for Heron and Basilisk, for Winged Snake, Benjamin, and those silly marmosets. For all his dear creations. For Madam Beast and the rest. And most of all, for Vivian.

He stood before the door. He did not need to knock. She had been waiting for him.

Zarah Trebbiano opened the door and regarded him coldly. "So. It *is* you. I did not think you would have the nerve to come here alone."

His mouth went dry. He licked his lips. "I need to talk to you, Zarah."

"Well, come in then." She turned away from him and walked back into the room. She was wearing a silk robe, dark blue embroidered with fishes, over what, he did not want to think. Her legs and feet were bare beneath its hem. Her black hair hung in shimmering, bouncing curls. The room was filled with her perfume. It made him forget all the things he intended to say. He stood in the middle of the room, holding the box, frozen.

She settled herself gracefully among the pillows on a couch, her legs folded beneath her. All around her was elegance and luxury in silken, brilliant colors. It made his head swim.

"Well, Michel," she demanded impatiently, "What do you want?"

What did he want? Confusion swamped him. He couldn't be clever. He couldn't be witty. He could only be honest. "I want you to leave me alone," he said.

"Hah! You come here to ask this? That I should drop the lawsuit, eh?" She rose to her feet, her eyes flashing. "You put me in the hospital with your evil magic! I nearly died! Such pain I suffered—have you any idea? Oh, no, you shall not get away with that!"

"I don't want to get away with it," he replied earnestly. "It was dreadful what I did to you. Of course I mean to pay—the hospital bills—whatever—"

"Oh, you will pay all right, Michel! I will break you! I will humiliate you! I will make you crawl and plead and squirm! I will *destroy* you!"

He looked at her with simple, frank incomprehension. "But, why?"

"Because no one does what you did to Zarah Trebbiano! Least of all a worm like you!"

He stood there, looking hurt, bewildered, but unwilling to back down. This annoyed Zarah Trebbiano. It was extremely annoying that he was here, looking at her that way, instead of hiding away from her, cringing in fear, waiting for her to descend on him like an avenging fury to drag him out into the open and tear him to shreds.

He spoke, earnestly entreating, "I am the same as I was before, when you said you loved me. I haven't changed. Yet before, you spoke so passionately about how you loved the way I was. Now, you say the most horrid, spiteful things about me. Why are you doing this? Why do you want to hurt me so?"

"Oh, Michel, you are a fool!" she exclaimed in exasperation.

"Yes," he nodded slowly, "I expect I am. I don't understand this hatred, this anger."

"You humiliated me! You lied to me!"

"I didn't mean to humiliate you, Zarah. True, I did lie to you, and I am sorry for that. I do hate having to lie. But you frightened me so. You see, for you it was all a kind of a game. You needed to conquer me, I suppose. A very pleasant and exciting game for you. But for me, it was terrible. Not a game at all. You wanted something I couldn't give. It would have meant my life, you see. I'm afraid I can't explain it any better than that. I don't suppose you understand."

"I understand that you are afraid of sex! You are afraid to be a man! Bah! You are not a man at all!"

"Oh, but I am," he insisted softly. "I am, indeed. Just not the kind of man you are used to, the kind of man you want. I cannot love you the way you want to be loved, Zarah. I tried to tell you that, but you wouldn't listen."

She glared at him. How could he do this, come here and talk to her like this? So gentle and reasonable. She wanted to hate him! She wanted to vent her frustration and anger at him! She didn't want this honesty, this open-hearted sincerity. They were too much the qualities that had fascinated her in the first place. They made her think of the eccentric, angelic boy she had fallen so desperately in love with, the brilliant artist whose mysterious creations had baffled and enthralled the world, with his droll wit, outrageously extravagant and at the same time impossibly innocent. She had been obsessed with him, determined that she should succeed where other women had not, to teach him the pleasures of being a man.

Yet here he was, more than ten years later, and he had still eluded her. He would always elude her. It drove her crazy!

"You tire me with your absurd talk," she said coldly, turning her back to him. "I wish that you would leave."

"Before I do, I want to give you this," he said.

"What is it?" she demanded, facing him scornfully. "A bribe? You think you can bribe me to drop my lawsuit against you with one of your stupid fabrications? Bah! I shall own them all when I am through with you!"

"No, not like this. This isn't anything I would ever sell. It's very special. It has substance. Please, take it." He held the box out to her. Her eyes narrowed. Her impulse was to reject him and his gift with scathing contempt. But she was curious.

"This is not a trick, is it?" she asked suspiciously. "I have had enough of your evil magic!"

"Oh, no!" he cried, shaking his head. "Nothing like that. That was dreadful. I was horrified by what I did then. It made me sick afterwards." He shuddered. "No, in fact, it is because of that awful thing that I made this for you. Please. Open it."

A plain white box. She held it, feeling a sense of excited anticipation that she did not want to feel. I will be disappointed, she told herself sternly, to keep her scornful frown in place. She lifted the lid.

Nestled in the box was a pure white bird.

"A bird?" she cried disdainfully. "What do I want with a bird!"

"She isn't just a bird, Zarah. She is a creation. She is yours. Go ahead, touch her."

The bird regarded her timidly with her ruby eyes, then cooed softly. Zarah touched the feathers of the creature's back. They were downy soft and warm.

"Pick her up," he urged her.

"Bah! It might make a mess!"

"No, she won't. Creations don't. Unless you feed them."

"What, you do not feed these creations of yours?" She stroked the velvety soft feathers. The bird cooed again, a sweet, trill.

"They don't need food. They just need kindness, that's all."

"What nonsense!" she said, but she gently took the bird out of the box. It settled happily in Zarah's hand, warm and soft. She could feel the tiny heart beating. Without meaning to, Zarah smiled. "A dove! Does she have a name?"

"I haven't given her one. You may name her whatever you like."

"But, how do I take care of her? Shall I need a cage?"

"No, but if you'd like to give her one, she'd be happy with it. As long as you take her out often and let her fly about. She'll keep you company. She'll sit on your shoulder if you like, or on your finger. If you talk to her, she'll understand. You can tell her all your secrets and she'll never betray them. But you must be kind to her. She'll get sick and lonely if you leave her alone too much. That's the one thing that creations must have. You must love them. If you do, they will thrive."

She could not keep the smile from her face. "And no droppings?"

"None," he promised. "You will be good for Zarah, won't you my little dove?" he said softly, tenderly caressing the feathers of her head. "Oh, but you are not my little dove anymore. Zarah is your mistress, now. All right?"

The bird looked from him to her knowingly, and cooed.

"You will take good care of her, won't you?" he asked Zarah anxiously.

"But, of course! What do you think I am? Such a sweet thing!" She frowned at him. "She will not disappear after an hour as the ring you gave me did?"

"No. She has substance. If you take good care of her, and are kind to her, she will stay with you all your life."

The dove pecked very gently at Zarah's fingers and she laughed. "Ah! It tickles! Oh, but she is too precious!" She looked at him. "Michel," she asked, "Why do you do this for me?"

He smiled at her tentatively. "Because I think that perhaps you do love me in your own way. And I am sorry I can't love you that way in return. What happened between us was so awful. I had to try to heal it somehow. I don't hate you, Zarah. I wouldn't know how. And if the money will help, you can have it. I don't mind. I do owe it to you for what happened. Just please leave me enough so that I can keep my house and take care of my creations and my cats. That's all I really need. And one other thing I'd ask. If you ever get tired of Dove, please send her back to me. Don't give her away to just anyone. And you mustn't ever sell her. That would be terribly wrong."

"I promise, Michel. But I do not think I shall ever tire of her. She is too lovely!"

"You are lovely, Zarah," he said.

"Oh, but now you are trying to charm me," she scolded him with a coy smile.

He shook his head. "It is only the truth. And I think perhaps I was in love with you once. I don't know how anyone could help it. But it was hopeless. And anyway, I wasn't lying to you when I said that I am in love with someone else now. Very, very much in love."

"Oh, no," she cried, "Don't tell me! Not that dog of a housekeeper of yours?"

"Please don't talk about Vivian that way. She is strong and clever, and she's done so many marvelous things. And she takes such good care of me. She's patient with me and my creations. And so kind. I really couldn't live without her."

"And she doesn't try to make love to you the way Zarah does, eh?" she said knowingly. "Very well, then, Michel. Go home to your housekeeper. I wish you happiness. And I shall call my lawyers and tell them to leave you alone."

"Oh, but you are entitled to something!" he protested.

"I think we are even, Michel. The words I threw at you were horrid, poisonous things. I am sure their sting pained you as much as what I suffered. Besides," she added aloofly, "I have no need of your money."

"Thank you, Zarah." He lowered his eyes. "I think I'd better go now."

"I am glad you came. It is better to part as friends. And I thank you most sincerely for your precious gift. I promise you I shall take the best care of her. Yes, I shall!" She kissed the dove on the top of her head, and the bird pecked her lips affectionately. Zarah laughed with delight.

"Good bye, Zarah."

"Good bye, Michel." She took his hand and then stood up on tip-toes to kiss his cheek lightly. It brought a flutter to his stomach, but he was no longer afraid of her.

When he was gone, Madam Trebbiano admired her dove with unrestrained pleasure. "What a precious thing you are! You shall go with me wherever I go. I shall be the envy of everyone! Oh, but do I not deserve it? Ah, Zarah Trebbiano, you are without compare! Such a fine and generous soul you have! So forgiving!" She danced over to the window, the dove perched on her shoulder. Looking out, she could see Archimedes Nesselrode getting into his car. She smiled sadly. "Ah, but there shall never be another like you. She is fortunate, that dog of a housekeeper of yours. Be well, my sweet Michel."

CHAPTER SIXTEEN

Resolution

"Where in heaven's name is he?"

None of the household creatures knew, but all were upset, in spite of specific instructions from their master to the contrary.

Heron stalked about the house, clacking her beak and shaking her head, losing feathers all over the place. The marmosets chittered anxiously, hanging about on the curtains and looking out the window. The cats roamed restlessly and hissed at one another. The basilisk paced up and down the long driveway, occasionally raising her head and howling in a mournful, rumbling way.

When the telephone rang at about ten o'clock Ms. Mare answered it with mixed eagerness and trepidation.

"Vivian, my dear, how are you?"

"Mother! Why, this is a surprise!"

"I simply had to call. The papers have been saying such troubling things."

"The press has exaggerated the situation monstrously," Ms. Mare replied with heat.

"They always do," her mother said soothingly. "That is why I was determined to call, to discover the facts. Do tell me what has happened! That is, if you are at liberty to do so. Are you busy? Is your employer around?"

"No, he is not, and I only wish I knew where he has gone!"

Catherine Mare listened sympathetically as her daughter gave her an account of the events of the past few weeks. Certain delicate details were of course omitted, but she told her mother more than she had told Frank Shekle because, after all, she was her mother.

"How awful it must be for you!"

"I shall bear up under it somehow," Ms. Mare said. "My greatest concern was what you and the Galbraiths would think of it all. It may prove to be an ugly trial."

"Don't worry, my darling, we are on your side of course. We all know better than to take at face value the ghastly prattlings of the newspapers."

"That is a relief!"

"You have grown very fond of your Mr. Nesselrode, haven't you?" Catherine Mare said.

"Yes, Mother, I have."

"Is the feeling reciprocated?"

"It is. Quite certainly so."

"I see."

"Mother, you needn't be concerned. Mr. Nesselrode is a complete gentleman in every way. Nothing has occurred or will occur of an inappropriate nature."

"Has...marriage been discussed?" she asked hesitantly.

"Yes, but I told him it was quite out of the question. There are certain issues which must be resolved first."

"Thank goodness!" the elder Ms. Mare exclaimed. "I'm glad you realize that."

"You brought me up to be sensible."

"Not that I would ever stand in the way of your happiness, my dear, but I would want to be assured that you and Mr. Nesselrode were not acting impulsively and had considered all the ramifications of such a match, particularly in light of his less than cordial relationship with his family."

"We have discussed that," Ms. Mare the younger assured her, adding, "However, I must warn you, our feelings for each other are quite strong and quite sincere, and we do suit each other admirably. I anticipate a permanent relationship of some sort. But we must weather this crisis first."

"It will be a test of your resolve," Catherine Mare said. "And of your commitment to one another. Rest assured, Vivian, that we shall stand by you in any case. Whatever you and Mr. Nesselrode decide for yourselves, you can be sure of our blessing."

Ms. Mare hung up the phone with a sense of relief which quickly dissipated. Knowing that her mother and the Galbraiths understood and supported her took a huge burden from her shoulders. But the absence of her employer rapidly filled the void.

Mr. Shekle's call came in the early afternoon.

"Great news, Ms. Mare! I just heard from Trebbiano's lawyers. She's instructed them to drop the suit. Just like that!"

"That's marvelous," Ms. Mare replied, trying to sound sincere, but chilled to the core. "Did they give any reason why?"

"Nope," Frank replied, "Just, 'Madam Trebbiano has reconsidered, and has graciously agreed not to pursue the matter.' Go figure!"

Ms. Mare hung up the phone. There could be only one explanation. He had gone to her.

She sat on the couch, stunned. Then she became angry. How *could* he? After all they had discussed! She thought she had made herself quite clear, and he had agreed, the matter had been settled, and now for him to go and do this, it was absolutely inexcusable! Unforgivable! She could not bear it. She would pack her bags now and leave. The thought of her Angel and that odious woman... no, it was simply intolerable. She would not be able stand it, knowing what he had done, throwing away his gift like that!

She was on her feet, half-blinded by tears, heading towards her room. How could he do it? Such cowardice, giving himself up instead of facing things and fighting back, choosing to let that wretched hussy blackmail him into submitting to her foul debased desires! Betrayal, that's what it was! He had betrayed her, his Vivian, their love for each other! How could she ever look at him again? How could she trust him? She would pack and go this instant!

She tripped over the starfish and stumbled against the newel post.

"Damn! You miserable, horrid, unnatural—!"

She sat down on the stairs and wept, something Ms. Mare hadn't done since she was a girl. It was just so awful, so unspeakably awful. Then she felt something against her leg. She opened her eyes. The grey Manx was rubbing against her. Heron spread a sympathetic wing over her shoulders. Winged Snake was coiled at her feet, looking up at her, and a marmoset held out a box of tissues.

"Oh, dear, I'm not behaving sensibly, am I?" Ms. Mare sniffled. She accepted a tissue and blew her nose. "This won't do at all. Not at all. I can't just walk out, can I?"

Heron regarded her with gentle reproach and Winged Snake raised herself up on her tail and waved about.

"I know, I do apologize, but I simply couldn't bear the thought of him...."

Heron squawked and ruffled her feathers.

"But why else would she drop the lawsuit? That must be what happened!"

Heron clacked her beak and looked at her sternly.

Ms. Mare sighed. Yes, she had to wait and find out the truth. That was the sensible thing to do. Not to rush off half-cocked. But she could no longer be sensible on the subject of Archimedes Nesselrode.

Precisely. Even if she did resign her post it would be no solution. She would never be able to forget him, or this household, Heron, Winged Snake and all the rest. Think what she would be giving up! There could never be a situation nearly so interesting. Nor another Angel.

That was it. She should never have allowed it to happen, for her heart to become involved. Her mother had warned her about this. It was a mistake to become emotionally involved with one's employer. Or with any man. When one's emotions became engaged one lost rational sense.

She would submit her resignation, but she would do so with dignity. She would wait until he returned, for he must return eventually, and she would listen to his explanation for his actions. Then she would inform him that what he had done was intolerable to her, and that she had to leave.

If she could.

Swamped with indecision, her efforts at rational decision flummoxed, Ms. Mare resorted to the one great certainty in life, that which could be relied upon no matter what catastrophe had ensued. She began furiously cleaning house.

A thought pricked her while she was scrubbing the tiles in the bathroom. What if he asked her forgiveness and begged her to stay? Would she forgive him? He might well have thought he was doing it for her, to protect her, and out of a misguided attempt to banish the darker side of his gift. He'd spoken sincerely of that. A tragically foolish mistake, but he could be terribly foolish.

If she really loved him....

Oh! How she *hated* that phrase! The universal excuse of pathetic females to remain in relationships eminently unsuited to them, the weapon unscrupulous men used to lever them into submission! Oh, you would forgive me if you *really* loved me! Bah! Not her!

She abraded the porcelain fiercely with sponge and cleanser. Love is a matter of mutual respect, not self-sacrifice! Curse the man who whines about unconditional love as relief from responsibility for his own actions, and curse the woman who lets him get away with it!

But what if the man truly couldn't help it? And what if he was really a dear?

Ms. Mare peeled off her rubber gloves and tossed them onto the vanity. Damn.

Up to her elbows in soapy water in the kitchen sink, she paused. Could she live with him as an ordinary man? Never mind the magic and the extravagances. What of the person inside? Was he worth her love? Her loyalty? Think of how he would feel, having given up his creative spark, humiliated himself to preserve all he cared about. How would she feel if she then spurned him?

She rinsed the pots and put them in the drainer, and wiped the counter sparkling clean. Even if he had committed that act of frightful folly, he did not deserve to be abandoned. That would be cruel.

She came downstairs from putting away linens to find Heron and Winged Snake carefully replacing the clean dishes onto the hutch, while the marmosets emptied the silverware out of the dishwasher, handing off the pieces to one another and placing them into the drawer. Ms. Mare watched the process. A dish slipped from Heron's beak and Snake caught it with her tail. One of the marmosets scuttled down to grab it, placing on the hutch where Heron indicated it should go.

She felt a smile tug the corners of her mouth. As she passed through the dining room she noticed the Bishop standing on the table carefully polishing his teapot. He looked over at Ms. Mare and raised his eyebrows inquiringly.

"You are doing a splendid job," she said in response, "Do continue."

With a satisfied nod, he returned to the task.

"You're all trying very hard, aren't you?" she said. They looked up. "I know, we're all worried about him."

Heron regarded Ms. Mare over her spectacles with reproach.

"Oh," Ms. Mare murmured, "I see." They were worried about their creator, but they knew he would return to them somehow, and would look after them and protect them, no matter what. They were not so sure about her.

Ms. Mare sighed. "My dears, I will not leave you. No matter what sort of foolishness your master has gotten himself into, we shall do our best to mend it. We will stay together and it will all work itself out somehow."

Dusk was falling when she saw the flock of gate-watch birds come flying over the house, singing their song of alert. Someone was at the gate. Breathless, Ms. Mare grabbed her coat and pulled on her boots, hurrying out the door. She called to the basilisk, but the beast wouldn't come. Ms. Mare stood in the chilly air, the light of the afternoon failing. Was it he? It must be he. But if it were not, if it were instead some pest of a reporter, the idiot might well try to get in and would run afoul of the basilisk.

She started down the drive. All they would need now was the added fuss of a reporter eaten by the basilisk. There would no doubt be serious repercussions.

Then she heard the joyful roar of the basilisk and relief swept over her. It *was* he! Mr. Nesselrode had returned, finally! Bouncing lightly from foot to foot to keep warm—as well as out of impatience—she waited for the Daimler to come around from behind the shrubberies that shielded the house from the road. The basilisk appeared first, prancing and pouncing like a huge, ungainly puppy, kicking up snow. The car followed. Ms. Mare was nearly frantic with anxious anticipation, fearing the worst.

He tooted the horn and waved to her gaily. That was an encouraging sign. Could it be that he was all right after all? And if he were, well then he certainly deserved a sound scolding for worrying them all this way!

"Mr. Nesselrode! Where have you been?" she demanded as he got out of the car.

"I told Basilisk I should be back before nightfall." He petted the creature's snout affectionately. "And I was as good as my word, wasn't I, dear old thing? Silly beast, were you worried about me?"

"We *all* were!" Ms. Mare said furiously. "What else could you have expected?"

"I left specific instructions with Heron to tell you not to worry. My, it's getting cold out here!"

"It is indeed! And here you are with no jacket! Mr. Nesselrode, you are impossible! Now get into the house before you catch your death!"

"Wait, wait, I have to get something from the trunk. I would have been home sooner, but I wanted to do some shopping. I don't get out much, you know." He opened the trunk and took out several parcels.

"*Shopping!*" she cried. "Why, of all—! I was worried *sick*! And Heron is practically molting! And after Mr. Shekle's call, why, I didn't know *what* to think!"

He shut the trunk, his packages balanced precariously on one arm, bags hanging from his fist. "Oh, and what did Frank have to say?"

"He called to tell us that Madam Trebbiano has dropped her suit. There is to be no further action against you."

The artist beamed happily. "Marvelous! She kept her word, then."

"She—" Ms. Mare gasped. "Then you *have* been with her!"

"Well," he said, "not in the Biblical sense." And he swept past her into the house humming gaily.

Ms. Mare stared after him, speechless. Then she cried, "Mr. Nesselrode!" and scurried after him. She chased him through the kitchen and into the hallway. "Mr. Nesselrode, will you *please* tell me what is going on!"

"The world is round," he sang, springing up the stairs, "the stars are in their heavens, and I do hope dinner shall be on time. I am *starving!*"

"Dinner shall be served at the appointed hour!" she shouted up the stairs after him. "And I shall expect a full explanation at that time!"

He leaned over the railing. "You," he said, "shall have it." And with that, he disappeared through the door up to the attic.

Ms. Mare glared after him. "Really!" She turned to see Heron standing in the doorway, stern and disapproving. "The things we are expected to put up with!" Ms. Mare said, and Heron gave a curt nod of agreement as they both went to the kitchen to start dinner.

* * *

The Bishop blessed the meal, waved his crook solemnly, and climbed back into the teapot. Ms. Mare put her napkin in her lap and said, "Well?"

Mr. Nesselrode's eyes twinkled. "I was, I think," he said, buttering a roll, "for once in my life, quite clever. And quite brave." And he proceeded to tell the tale of his day's adventures, with occasional flourishes of his fork and long pauses to enjoy a bite of food. Ms. Mare listened with a sense of admiration and amazement, liberally mixed with alarm that he should have attempted such a thing.

"Why didn't you tell me?" she demanded.

"You wouldn't have let me do it," he replied, twirling a forkful of pasta and popping it into his mouth.

"True," Ms. Mare admitted. "But that dreadful woman...she might have done something awful to you."

"And risk another handful of scorpions down her dress? I thought it unlikely. But really, she's not such a terrible person. I knew there had to be a way to reach her."

"Still," she said, "it was a appalling risk."

He grinned at her proudly. "I *was* brave, wasn't I?

"Yes," she said, smiling back at him. "Very brave, indeed."

"And you're impressed with me?" he asked hopefully.

Ms. Mare sighed. "Mr. Nesselrode, I have always been impressed by you."

He laughed with delight.

"So," she said, touching a napkin to her lips, "Now that you have nothing to fear from Madam Trebbiano anymore, will you be making regular public appearances again?"

He shrugged. "I think from time to time. It is such fun. And it would please Frank so much if I did. I think I owe Frank that. He has been very good to me."

"Frank Shekle has been more than amply rewarded for his pains, I'm sure!" Ms. Mare declared.

"Oh, but money doesn't matter. One can throw money around all over the place and still be detested. It's all the rest of it. That's what makes the difference."

"I expect you're right," she said, marveling at him.

"By the way," he said, a devilish gleam in his silver eyes, "I hope you haven't much planned for tomorrow."

"Well, I...," she started. "But it's not a full moon."

"Doesn't need to be," he replied cryptically, "for what I have in mind!"

CHAPTER SEVENTEEN

A Sensible Arrangement

Ms. Mare climbed the stairs to the attic, following the toad butler. She had been in the middle of hanging up laundry, but the toad was most insistent that she must come. So she asked Heron to manage as best she could and sternly ordered the marmosets to help and to behave themselves. Heron was quite clever with her beak, but could only do so much, and the marmosets just couldn't seem to keep their minds on any task for too long. It really wasn't a good arrangement, and there were times when Ms. Mare felt completely overwhelmed. It didn't help to be summoned away in the middle of things, but if her employer requested her presence then she felt obliged to do as she was asked.

She stood amidst the maze of treasures and clutter, the dust and the furtive rustlings, and a smile caught up with her. As momentarily annoyed as she was to be called away from her work, it was a thrill to be up in this place of curious wonders. It seemed as if the outside world ceased to matter, that this was a world apart. She saw the peacock, his fan of brilliant feathers spread, preening himself proudly at the top of the spiral staircase. A pair of okapi raised their oddly snouted heads above a stack of crates to regard her curiously. The sea horse who had played so marvelously the night of the waltz leaned over to greet her. His tail was curled around a ladder leaning against an attic beam. He waved his prehensile fins at her. Ms. Mare waved back.

The toad led her to the center where the artist worked, then bowed and took his leave of them. Archimedes Nesselrode greeted her. He was dressed in a paint-smeared smock that was too big for him, hanging off his shoulders and torn at the sleeves. On his feet were sneakers held together with tape. Only the lower legs showed of his pants, but she knew them to be threadbare at the seat with holes in the knees, because she had, reluctantly, laundered them instead of throwing them out. She had asked him if he wouldn't allow her to get him some decent clothes but he wouldn't hear of it. These were comfortable, he said.

"Ms. Mare! Do come and see this. I wanted you to be a part of the process, since I am creating her for you."

"For me?" she asked, coming over to inspect the jumble of odd bits and lumps.

"I've got it all worked out and quite clear in my mind," he said, gesturing to the table, where a scattering of sketches were spread about. On the easel was an image done in pastels of some octopoid creature. "But since she will be yours, I thought you ought to have some input as to the final touches."

"Mine?"

"Yes, indeed. I should have done this long ago." He wound a piece of ribbon around a wire. His hair had been hastily combed, his part all askew, and odd strands were hanging in his face. He sat back on his heels. "So, what do you think so far?"

He stood up and gestured to the collection of what appeared to be junk and left-overs. The central lump, a busy construct of wires and cloth, yarn and rubber, was about the size of an end table. From it ran several strands of rope and wire, wound around themselves in loose coils. Woven in were bits of foil, colored cardboard, straw and cellophane.

"Forgive me, but I can't really make out what it is supposed to be," she admitted.

"Come, come," he said, gesturing her over to the table. He held up a sketch of an octopus holding a spoon and a bowl, a broom, a paint brush and a basket full of laundry. "Do you see now? She is to be the new maid. Subject to your orders, of course. I wouldn't know how to make her so that she would be as clever as you. She'll have to be taught and kept track of. But then you'll be free to do more of the things you enjoy. To work in the garden, if you wish, or to read, or..." He smiled at her shyly, "To assist me, if you feel so inclined."

"A new maid?" she echoed, staring at the sketch and then at the heap on the floor. "This?"

"You need help, I know," he said, "And the others aren't really suited for it. I didn't make them to be, although I know Heron does her best. I thought an octopus would be an admirable design for the job." He picked up a couple of other sketches eagerly, showing her images of tentacles curling, grasping, manipulating. "You see? She will be able to handle anything, to do anything, several things at once, in fact. She'll reach to the highest shelf without a stool, and reach behind things where a person might have difficulty. She will be very strong, able to manage heavy loads or move furniture. Yet have the most delicate touch, able to use a needle and thread quite skillfully. Once she's taught how, of course." He looked at Ms. Mare hopefully. "I've tried to think of everything. I hoped you would be pleased."

"My word," she murmured. "Well, it certainly sounds quite wonderful. But I'm still not sure I understand...." She looked towards the tangle caught in mid-writhe in front of them.

His eyes glittered. "That is what you shall see! Do you want to?"

"Oh, very much! Did all your creations start out this way?"

"All the ones of substance," he said. "Not exactly like this, of course. They are all unique, requiring unique materials. That's why I need all this." He waved his hand around at the motley collection of the attic. "I never know what I'll want until I get going on it."

"I see," she said. "So, what am I to do?"

"Ah!" he exclaimed, rubbing his hands together. "First, I want you to go and explore a bit. Don't get lost, mind you. Give a yell if you do. But find something you like."

"What sort of thing?"

"Anything. A bit of yarn whose color strikes you, a ribbon or a piece of cloth. A feather. A pebble. A glass. A hat or a shoe. Anything! Whatever catches your fancy. Pick it up, and see if it feels right. Then bring it to me."

"How shall I know if it's right?" she asked him helplessly.

He smiled at her. "That is what we are going to find out."

"But, Mr. Nesselrode—"

"Go on, just go looking. I'm eager to see what you choose."

"Anything?" she asked again.

"Anything," he confirmed with a nod.

Feeling a sense of excitement, even though she had no idea what she was looking for, Ms. Mare set off tentatively into the maze. There was so much to look at, so much to choose from that she felt quite overwhelmed. She peeked into a box and found it contained old photographs. Another had bits of string. She considered a jar of smooth stones, then a chest of costume jewelry. She found a collection of long coils of soft tasseled rope, such as what one might use for a bell-pull. Might this be appropriate for an octopus? The gold was rather pretty. She picked it up. Did it feel right? Good heavens, how would *she* know? She'd never done anything like this before. She had a knack for arranging flowers, and she had good taste in clothes and linens, and could pick out curtains or upholstery, but beyond that, she had no real artistic sensibility. Oh dear, she didn't want to be a disappointment to him. But she really had no idea what she was doing.

Then her eyes settled on a conch shell poking out of packing material in a box. She carefully eased her way among the piles to reach it and picked it up. The outside was shades of honey brown and gold, dark striped and spotted and delicately spiraled, with a smooth, pink interior. Rather feminine, yet hard; not brilliantly colored, but still lovely. Something about it captured her imagination. Yes, for a poor octopus who would never know the sea, never roll about beneath the waves, whose fate was to be a servant in a land-locked household. Oh, yes. She should have a beautiful bit of the ocean within her heart.

It took Ms. Mare a few moments to find her way back to the center with her prize. She found the artist winding bluish-green crepe paper around one of the arms. "Mr. Nesselrode, will this do?" She handed him the shell.

He turned it over in his hands and his eyes sparkled. "Oh, Ms. Mare. Oh, yes." He looked at her, his expression warm. "It is perfect. Perfect. You do have a talent for this." He laughed with irrepressible delight. "Oh, this is splendid!" He knelt down next to the creation and carefully peeled back a bit of the wire and yarn mesh on the outside. Then he pushed the conch shell into the inside of it, arranging it just so, adjusting the placement a few times, then sitting back on his heels to consider. He got up and raced off into the stacks, returning after a moment or two with a handful of greenish coils of rubber. He went back to work on the creation's interior. "Ms. Mare, would you hand me that please?" He pointed, one arm remaining buried in the creation's innards.

"This?" she asked, holding up a spool of silver cord.

"Yes, and the scissors. On the table."

It took her a while to find the scissors under the sketches and among the rest of the paraphernalia. "All right," she said at last, "Here you go."

"Good. Now cut me a length. Just pull some off the spool. Yes, that's enough. Good. Thank you. Another please, a little longer. Good. Yes. One more. That seems about right." Finally he nodded, and replaced the outside mesh to close it, bending it carefully back over the opening. "There! Now, if you would, Ms. Mare, assist me in wrapping the arms."

"All right," she said. She watched what he was doing, then took up a roll of crepe paper and began doing the same. "Is this right?" she asked.

"Just fine, just fine. Use the orange if you run out of the turquoise."

"It doesn't matter—"

"It's all just as it should be," he assured her.

She finished one arm, tucking the end of the paper into a fold as she observed him doing, and she started on another arm. "Is this really going to become something alive, like Heron or Winged Snake?"

"You'll see!"

When they had finished wrapping the thing, he went to his table and pulled a heavy box out from underneath. "Next," he announced, "we must cover her in clay." He dug through the plastic inner wrap of the box and pulled out a handful of terra cotta clay. "Now, you must knead the clay in your hands until it becomes soft, like this." He demonstrated, working the clay back and forth with his nimble fingers. She took out a piece of clay and tried to do likewise. She found the clay surprisingly hard, and marveled at the strength he must have in his fingers to work it with such apparent ease. She would not have guessed those slim fingers, those delicate hands, would possess such strength. She pressed and pulled at the clay and finally began to soften it.

"Now," he said, "you must take the clay and smooth it over the surface, like this."

But here she found she was unable to follow his example. No matter how hard she tried, she could not get the clay to adhere to the surface and smooth out. She finally gave up. "I'm sorry, Mr. Nesselrode. I simply can't manage it."

He frowned, then shrugged. "Hmm. Oh well. Never mind. Just leave that part to me. There's something else you can do. Bufus!"

The toad butler appeared.

"Would you be so kind as to show Ms. Mare where she may find bolts of cloth? Not the scraps, but the bigger lengths."

The toad butler nodded.

The artist said to Ms. Mare, "Pick out something for the outside. Something nice, but practical. Something good to look at, that would be pleasant to touch, but wouldn't tear easily. Oh, you'll know."

She nodded, and followed the toad. "Take your time," he called after her. "Applying the clay will occupy me for quite a while."

She wandered about in the places the toad took her, looking into trunks and inspecting the contents of shelves, becoming distracted by all the other things she found. She was enchanted by the discovery of a chess set of exquisitely carven wood which, instead of the traditional pieces, had Spanish conquistadors and Aztec warriors. "I must ask him if he plays chess!" she thought to herself. There was a teakwood chest filled with polished, semi-precious stones. She began looking through them, admiring their beauty. She found first one, then another piece of snowflake obsidian, nearly perfectly round and flattened. Something about them held her interest more than the other, more brightly colored stones. She imagined them coming alive, the static snowflake patterns in the deep black becoming the sparkle of intelligent eyes. With a decisive nod, she put them into her pocket.

Then she remembered her mission. She looked over several bolts of cloth, shaking her head. None of them would do. "Are there any more, Bufus?"

The toad bowed and took her over to a corner. The dust was rather thick here, but she was able to unroll enough to see what the material was really like. There were several shades of vinyl, or something smooth and leatherish like vinyl, and she nodded slowly. Here was a shade of pearl grey that seemed right. It was textured slightly, and felt like smooth skin. Yes, this was what an octopus ought to feel like. But not wet and slippery, like a creature of the sea. Dry. Tough, but not rough. A pleasant, natural color. Yes, this would do.

She returned to the center—it was becoming easier to find her way around—and discovered that the artist had finished covering the main body of the creature and was now working on the arms, a slow, painstaking process. "Mr. Nesselrode, do you think you could use these?" she asked, showing him the stones in her pocket.

He looked up, blinking. "Eh? Let's see." He examined them. His mouth slowly opened in astonishment. He got to his feet, still staring at them.

"I thought," she suggested hesitantly, "perhaps, for the eyes?"

He stared at her. "You thought—?" He turned to look at the octopoid lump of clay-covered hodge-podge. He fell to his knees and very carefully positioned the stones, working them into the clay and shaping the clay around them. He stood back. Now, instead of a mere lump, a creature regarded them silently with bright black eyes. He clapped his hands together and giggled with delight. "Perfect!" he squealed.

"Oh, and I found this," she said, gesturing to the toad, who carried the roll of pearl-grey material. She took it over to show it to him. "The outside is rather dusty, and the material has cracked a bit, but inside the roll it looks quite usable. I thought it an appropriate material, a nice color. What do you think?"

"I'd forgotten I had this," he murmured. "That's the problem with acquiring so much. One can't keep track...." He caressed his clay-smeared fingers over the surface of the material. "Of course. Just the thing." He looked up at her. "Perfect. Oh, Vivian, it is *perfect!* *You* are perfect! Oh, bats and cuttlefish, I do *adore* you!" He took her face in his grubby hands and kissed her. It took her breath away.

***

She sat on the stool and watched him work, marveling at him. Vague pricks of guilt—not to mention hunger—reminded her that it was well-past lunch time and she ought to go and see about dinner. But she didn't want to go. She just wanted to sit there and watch him.

His hair tended to fall in his face as he bent over the arms of the octopus, shaping the delicate tips of the tentacles and the cups that lined the bottom. He would absently reach up and tuck his hair behind his ear, getting clay in it as a result. At one point he scratched his nose, and left a terra cotta smudge across it. He was absolutely absorbed in his task, his sinuous fingers dexterously shaping the clay. It seemed to respond to his touch with an almost conscious cooperation.

Amazing, she thought to herself. He is amazing. A dreadful mess, but utterly amazing. Dear me, I do love him so awfully much!

He sat back on his heels. "There," he said. He got up, walking slowly around it, scrutinizing his work minutely, bending to touch up a spot here and there. "She's shaping up rather nicely, don't you think?"

Ms. Mare nodded. "Simply marvelous. I can't wait to see what will come next."

"The next step," he said, coming over to the table, "I'm sure you can help with. We'll need to cut the fabric for the final covering into sections, and—" Little Benjamin came down and landed on his shoulder, squeaking softly into his ear. "Eh? Is it? Oh, dear. Well, all right." He turned to Ms. Mare. "It seems it is time for dinner. I expect we'll have wait to finish after that."

"Is it that late? Gracious! I haven't done a thing for it!" She jumped off the stool. "I'm terribly sorry, Mr. Nesselrode, I'll get right to it."

"Well, after all, it can't be helped, can it? I'll give you a hand. Dinner shan't be formal tonight, what do you say?"

"Excellent idea, Mr. Nesselrode. So long as the Bishop isn't offended."

She got out bread and cold chicken for sandwiches. In flagrant violation of custom, they ate in the kitchen, and fed the cats likewise. The Bishop was indeed offended, and stood on the table, glaring at them from the dining room for several minutes before pronouncing a dire phrase or two in Latin and storming back to his teapot, muttering to himself. Ms. Mare and Mr. Nesselrode grinned at each other and laughed, feeling terribly naughty, and they tossed bits of cold chicken from their sandwiches down to the cats.

When they were finished, he took her hand. "Come on, let's go."

"But, I haven't cleaned up yet," she protested.

"Oh, leave it. Come on!"

"But the cats and the marmosets will make a dreadful mess of things if they aren't put away."

"Oh, pish," he said. "This is more important. Come!"

She sighed, smiling in spite of herself, and went along. He pulled her up the stairs and she felt like giggling. They were like delinquent children getting away with something. They returned to the attic, to the unfinished creation.

"Now!" the artist said, rubbing his hands together in anticipation. He took careful measurements and marked the fabric, then gave her a pair of shears. She cut the pieces out and he began to place them over the clay. At first she was too absorbed in cutting the pieces of fabric out as precisely as possible. She didn't notice what he was doing. When she finally did, she stopped working and stared.

The artist was laying the pieces carefully over the clay, smoothing them into place with his fingers. As he added it, every piece settled cleanly and snugly into place and blended seamlessly with the piece next to it. Each join seemed to vanish under his touch. Not a single seam was visible. She watched closely trying to see how he did it, but was baffled. All he was doing was touching it.

"Here," he murmured, "Around the eyes. This will be tricky. Could you please cut me just the narrowest strip? Slightly crescent shaped. No, just a bit smaller. Ah, that's it. Another. Make the curve just a bit tighter.

Like this." He formed the shape in the air with his finger. "Good, good!" He sat back. "There!"

The pearly grey octopus regarded them with serene dark eyes.

"She's lovely," Ms. Mare said. But still, it was just a large doll, however skillfully made. It wasn't yet alive. "What now?" she asked.

Mr. Nesselrode walked around the inanimate creation, scowling critically. "Is she quite ready? Is she perfect? Examine her carefully, if you will. Once I've finished her, that's it. She can't be changed." He returned to his sketches and his pastel portrait. "Have I forgotten anything? I feel like I've forgotten something."

"I can't see a thing wrong with her," Ms. Mare said. She counted the number of suction cups on each tentacle, examined the tips of the arms, looked into the eyes, searched the skin for flaws. "Honestly, she seems quite perfect."

"Horrors!" he exclaimed suddenly, "She hasn't a mouth! Bless my knickers, how could I forget such a thing?" He grabbed a narrow blade from the table. "Ms. Mare, could you please tip her back a bit? I need to get underneath. Don't worry, old thing, this won't hurt a bit."

The creation was remarkably heavy. Ms. Mare picked it up carefully, not wanting to damage it in any way, and leaned backwards. He worked for a moment or two underneath it, at the junction of the tentacles. "Mr. Nesselrode, do be as quick as you can, or I'm afraid I may drop it on your head."

"Just a moment. Let's see. There, and then—there. Smooth this out. Oops! There we go. All right, Ms. Mare, let her down."

"Oof! Substantial to say the least!"

"She's nothing compared to Basilisk. I had to put *her* together in the barn. Wouldn't fit in here. I had to carry every blessed thing I needed out there. And so many delays! I didn't have half of what I needed. I had to stop working every few days and wait for things to be delivered. And of course, I didn't have a moment's peace until she was finished. Poor Heron did her best to keep me from flying off the handle. What I wreck I was! Oh, I am glad those days are past!" He turned to look at Ms. Mare fondly. "I have you with me, now."

She took his hand. "And the best days are yet to come," she said.

"I believe you are right. Vivian. My dear Vivian."

"My Angel."

He gave a short, high-pitched laugh. "Bless us, it must be getting late! The moon must be up!" Then he glanced at the inanimate octopus and grinned. "Shall I finish her?"

"Please do!"

He took Ms. Mare over to the stool by the table and sat her down. "Watch this," he said. Turning, he took a deep breath. He pressed his fingers together and walked slowly over to the creation, an expression of fixed intensity on his face. Then he dropped to one knee, picking up a tentacle. His eyes half-closed, he stroked his fingers over it. Gently caressing the grey skin, he worked his way up the arm and down another, slowly, lovingly. He began to murmur very softly to it, too softly for her to make out the words.

She held her breath, watching him, fascinated. Her eyes widened. The grey vinyl fabric was beginning to change character subtly, beginning to look more pliant, more soft. She gasped as she distinctly saw the tip of a tentacle twitch. The artist put his arms around its great head, pressing his cheek against it. He stroked it tenderly, whispering to it. His fingers touched its eyes gently, and then he passed his hands over them. They grew liquid and luminous. The tones of his voice were praising, coaxing. The arms of the creature began to move, to curl and flex.

He continued to caress it and murmur softly and lovingly to it. Its arms, like those of a child waking to the touch of an adored parent, reached towards him and curled around him. A soft whistling sound came from the creature as it embraced him. Its arms explored his face and body, touching him with curious interest. The large eyes looked into his and he smiled in response. Then he laughed, "Oh, my beauty! What a fine thing you are! We are so happy to see you! Do you feel quite right? Have I done it all the way I should? You are alive, yes! How does it feel? Quite nice, I hope. Oh! But you're tickling me! Do stop! Look around you. Move a bit. See how it all feels."

The octopus raised herself up on her arms experimentally, testing how her limbs worked. She turned and saw Ms. Mare. Following Mr. Nesselrode's example, Ms. Mare smiled at her warmly. "Hello, there. Yes, you are a beauty. I hope we can become great friends."

He came and stood beside Ms. Mare, introducing her. "She shall be your mistress. Oh, we are *so* delighted with you! We need you very much, you see. To help us. It's been so difficult, but now you are here. You are strong and clever. You'll learn that soon. How proud you will be of yourself when you discover all the things you can do! And how grateful we shall be for your help. Ms. Mare shall teach you. I will too, but she will be with you the most. And there are many others you will meet. Welcome to life, my lovely Octopus!"

The creation whistled softly, moving carefully, going to Ms. Mare and gently touching her face with the tip of a tentacle. She began exploring the items on the table curiously, picking them up, clumsily at first, but with increasing skill as she learned how to use her limbs. Ms. Mare watched in fascination, this being which she had seen grow from a seemingly random collection of junk into a living, feeling thing.

"We shall let her stay up here for a day or two," he said, "Let her get accustomed to herself. Then we can bring her downstairs and you can begin training her. You'll be very gentle with her at first, won't you?"

"Oh, of course!" she assured him. "I'll treat her with the utmost respect and concern. After all, she's quite like a newborn child, isn't she?"

"Oh, yes, that she is, absolutely! Rules and expectations must be clear and reasonable." He sighed. "A pity I wasn't more disciplined with the marmosets. Ah, well. One learns." He frowned and said anxiously, "You do like her? She is suitable?"

"She's absolutely marvelous!" Ms. Mare said, smiling. *You are marvelous,* she thought. She felt so in awe of him, that he could bring life to lifeless things this way. What miracle, what divine touch, had gifted him with this power?

"Oh, Angel," she whispered softly. He seemed not to have heard her, grinning proudly at his newest creation. Twice today he had called her by her first name. Their relationship was changing.

***

It had snowed again, and the roads were slippery and difficult. Ms. Mare had taken longer with her Thursday errands than usual, and was relieved to return home intact with no dents to the Daimler. The basilisk greeted her at the gate and followed the car back to the house.

"Octopus, I would appreciate a bit of help!"

The agile grey creation came out the door, slithering down the steps, offering arms for her to fill. "Thank you. Now, into the kitchen, mind you don't bang the bags together. There are glass bottles which could break and fruit which is liable to bruise. Careful going through the door!" Octopus was very eager to please, and quick to learn, but had to have everything explained to her. It was slow going. And no matter what, it would still fall to Ms. Mare to run the errands in town. It would not do to send an octopus, regardless of its intelligence and competence, to the store to purchase one's groceries. There would certainly be talk.

Heron was waiting in the kitchen. She began relieving Octopus of her burdens.

"Thank you, Heron," Ms. Mare said, "but I can manage."

The bespectacled bird clacked her beak firmly, and Octopus bobbed her large head.

"Well, it is very kind of you to offer, but—"

"Vivian."

His voice startled her. It was the middle of the day. Ms. Mare turned to see Mr. Nesselrode standing in the kitchen doorway, dressed quite nicely by his standards; not a single hole or frayed cuff. "Could you please come with me?" he asked. He sounded a bit breathless.

She looked at him curiously. "Why, of course. Where are we going?"

"Just into the other room. If you would be so kind."

He seemed both eager and nervous, his voice a notch or two higher than normal, an unusual flutter in his gestures and bounce in his step. She followed him into the living room. The little table by the window had been laid out with fresh linens. A crystal vase held a single rose. There were two glasses and a bottle of champagne on ice.

He held the chair for her. "I know this is quite irregular," he said, "but it seemed to me the only proper way of doing this."

"Indeed!" she exclaimed. "Very irregular! In the middle of the afternoon when I've chores to do!"

"The others will take care of everything," he assured her. "I've talked it over with them, and planned everything out... that is, depending...." He took a deep breath. "Please sit down."

"Very well," she said, settling in the chair and smoothing her dress. She touched a hand to her hair self-consciously. "Now, what is this all about?"

He sat down across from her, reaching across the table to take her hand. "Ms. Mare," he started, then grimaced, forcibly correcting himself, "Vivian, a great deal has happened in a very short time. We have shared quite an adventure."

"Indeed, we have," she agreed.

"You have shared in my work and proven yourself to be a very able assistant. You have been invaluable to me in many ways, making up for what I lack, which I fear is a great deal. You have seen the very worst in me, and yet you remain loyal and devoted. You...." He paused, struggling for words. "Oh dear, this is so very difficult for me to do, and yet I must do it!"

"Do what?" she asked gently, mindful of his obvious discomfort.

"I... I... I want to ask once again if you... that is... to be... oh *bother!* " He took a deep breath. She waited patiently.

"V-Vivian, I am asking for your hand in marriage. In the daylight. With everything quite real, and nothing insubstantial. It's all quite plain and ordinary, and the others assisted me, because I am not used to such things. But I must learn, because that is what marriage is, as you pointed out to me, a matter for daylight as well as moonlight, and oh, I am so useless when it comes to practical matters, but I swear I will do my best, and—"

"Angel," she said, "I accept."

He blinked at her. "You do?" Elation brightened his face.

"I do, with the understanding that there is still a great deal that we must discuss," she said.

"Yes, of course!" Suddenly, he began groping about his pockets. "Ah! Then, perhaps, you will accept this as well?" He held out his hand. In it was a small box containing the star sapphire ring.

She took it out of the box, holding it to the light and turning it. A very fine setting and a lovely stone, but lacking the ethereal quality of the insubstantial ring she had worn before. It had the solid sense of ordinary matter. Just as it ought to. "I accept it," she said, slipping it onto her finger, "along with your proposal."

"Praise the numina!" he cried, rising up and leaning across the table to kiss her, nearly knocking over the glasses and the ice bucket with the champagne.

"Careful, Angel." She reached out a hand to steady a glass.

"Oh, dear. It is so different from moonlight. I feel so dreadfully clumsy! But, you don't mind?"

"Not at all," she assured him.

He grabbed the champagne bottle. "Then it is time for this! It is quite real. I purchased it when I was out. I felt so marvelously sure of myself after my meeting with Zarah. I was very clever and brave, wasn't I?"

"You handled the matter with Madam Trebbiano masterfully," she praised him.

He gave a little giggle. "I did, didn't I?" Then he frowned and sighed. "But I can't seem to master this bottle."

"Allow me, Angel."

"Oh, Vivian! I do so need you! I've tried to do this all without creating a thing. Even the rose is real. Well, it is silk. I found it in the attic."

"It is all very lovely, and I am charmed." The cork emerged from the bottle with a pop, and she poured.

"It isn't as splendid as I would have liked, but it had to be this way. And after all, it did work. You said yes." He took his glass and raised it. "To daylight, then."

"And moonlight," she added, raising hers.

They drank the toast, and then he reached behind the ice bucket and took out a small wooden box. "This is real as well, from the attic." He opened it, and familiar music began to play.

"The waltz!" she gasped.

"Yes, this is where I got the idea for it. Such a pretty tune." He smiled at her. "Shall we dance?"

"I'd be delighted."

They got up and he took her in his arms, leading her for a few turns around the room. Just the ordinary living room, just their ordinary clothes, nothing more extraordinary than a couple of cats to observe them. No grand orchestra to guide their steps, just the tinkling tones of an old music box. But it was all it needed to be.

Furtively, the marmosets peered around from behind the curtains. Heron and Octopus stole a glance from the kitchen and nodded with approval. Winged Snake peeked up out of her nest by the fireplace and hissed happily, and from the dining room, the Bishop lifted the lid of his tea pot and murmured a blessing in Latin.

END

CPSIA information can be obtained at www.ICGtesting.com
Printed in the USA
BVOW04s1059061113

335482BV00006B/13/P